DO NO HARM

THE MEDICAL STUDENTS
BOOK ONE

JAMES COHOON

Relax. Read. Repeat.

DO NO HARM (The Medical Students, Book One)
By James Cohoon
Published by TouchPoint Press
Brookland, AR 72417
www.touchpointpress.com

ISBN-13: 978-1-952816-02-4

Cover Design: Colbie Myles

First Edition

Printed in the United States of America.

To the love of my life, Rozanne, and our two amazing kids- Kristin and Travis- who make my world complete.

PART I

Chapter One

Ted Nash needed some extra spending money. His allowance barely covered his beer, marijuana, and parking ticket expenses. And jobs were for suckers.

He backed his dad's old Porsche out of the driveway and drove slowly down the street looking at the multimillion-dollar homes in his well-manicured Pacific Palisades neighborhood. One of the benefits of his father's many hedge fund business trips was that Ted could use any of his father's cars besides the BMW 530 that he received seven years ago as a high school graduation present.

Having lived in the prestigious Riviera section of the Palisades for most of his life, Ted knew many of the people on the street. They were all one-percenters. Many of the kids were like him, with absentee professional fathers and overbearing, clueless mothers. Near the end of his street, however, lived a family that did not seem to belong. Ted often saw Mr. Preston outside in the front yard playing catch with his 8-year-old son Matthew. Sometimes Ted observed Mr. and Mrs. Preston walking around the block holding hands— usually with Matthew in tow. One weekday morning, when Ted was driving home after an all-night party, he witnessed Matthew and his father kicking the soccer ball around in the neighborhood park. Apparently, Mr. Preston did not have to travel constantly for whatever job he had. The father, mother, and son seemed to have stepped out of an episode of a 1950's family TV show. In fact, Ted often mused that the Matthew bore an uncanny resemblance to Wally Cleaver from *Leave it to Beaver*. Ted hated that show.

Ted coasted almost to a stop as he neared the Preston's home. He stared at the open second-story window and wondered how much cash was just sitting inside for the taking.

Ted knew that his mother kept a small 9 mm Glock handgun hidden in wooden box under her bed. His parents had never told him about it, and he was quite certain that they did not know that he had found it years before—and that he had even fired it in the basement when he was alone in the house. He had taped an old towel around the barrel. Although the sound was muffled, he still enjoyed the feeling of power that he experienced after every shot. He determined that when he turned thirty and got his first trust fund payment, a secret-agent's Beretta M9 pistol with a titanium suppressor was going to be at the top of his must-have list.

Because Ted was an inherent coward with an aversion to even potential confrontation, he planned to rob the Prestons when no one was home. Besides, he couldn't afford to be caught. What would his parents say? His father had already warned that Ted was out of second chances.

His misadventures in high school were forgiven with a stern talking to and perhaps a temporary suspension of privileges. However, when he was expelled from UC Santa Barbara for date rape, on top of two DUI arrests, his father had threatened to cut him off completely. As was Ted's habit, he used his mother to mislead his father and soften the punishment. Clara had gone to her husband with Ted's flimsy defense. "Theodore, Ted was railroaded by those prudish administrators. You know how those college girls are these days. She probably seduced Ted and then regretted it later. We are his only parents. We have to believe and support him."

Back in his childhood bedroom for the last seven years, he had used his free time playing the latest violent video games and watching crime shows. He had noticed that TV criminals cased a joint before breaking in, so Ted did the same. In his favorite episode of NCIS, the burglar watched the victim's house 24-7 for several weeks. But Ted didn't have that kind of dedication, and he didn't want to miss dinner. So, for three evenings in a row, he sat in the Porsche across the street from the Preston house so that he could observe who went in and out. It would have been monotonous, but he passed the time by dictating suggestive questions to Siri on his iPhone and chain-smoking designer cigarettes that he had stolen from 7-11. He did not want to leave a trace of his smoking habit in the car, so he kept the windows open and littered his butts on the street next to the curb.

Each night he saw the entire family moving around in the house through the undraped windows.

"This is ridiculous," Ted thought. "Don't they ever go out at night?"

Ted decided that he didn't need to waste any more of his time doing surveillance and concluded that he should simply pull the job in broad daylight when the parents were at work and Matthew was at school. He would just watch each member of the family leave the next morning, and then have the house to himself. With the plan in mind, he went home, said goodnight to his mother, and went upstairs to his bedroom. After the *Late Show* and his usual bedtime snack of beer and nachos topped off with a joint, he had a very sound sleep.

The next morning at 7:30am sharp, Ted walked down the street and positioned himself in a stand of eucalyptus trees in the yard next door to the Prestons. Sure enough, almost immediately he saw Mary Preston get into her silver Prius and drive off to work. She looked to be about 35, older than what Ted usually went for, but she sure was pretty. He couldn't help but think about how great she looked in that mid-length grey flannel skirt, matching blazer, and knee-high black leather boots as she walked to the car. Soon thereafter, Matthew came out of the house and was picked up by the private shuttle bus hired by the parents of the area to safely transport their precious children to local elementary and middle schools. Finally, within twenty minutes, Grant Preston, dressed surprisingly casually, hopped into an old MGB, and drove off.

Ted waited another minute or two before he came out of the trees. Seeing no one else on the street other than gardeners in old pick-up trucks, he scurried the few feet to the Preston's long cobblestone driveway and stared at the front of the house. A tall wooden trellis, covered with some sort of vine, flanked the left side of the front door and extended up to the roof. The trellis looked sturdy enough for climbing. He saw what appeared to be a cracked-open bathroom window on the second story right next to the vine. The rustic cobblestone lane passed under a rose-covered archway alongside the mansion leading to a circular parking area and garage behind the house.

He had it all planned out. If every door was locked, he would look for an accessible window on the back side of the house. If that failed, he would make sure the coast was clear, and then he would climb up the front yard trellis to the bathroom. Nothing could go wrong.

With his typical false bravado, Ted straightened up, took a deep breath, and said aloud to no one, "Let's do this thing!" As he made his way to the backyard, Ted patted his mother's handgun which he had jammed in his pants pocket. The pistol was digging into his thigh. He wished he had one of those fancy shoulder holsters that James Bond always wears.

His mind wandered thinking about how much money he would find. He still had not decided what he would do if he found a bunch of jewels. Would he take them and pawn them? He wasn't quite sure how to do that, but it couldn't be too difficult. He decided to play it loose. He could always take the jewelry and figure it out later.

The backyard was amazing. It looked like a park with a swing set and a little wooden fort. He imagined that Mr. Preston and his son had built the fort together. For some reason that thought caused Ted to reconfirm that the Prestons were the perfect choice to contribute to The Theodore Alexander Nash III Amusement Fund.

Ted couldn't believe his good luck when the first door that he tried opened right into the kitchen.

"What fools they are to leave this place unlocked when they are gone," Ted thought to himself as he glanced at the untidy counters.

"And they just left the breakfast dishes on the table," he muttered. "This must be their maid's day off."

Ted found the stairs to the second-floor bedrooms. The burglars in the movies always found valuables in nightstands and dresser drawers so he figured he would start in the master bedroom. As he walked into the expansive room, he saw a large photo of the family hanging over the unmade king-size bed. The boy in the photo looked to be about five years old. Matthew and both parents were sporting summery white linen clothes and perfect smiles. They looked like the happiest family in the world. Mrs. Preston looked particularly attractive in her billowy white skirt and blouse. Ted decided to start his search in her underwear drawers.

Ten minutes passed, and Ted had only made it through the top two drawers of different kinds of bras. He held up the frilliest one and looked again at Mrs. Preston on the wall. He lustfully pictured what she would look like while wearing that bra. He then opened the third drawer and found some very sheer panties. He held them up to the light from the window. While in this trance-like state, he heard a downstairs door open. Before he could think to drop the panties, he heard footsteps coming up the stairs. *This was not part of the plan.* Before he could devise an escape, Mr. Preston was standing in the doorway to the bedroom holding a Starbucks cup with a puzzled look on this face. His confusion quickly turned to anger.

"What are you doing here?" Mr. Preston exclaimed. "What do you want?" Ted froze.

Mr. Preston squinted and looked more closely at Ted. "Hey, aren't you the Nash boy from down the street?"

Ted stared at Mr. Preston and then looked down at the panties in his left hand. Without another word he reached his right hand into his pants, pulled out his mother's gun, and fired three rounds. The second and third chest shots were unnecessary because the first bullet had crashed through Mr. Preston's skull.

The sound of gunfire brought the local police within minutes. One police cruiser with two officers drove directly to the Preston residence while Officer Mahoney in another cruiser combed the surrounding streets. Ted tried to escape by cutting through the backyard to an adjacent road that had direct trail access to Will Rogers State Park where he could disappear into the hills. Officer Mahoney swung his head from side to side as he drove down Capri Drive looking for a suspect. As he came up to Casale Road, he looked right and saw nothing. He then looked left and spotted what appeared to be a jogger in street clothes running down the narrow, paved road. Mahoney lost the runner as Casale curved sharply out of sight. He got on his radio.

"Possible shooter running down Casale towards the Sullivan Fire Road entrance to the park. Am in pursuit. Backup requested."

Officer Mahoney turned left and drove up behind the runner who was sweating profusely while huffing and puffing. The officer put his right hand on his holstered service revolver. He then drove up beside the slow runner.

"You! Stop right there!"

Before Mahoney could say anything else, Ted blurted out, "I didn't do it!"

Mahoney pulled his gun and pointed it at Ted, getting out of the car.

"Spread your legs and put your hands on the hood!"

As Ted leaned over, Mahoney saw a gun protruding from the waistband of his pants. Ted gawked at Mahoney, who was eyeing the gun.

With his mouth open gasping for breath, Ted wheezed, "Officer, that is my mother's gun. Will you drive me over to my house so I can put it back before she gets home? I don't want to get in trouble."

Chapter Two

At the local police station, Ted loudly proclaimed his innocence. He used his sincere face and asserted that he was being framed by some unknown person for some unknown reason. All of a sudden, the gun did not belong to him or to his mother. He had no idea how it got in his pants.

The handcuffs were tight. Ted clamored for the police captain to call his mother. She could get them to remove the handcuffs and get him released. She knew people.

Clara Nash took the call on her cell while she was at her weekly ladies' luncheon at *The Water Grill*, her favorite restaurant in Santa Monica. She was enjoying the latest gossip when her cell phone buzzed, the word *Police* on the screen. She turned away from the table to take the call. Clara listened in silence as a gruff desk sergeant notified her that Ted was under arrest at the Palisades police headquarters. She whispered, "I'll be right there," and ended the call.

The table went silent as four pairs of eyes stared blankly at Clara.

Her closest friend, Mollie Robinson, whose husband owned the Lane Helicopter Company, put her hand on Clara's. "Clara, what is it? Is everything okay?"

"I'm so sorry," Clara mumbled. "I have to go."

Mollie leaned into Clara and said in a back-stage whisper, "You can't go now. I was just going to tell what I heard about Mary Beth Williams. My hairdresser told me she overheard that Mary Beth and her pool boy—"

"I would love to hear about it, but that was my caterer. You know how I'm throwing a big surprise party for my husband this weekend. Apparently, there is some problem with the wines I ordered." Clara stood and pushed in her chair before anyone could protest. "See you all soon!" Clara said with a half-hearted wave as she walked away.

Clara drove as fast as she could to the station, wondering what trouble her son had gotten into this time. Upon her arrival, she snapped her neatly manicured fingers and demanded to speak with the chief or captain or whoever was in charge. She firmly stated to anyone nearby that her Teddy was a good boy who would never do anything that was against the law. He was to be released immediately or else. No one at the station was too concerned with what the *or else* might be. After listening to several minutes of Clara's boisterous threats from his office, the police chief came out to the front desk and politely informed Clara that Ted had been booked and jailed as a murder suspect. He would not be released. Clara stormed out of the station, determined to clear up this terrible misunderstanding. There was no way that her precious son could have committed such a crime.

Ted's father was involved in an important business meeting in London when his wife began texting and calling him. Theodore Alexander Nash II was not happy about the disturbance. His wife knew full well that she was not to interrupt him during the workday unless someone was dying or, preferably, was already dead. He reluctantly answered the phone. Clara was hysterical.

"Theodore! You have to come home now! It's Ted!"

Mr. Nash sighed. "What now?"

His wife sobbed through the story about how their Teddy had been arrested and how they were saying he killed someone. Mr. Nash was a man of few words and he did not waste any with his wife.

"Clara be quiet please and listen to me. Hang up the phone so that I can call our lawyer."

The Nashes' personal attorney, Joseph Banks, was not a criminal lawyer and was smart enough to know that the defense of a murder charge required the services of the best, and that meant 42-year-old Los Angeles celebrity trial lawyer, Gregory Murtaugh. Although nicknamed 'The Sleazebag' by prosecutors throughout the state for his immoral, if not unethical tactics, Murtaugh had a successful track record defending the most famous and wealthiest felony suspects in California. With his slicked back hair, charming good looks, and $2,000 navy blue suits, Murtaugh was a favorite of the TV guest circuit. Banks arranged for Murtaugh and Mr. Nash to talk within the hour. Of course, Murtaugh agreed to handle the case, as soon as the delicate matter of his huge fee had been discussed and then wired to his Beverly Hills office.

Murtaugh had his driver take him to the local Podunk jail to meet privately with Ted. Murtaugh walked in like he owned the place, flashing his winning smile—the one he used in courtrooms full of easily-manipulated jurors—to all the cops and administrators. In return, he got the usual 'if looks could kill' gazes that he expected. He was not a favorite of law enforcement. Maybe that was because he typically defended his guiltiest clients by using what he called the Johnnie Cochran approach—label the police as bunglers, liars and incompetent oafs.

When Murtaugh first laid eyes on Ted, he took an instant dislike to his client. Ted looked like a cross between a moron and an entitled jerk, wearing a stupid expression along with argyle socks and tennis shoes. *Who dresses like that?* Worse yet, he looked arrogant enough to think he would never face any consequences, whether or not he was guilty. The final result, Murtaugh supposed, of growing up in Riviera with more money than parental attention.

Initially, Ted would not even admit he was in the Preston home, much less that he shot anyone.

"Hey man, I was just out for a jog when some crazy cop pulled a gun on me. If you are my dad's lawyer, you need to get that cop's badge. He should be kicked off the force." Murtaugh said nothing. He just let Ted ramble. Within minutes, Ted's story changed to the claim that he went to the Preston home to ask about doing yard work for them.

"When I knocked on the door, no one answered. The door swung open, so I got worried. I called out, but no one answered. I went upstairs to look around and stumbled upon Mr. Preston's body. I was freaked out! I saw a gun lying on the floor and picked it up without thinking."

Murtaugh stared at his client.

"Seriously Ted?"

Ted started to fidget and fiddle with his hands. He licked his lips while cracking his knuckles one by one.

"What if it was an accident? What if I was just trying to scare him into not telling my parents that I was there? What if I shot the gun but I didn't mean to kill him?"

Murtaugh stared some more. "I'm your attorney. If you aren't going to be honest with me, this conversation is over. What's it going to be?"

"Okay! I'll tell you how it went down, but you have to get me out of here, boss. They have me locked up with real criminals. I'm sure my dad is paying you a lot of money. How long before I can go home?" Ted started to get up from his chair.

Murtaugh sighed and seethed at Ted, "Sit your sorry ass down and shut up."

He wondered to himself why he ever got involved in defending rich degenerates for a living. He mentally shrugged as he remembered his home in Tuscany, his yacht, and his two ex-wives, not to mention his current young trophy wife. She had a body that didn't quit, but neither did her spending.

The next meeting was with Assistant District Attorney Marcie Livingstone, whom Murtaugh knew well. Ms. Livingstone saw no reason to hide the ball.

"Greg, no sense blustering on this one. Your client was caught with the murder weapon in his possession, powder burns on his fingers, and Mrs. Preston's panties in his pocket. His fingerprints are all over the master bedroom where Mr. Preston was found with three bullets in him. The bullets were fired from your client's gun. This is murder one and there is just nowhere for you to go. We will hand over everything we have so you can have your people check it out."

Murtaugh had to think fast.

"Marcie, I talked to Ted Nash personally. He's a good kid from a good family. It was a terrible accident. He had this stupid idea to rob the Preston house when no one was home. Preston came home early and surprised him. Ted panicked, pulled out his mother's gun to frighten Preston so that he wouldn't call the police. Ted had never shot a gun before. The gun went off by accident. Ted got scared when he saw Preston might have been wounded. So, he ran away. He is innocent of murder. Manslaughter at most. And you know I wouldn't bullshit you."

Marcie rolled her eyes and had to work hard to stifle a laugh.

Despite his bluster, Murtaugh knew that his client was looking at a guilty verdict and death row. He was going to have to use his skills not for a trial but to convince the Nash family that they needed to take a plea deal for life in prison, assuming Murtaugh could get Marcie to recommend a plea to the Prestons and to the Judge.

After much debate and angst, both Mr. and Mrs. Nash were on board with doing whatever was necessary to keep their only child alive. They knew that they could convince Ted to enter a plea. They would worry about getting him out of prison later. The problem was that the Preston widow might push the DA into a death sentence trial. Clara Nash had to admit to herself that if the roles were reversed, she would scream from the rooftops that the killer of her husband had to die.

The Prestons were long-time members of the local nondenominational church. Pastor Eagleson was one of the first to offer comfort to Mary and Matthew. Mary and Eagleson spent many hours together in the days following the tragedy talking about God's will and the afterlife.

Family friends and relatives chimed in with platitudes about how Mr. Preston was in a better place. Mary's brother, Dr. TJ Wilson, vowed to help raise Matthew. After she cried until there were no more tears, Mrs. Preston resolved to focus on Matthew.

Ms. Livingstone was politely pressing her to discuss the question of whether she wanted the State to seek the death penalty. At first it seemed like a no-brainer—especially when the investigating detectives reported that Nash had rifled through her underwear and then shot the love of her life and the father of her adored son for no reason whatsoever. But Ms. Livingstone issued a caution.

"Mary, you need to know that there is no way to ever predict how a jury will decide a request for the death penalty. Especially here in California where there is a strong anti-death penalty sentiment. And if the jury were to buy Nash's story that the shooting was accidental, then he might only serve a few years for manslaughter. That would be a real travesty."

Moreover, Mary's church was on record as strongly against the death penalty. Pastor Eagleson, in his soothing baritone voice, counseled her in the ways of the Lord.

"Mary, every single human life is a precious divine gift and we don't have the right to play God. It is natural to want vengeance against those who have harmed us. But we both know that vengeance is the exclusive purview of the Lord. Ted Nash needs to have a full lifetime of opportunity to repent his sins. Asking for his death would haunt you forever. And don't forget about Matthew. How will he feel ten years from now when he is old enough to understand that his mother was responsible for the taking of a human life?"

More important to Mary than the religious philosophy of her spiritual advisor, however, was that she did not want a lengthy trial and subsequent appeals to be the focus of the next decade of her son's life. There was already a lot of press surrounding the murder—*spoiled ne'er-do-well son of super-rich family kills neighborhood husband and father*. The news anchors had already reported in hushed tones the private details of the Preston family. The whole world now knew that Grant Preston had come from nothing, that he had created and sold a next-generation browser, and that he had spent most of his days since then working from home to assist various non-profit charities. The morning of his murder, he had simply followed his daily routine of stepping out for coffee before sitting down to work in his den. A full-blown trial would be a media circus. Mary would do anything to protect Matthew from further trauma. But before she got back to the district attorney's office, she had to discuss the issue with her son.

"Matthew honey, we have to talk about how Ted Nash is going to be punished for killing your father." It turned her stomach to even verbalize Nash's name. She felt chilled to the bone even though she had turned the thermostat to almost eighty. "We can ask that he be put in jail for the rest of his life or we can ask that he be put to death for what he did," she said noncommittally.

Matthew did not need time to reflect. His heart was filled with rage. "He should be killed just like he killed Dad. Why should he get to live the rest of his life?"

Mary tried to disguise her agreement as she continued.

"Pastor Eagleson says that Jesus would let Nash live and so we should too. Pastor believes that dwelling on our hate will make us miserable and that your father would not want us to do that. I know this is hard to understand, but all I have to hold on to now is you and our faith."

Matthew listened for what seemed like an eternity. He nodded at all the appropriate times. He knew that his mother was going to follow the wishes of the church. Matthew did not doubt the sincerity of their pastor. But Matthew also remembered what his father used to say: "One can be sincere, and still be sincerely wrong." Matthew and his mom cried together while holding each other so tightly that he could hardly breathe. He couldn't bear to see his mother cry. Matthew retreated to his room and closed the door softly. He was only eight, but he knew what was right and what was wrong. What was wrong was letting a cold-blooded killer live. What was right was justice, punishment of evil, and yes, retribution.

Although he knew he could never share his dark thoughts with his mother, Matthew began imagining how he was going to someday, somehow, snuff out the life of Theodore Alexander Nash III.

Chapter Three

Matthew felt like he was leading a double life for the next 10 years. Everyone at school and church, and all his social contacts, knew the tragic circumstances of his father's death, but to the outside world, he was the well-mannered young man, the straight-A student, and the outstanding athlete. He knew deep inside that he did not have the brilliant intellect of his father, but he made up for it with hard work and singular determination. His coaches exclaimed over not just his natural athletic ability but also his willingness to be coached even though he was the best player on every team.

Matthew doted on his mother more than ever. He was as kind and supportive as any son could be. He continued to go to church with her and quietly sat through sermons about the virtues of forgiveness. He tried hard to be the perfect child for her so that she never had to worry about him in any way. No teenage temper tantrums to upset her. No academic troubles. No fighting with other kids. And no girlfriend dramas. Plenty of girls made it clear that they were interested in a committed relationship, but Matthew always kept things low-key and distant. He didn't need the complications of a steady girlfriend. He didn't need any outside conflicts. His internal fury, fueled by his daydreams of avenging his father's death, was all he could handle.

His mother had never remarried or even dated. The only man that Matthew ever saw on a regular basis was his mother's unmarried older brother, Dr. TJ Wilson. Matthew had become very close to his uncle over the years. The three of them often had Sunday dinners together during which Uncle TJ would discuss his surgery practice and the wonderful world of medicine.

His mother kept busy with the Grant Preston Foundation, which she had created to continue the charity work for which her husband was known. As a high school senior, Matthew reluctantly accepted a position in the foundation as the head of the Youth Against Poverty division. He did not necessarily believe in the philosophy of his post, but he dutifully performed the functions in order to honor his father and to make his mother happy. The role that galled Matthew the most was when he and other teenage sons and daughters of wealthy parents ventured into low-income neighborhoods to talk to preteens thought to be at risk of becoming criminals. Matthew enjoyed the interactions with the young kids and tried his best to leave a lasting impression on those that he tutored. But he understood that most of the other tutors merely considered these excursions as college resume builders. After their one-hour sessions, they hurried back to their mansions in the comfort of tank-sized black SUVs, never to think again about the impoverished or the disadvantaged among us until the following month. Matthew scoffed to himself about the misguided stereotyping of the inner-city kids. After all, Ted Nash had grown up with every advantage imaginable.

Matthew was going to graduate from high school in a few weeks and everyone, including his mother and uncle, was waiting for Matthew to decide which college he would choose. He was inundated with letters of acceptance. College coaches were recruiting him for both football and baseball. He had received multiple scholarship offers—some based on his athletic prowess and some based solely on his hard-won academic credentials.

Matthew played along, but in the secret world he had created inside of his head, he had no intention of going to any college whatsoever. Not a day had gone by since his father's murder that Matthew hadn't fantasized about killing Ted Nash who was serving his life sentence in San Quentin prison near San Francisco. He came up with any number of fantastical ways to infiltrate the prison so that he could shoot Nash in the head, stab him in the heart, or strangle him with his bare hands. When he was younger, the ideas involved everything from committing a crime so that he could become Nash's cellmate to becoming a food server in the prison lunchroom. As he got older, he thought about tricking his way in by impersonating a prison official or a law enforcement officer.

His current ideation was that maybe he could become a prison guard, which required only a high school diploma—that would put him in the proximity of the prisoners with a gun in his hand. As he lay in bed many nights, his mind would conjure up one scenario after the other as to how that would play out. His favorite fantasy was that once inside the prison, he would use his wealth to bribe the other guards in order to finagle his way into Nash's cellblock. Then he would empty his gun into Ted's head. But that would mean his own prison sentence, which might be a bridge too far for the sanity of his mother. If he had to use a gun, he would, but a better plan would be to smash Ted's head in and make it look like the killing was the work of some inmate with a grudge. This way, Matthew could accomplish his goal without having to spend his own life in prison.

Matthew had already found that he was a pretty good shot. One of his football teammates had his 16th birthday party at a shooting range and Matthew had won the prize for the most center target shots. Since that party two years ago, he had been going with one or another of his friends at least once a month to practice his marksmanship. These trips were kept a secret from his mother— she would never approve. She had only reluctantly allowed him to do martial arts for the last 5 years, based on Matthew's claim that the lessons were for self-defense only. His Taekwondo instructor taught him how he could protect and defend himself in case of an attack, but Matthew was more interested in learning how the same moves could be used to beat another man into a bloody pulp, before shooting him.

Although Matthew had yet to come up with a foolproof plan to exact his revenge, he was positive that spending four years in college was not going to further his goal. He had to figure out a way to break it to his mother. Perhaps his uncle could help soften the blow.

Matthew made the call on the special cell number that he was supposed to use in case of emergency.

"Hi Uncle TJ."

"Matt, are you okay? Is anything wrong?"

"No, I guess I should've just called your office and left a message for you. But I wonder if you have time to meet sometime this week for lunch. I need your help with something."

"How about tomorrow at Big Dean's on the pier?"

After he hung up, Matthew looked at the graduation gown hanging in the corner of his room.

"Just a few more weeks and the charade of high school will be over," he thought. For his graduation present he was going to ask for a week-long trip to San Francisco. He knew that San Quentin offered abbreviated public tours every weekday. He had to get familiar with the place.

Chapter Four

Dr. Wilson found Matthew sitting at one of the back tables at the *World-Famous Big Dean's Cafe.*

"Hi Matt. Why are you sitting way back here? You usually like to sit at a picnic table out front to people watch," he said with a chuckle.

"Oh, I just thought this would give us a little more privacy. I have something kind of important to discuss."

"Well, let's order first. God did not intend for important matters to be discussed on an empty stomach."

Matthew smiled. "Whatever you say, Uncle TJ."

Over hamburgers and chocolate shakes they chatted about the upcoming graduation ceremony and the after-party for the 142 graduating seniors. Matthew had not paid too much attention, but he had heard that the class had rented a Palm Springs residence that had a huge pool with a water slide. Of course, the food would be catered, and a private party bus would transport the kids in luxury to and from the all-night event.

"That sounds like it will be pretty wild," said Dr. Wilson. "Some of your classmates might try to have a little too much fun. You be careful, son."

"No worries. I'm only going because it's expected. I actually have other things on my mind. That's why I wanted to talk to you today."

"Sounds ominous." Dr. Wilson was getting a little worried. "Ok, what's going on with you?"

"Well it's this whole college thing. I just don't feel ready. I was thinking that I should take a gap year or two and think about what I want to do."

Matthew had figured that he needed to broach the subject with baby steps. The first goal was to get his mom on board with putting college off. He would later drop the bombshell about wanting to be a prison guard.

Although Dr. Wilson was relieved that Matthew wasn't reporting that he got a girl pregnant or that he was into drugs, he was not a fan of the currently fashionable idea of indefinitely 'bumming around' in order to 'find yourself.' But as Matthew's father figure, he felt a duty to hear him out.

"Well, what do you have in mind instead of going to college?"

"I'm not sure yet. Because I got drafted in the 10th round of the baseball draft, I was thinking I could try to play professionally instead of playing in college. Playing some minor league ball would give my mind a break. Or maybe I could go to Europe to practice my French. Or maybe travel around and see more of America. In fact, I was thinking about spending some time up in Northern California."

"Matt, I agree that you need to take some time off. Have some fun this summer! You have been working awfully hard. But I am concerned that you would later regret it if you didn't take advantage of all the opportunities that are in front of you right now. You have your pick of colleges. And, as you might have guessed, I was hoping that you would decide to pick Stanford, my alma mater, for your undergraduate education. And while we are on the subject, this is a good time to tell you that my dream has always been that you would decide to go to medical school. And then come practice with me! I know you have the mental fortitude for medicine, and I bet that you'd make a wonderful surgeon."

Matthew was surprised. Dr. Wilson was like a surrogate father to him but had never mentioned a career in medicine.

"I don't know about that. All that blood. And what about when your patients die?"

"Yes, that does happen. But remember, life begins at the end of your comfort zone. And even if you don't want to be a surgeon, there all kinds of doctors and we need them all."

Dr. Wilson decided that this was the time to make a strong pitch to Matthew.

"Look Matt, you can and should do what you want with your life. Your mother and I only want you to be happy and fulfilled. But give doctoring some thought. I know how important volunteering and helping the less fortunate is to you. Without trying to put too fine a point on it, there is no more noble profession than medicine. It is said that doctors bridge the gap between science and society, and they really do. Think about all the physical suffering that can be alleviated with the right care. And not just in our country. Many doctors from America go to countries rife with poverty and disease in order to make a real difference. Remember the recent Ebola virus scare? So many American doctors volunteered to go to Africa to treat the disease at its source, that many were turned away."

Matthew listened politely as his uncle continued.

"And there are so many things you can do with a medical license to help society. Sure, there are lots of doctors like me who treat folks who show up in their clinic or the hospital with some disease or injury. But there are also many physicians who devote their lives to helping those who do not have a voice—the mentally infirm, young children, older patients with Alzheimer's disease. Everyone is entitled to medical care but not everyone can get it. The world would be a better place if you lent your considerable talents to the quest for the expansion of quality medical care."

Dr. Wilson did not want to ignore any idea that might appeal to Matthew, so he even mentioned those medical professionals who have made tremendous contributions to mankind through medical research.

"And where would we be without the revolution in medical knowledge resulting from the tireless efforts of researchers to understand, prevent and cure diseases? Think of the increase in average life expectancy thanks to advances in medical care. Many of the cancer treatments that we take for granted today are the result of years of medical research and clinical trials. Medical research, more than anything else you can think of, increases the quality and duration of life in our society. You could be a part of that."

Later that evening Matthew was lying in bed unable to concentrate on anything except the complicated strategy he needed to employ with his mother. He was replaying in his mind the conversation with his uncle.

He suddenly bolted upright as he muttered aloud, "Hey, wait a minute!"

He picked up his laptop and knew exactly what search terms to use.

Within two hours, Matthew had found everything he required. Uncle TJ was only partially correct about accessibility to medical care—while millions of law-abiding and deserving Americans have been denied access to even minimal health care, imprisoned rapists, murderers, and violent gangbangers have been enjoying free unlimited medical care from some of the best doctors available for any malady, injury or disease.

Matthew discovered that the good taxpayers of California recently paid for a brand-new hospital at the San Quentin prison at a cost of $136 million. The prisoners are entitled to receive medical, dental, and mental health care at no cost, and they certainly take advantage of that benefit. Statistics showed that about 70% of all California state prisoners made regular use of the prison medical system.

The unfairness of this distorted arrangement angered Matthew, but there was a silver lining— he imagined that a large prison with a big new hospital would need lots of doctors. He was correct. He learned that San Quentin has more than 15 full-time doctors and more than 100 nurses to treat its fluctuating inmate population of up to 5000 inmates. Plus, many other specialty physicians including surgeons, podiatrists, and ophthalmologists come in on an as-needed basis. He could be a prison doctor and have unfettered access to prisoners. He, Matthew Preston, could be face-to-face with Ted Nash.

Matthew then checked out the medical schools close to San Quentin. He chuckled under his breath when he saw that Stanford Medical School had a long and storied relationship with San Quentin prison. Stanford alum Dr. Leo Stanley was the chief medical officer at San Quentin between 1913 and 1951, except for the period he served in the Navy during WWII. In 2008, the chief physician at the prison was invited to be the keynote speaker at Stanford's Fall Forum, the annual showcase for medical student service projects. Stanford undergraduate students had even formed a group called the Stanford Prison Forum which sends students to San Quentin to take classes with prisoners. Matthew was certain that none of these virtue-signaling students had ever had a family member who had been a victim of violent crime. In any event, it looked like going to Stanford University would be a good first step towards becoming a prison doctor at San Quentin.

The next day, Matthew asked his mother to invite Uncle TJ over to dinner as an early pre-graduation party. The three of them had Matthew's favorite meal—sweet-and-sour spareribs with a pile of steamed brussels sprouts. Just as they were about to start on the homemade lemon sherbet dessert, Matthew declared that he had made a college and career decision.

"Mom, Uncle TJ, I've decided to go to Stanford for college."

Both Mary and TJ broke out in big smiles, but before they could say a word, Matthew blurted out the rest of his news.

"And I want to be a doctor. I want to go to Stanford Medical School just like Uncle TJ!"

After many high fives, hugs, and shouts of joy, Matthew said, "I'm going to notify Stanford of my decision right now. I can't wait to get started."

"Oh honey," his mother said, "your father would be so proud of you. Think of how you will be able to impact the lives of your patients."

"I know," chuckled Matthew as he rubbed his hands together. "I can hardly wait."

PART II

Chapter Five

The Stanford campus was beautiful with tons of palm trees, fountains, and bikes. As a group, the undergraduate students were brilliant. Much smarter than he was. Matthew knew that he needed to get top grades in order to gain admission to the medical school because historically there had been at least 7,500 applications for only 102 places in each entering class. He worked his butt off. He rarely went to parties or other events at the school. Instead, he spent most evenings in a quiet corner of the Green Library. The only extracurricular activity he enjoyed was playing on the baseball team—the coach had virtually begged him to take the job of starting center fielder. Matthew went home to visit his mother as often as he could but even those visits were few and far between because he needed to keep his nose to the grindstone.

Matthew allowed himself only two non-school related activities. Neither was socially based. In fact, both were solitary endeavors. The first was exploring Stanford's underground system of steam tunnels. Most of the grates were bolted down years ago but Matthew was told by a baseball alum where a secret entrance still existed. With only the aid of a flashlight, he liked to wander through the dark passages, think about his father, and plan his revenge.

The second activity was visiting San Quentin and the surrounding area. He was shocked when he drove up to the maximum-security correctional facility for the first time. It looked like any other ancient government facility, but the old building walls were surrounded with trimmed trees, flowers, fountains, and lovely grounds. Surely California bureaucrats had better things to do with the public's money than to beautify a holding tank for criminals, but apparently not. And he had already learned from his online research that San Quentin spared no expense to make the prison a wonderful place to live, including a baseball field, basketball courts, tennis courts, a track, and unlimited weightlifting equipment. Matthew cringed when he thought of all the public schools that were lacking these high-end amenities.

He was on a mission to familiarize himself with the layout of the buildings and terrain. He could not get into the cellblocks of course, but as a member of the general public, he was allowed entry into the on-site museum inside the gates, which had basic maps and photos, giving Matthew insight into the location of various structures. The curator of the museum, having been employed at San Quentin for decades, was a font of information. With a smile and enthusiasm, he told Matthew that the prison had opened in 1854 and that many of the country's most notorious criminals had been imprisoned and put to death there. Matthew was shown a replica of the gas chamber which had been used before the changeover to lethal injection. One of the most notorious criminals to be put to death was inmate Robert Wells, who was enlisted to help build the gas chamber in 1938. After his parole, he murdered three people, so he was returned to San Quentin where he was put to death in the chamber he had helped to construct. Even today, San Quentin houses all of California's death row inmates. Although, courtesy of the California court system, virtually no one is executed anymore.

Another thing Matthew felt compelled to do was to simply watch the facility. Sometimes he would park his car on a deserted hill several miles away. From that vantage point he could look down and study the grounds and the people walking around inside the fifty-foot tall stone walls topped with barbed wire and guard towers. Other times he would rent a small boat and cruise by the San Francisco Bay side of the prison. He wondered as he stared, "What's Ted Nash doing right now? With any luck, getting gang raped. More likely, however, he's laughing it up while playing poker with a bunch of other vile animals. Where does he sleep? Where does he get his medical treatment?" And most of all, "What will be the look on his face when I kill him?"

The required courses for a pre-med major were rigorous, and Matthew did not have the strongest background in the sciences. Many of his high-school classmates had taken advanced placement courses in physics, chemistry and math, while Matthew, like most athletes, had chosen subjects such as basic science, required language, and shop class. Therefore, at Stanford, he took advantage of extra help sessions for helmet-sport athletes and made friends with the teaching assistants who could help him focus on what to study for the tests. And Uncle TJ always made himself available whenever Matthew called with science questions. Matthew probably talked more with his uncle than his mother during those four years.

Crafting a transcript with stellar grades, although extremely difficult, was only a third of the medical school entry battle. He also had to do well on the standardized Medical College Admission Test, known as the MCAT, and he needed to draft a compelling personal essay as part of the admission process. Matthew did not like to take advantage of his family wealth but there were times when he was glad that he had almost unlimited resources. He hired the best MCAT tutors on every subject and he spent months learning the secrets and tactics of this test of substantive knowledge. With all of that help, he performed just well enough so that his score would not disqualify him from consideration for admission to the top medical schools.

The personal essay was emotionally exhausting. He knew that the Stanford School of Medicine, like many of the highly ranked academic institutions, wanted a diverse group of medical students based on race, gender, economics, and even geography. As a white male California resident from a wealthy family, Matthew knew that he did not qualify as a traditional victim of society. In order to draft a compelling statement, he had to describe in detail his life circumstances growing up as the only child of a murdered father. In a deliberate, almost contrived manner, he chose to elaborate on the obvious such as the missed life milestones like graduations, birthdays, and Christmases. He could not bear to share the more important things that he had lost growing up fatherless. He refused to script an essay about the inability to talk to his father about the birds and the bees, about not being able to share with his father the joy of the winning hit in a championship baseball game, and about missing his father's advice and wisdom regarding how to be a better man. In short, he wrote what he thought would play well with the admissions officers without giving away his innermost feelings.

The day Matthew saw an email on his phone from the Dean of Admissions at Stanford School of Medicine, he had ordered a large black Starbucks coffee and was just about to take the first sip. He wanted to open the email when no one was around. He walked as fast as he could to his secret spot in the back stacks of the library. He sat down and opened the email. He read it the first time quickly and then read it twice more, very carefully.

He called his mother from the stacks. As soon as she picked up the phone, he almost yelled.

"Mom, I got in!"

Chapter Six

The week before medical school classes are set to begin, Stanford, like most medical schools, has the traditional White Coat Ceremony for the incoming congregation of future doctors. Considered to be a symbolic first step to mark the long journey ahead, this pageantry, although somewhat archaic, is meant to be a fun icebreaker to help ease the tension of the competition and uncertainty inherent in medical school.

This was going to be Matthew's first opportunity to meet his other 101 classmates. Attendance was mandatory. Matthew was not too excited about it, but his mother and uncle were ecstatic. In the days leading up to the big day, TJ just kept repeating every twenty minutes, "Matt, we are so proud of you." Mary did not say much but she couldn't resist squeezing his shoulder or tousling his hair whenever she walked by.

Mary had insisted that Matthew buy a new blue suit for the occasion. At 6'2" and a solid 210 pounds, combined with his Wheaties-box face, Matthew looked more like a young congressional candidate than a first-year medical student. Mary and TJ dressed up as though they were going to a presidential inauguration.

They flew into San Jose and made the short drive to the Stanford campus.

TJ apologized that his rental car, although luxurious, was quite cramped for three people. Matthew dutifully squished himself into the back seat like an adolescent so that his mother could sit up front. Once they arrived at the school, Matthew split off to assemble with the rest of his class while Mary and TJ found the large auditorium where the ceremony would take place. It was an unseasonably cold evening but the two of them stood shivering outside the large wooden doors near the front of the line so that they could get seats as close to the stage as possible.

Matthew slowly entered the anteroom full of mostly twenty-something men and women. There was a table filled with small plastic cups of poured champagne. Waiters walked around with trays of exotic hors d'oeuvres. The aspiring doctors were a rainbow of color. It looked like every ethnicity and country in the world were represented by these students. Most of the men wore suits and were standing in small groups eating and looking as uncomfortable as middle school boys at their first dance. He saw only a few white males and he counted his blessings that he was able to be admitted into this mix.

The women were an entirely different story. They were also of every ethnicity but most of them were wearing what seemed to Matthew to be cocktail party attire—short, form-fitting dresses. Matthew and his college friends used to call this fancy attire 'TV weather girl outfits.' Some of the costumes were as reflective as well-cut diamonds. The young ladies looked like they could provide temperature forecasts on the local evening news—and then afterwards go clubbing in Hollywood. And these women were flitting around the room like social butterflies at a sorority pledge dance. Matthew observed that none of the female students were eating any of the food—likely for fear of spotting their fabulous ensembles or, more likely, for fear of not being able to squeeze into the outfits the next day.

The women not only *seemed* to outnumber the men based on activity and volume, but Matthew knew from Stanford's website that there was indeed a distinct discrepancy in the gender ratio. In his class there were 55 women and only 47 men. Under other circumstances he would have enjoyed the potential possibilities, but he had no time for such a diversion.

To blend in, Matthew politely wandered from one small group of guys to another getting names and basic background information.

"Hi, I'm Matthew. Any idea what the plan is here?"

"Just waiting for Dean Masterson to arrive and get us lined up for the procession, I think. I'm Scott. Where are you from Matthew?"

"Not too far from home—I'm from LA. You?"

"New York City. Just got in yesterday. A whole different vibe here."

"I bet." As they talked about how they both came to be at Stanford, several other students jumped in and out of the conversation. Matthew was hoping that the ceremony would get underway so that he could graciously bow out of the conversation. Scott seemed to be able to talk endlessly about how primary care in poor neighborhoods was the only honorable course for a doctor these days.

Just as Matthew was waiting for Scott to come up for air so that he could move over to the snack table, Miss Torrey Lane Jamison walked up holding a glass of champagne in one hand and some sort of hors d'oeuvre in her other hand. With a mischievous smile, she whispered,

"Hey you guys. Have you tried these stuffed mushrooms? They are fantastic!" Then she made the universal gagging gesture with her finger in her open mouth. "Not!"

Torrey, like the other girls, was wearing something short and summery. But her dress was very different, even to Matthew's untrained eye. Hers was a modest cut—not formfitting, sparkly, or revealing. Her shoes were flats instead of the four-inch high heels popular throughout the room. She was petite but fit, probably only about five-three, with a blond pixie haircut that obviously needed little professional upkeep. If she wore any makeup, it was minimal. Despite her lack of decoration, Matthew thought Torrey was non-traditionally cute with big light blue eyes. He noticed a tattoo on the back of her left shoulder, but he couldn't make out what it said. She had one other characteristic about her that was hard to miss—she wasn't shy.

"I've got five bucks that says Dean Masterson is late because he's watching the end of the Giants game. I saw before I came in that it was into extra innings."

No one offered a response, so she continued.

"After this wingding is over, who's up for beer and pizza?"

Matthew could not help staring at her. On one hand, she seemed totally out of place here, but on the other hand she had a manner and fearlessness about her that he couldn't help but admire. Matthew could only surmise that she must be really smart if she got into this top-tier medical school with minimal social graces and no noticeable financial backing.

Dean Masterson soon arrived. There was no mention of any baseball game. The dean was taken aback by the apparent short attention span of the future doctors of America. Just getting them to line up in alphabetical order was akin to herding cats. The dean almost had to shout his instructions about what was going to happen during the ceremony in order to be heard over the cacophony. They were to file into the auditorium, in order, and sit in the assigned rows reserved for them. After remarks by administrators and various deans of the school, each future doctor would be called up on stage where a dean would help each of them into a brand-new white lab coat with his or her full name, and the words *Medical Student*, embroidered on the front. They would each also receive their very own shiny new stethoscope. Finally, as a group, they would recite the Hippocratic oath. Matthew was not looking forward to that part of the evening.

Every seat in the auditorium was filled. And every spouse, parent, and special friend seemed compelled to document every moment of the proceedings. As the students walked down the aisles to find their reserved spots, cameras clicked, and videos whirred. Mary asked TJ to do the honors, so Dr. Wilson had to watch the procession through a lens finder. Dean Masterson opened the festivities with a few sentences about the obvious group diversity. "One fifth of you were born outside of the U.S. You come from 28 different colleges and universities. 15 of you already have advanced degrees. 21 of you have published research. We have two members of the Screen Actors Guild and a former Pasadena Rose Parade Queen. We have seven varsity college athletes, including two national champions and a winner of the Kona Ironman. And I am proud to say that this year we have two more undocumented immigrants—one from Mexico and one from Brazil." The last statistic brought thunderous applause. Matthew couldn't help but wonder whether these same students would be so happy if they had been one of the two qualified American citizens who had been denied a place in the class. The Dean continued, "Many of you have already done amazing things in your short lives and the education you receive here will enable you to do even greater things in the future—whether it be primary care in under-served areas, research, emergency medicine, or in a discipline not yet discovered."

The dean was sure that this group of young men and women were destined to do extraordinary things in their careers to make their families, their school, and themselves proud. He gestured to the parents and other family members in attendance. "And these students know that they did not get to this point on their own. The parents in this room helped to shape them and make this day possible. You probably will never know how much your sacrifices and assistance are appreciated." On cue, the 102 students rose, turned around to look at their family members, and broke into thirty seconds of cheering and clapping. Matthew found his mother and uncle in the crowd, and he teared up. He wished, for the millionth time, that he could share such special moments with his father.

The several other speakers were from different administrative branches within the school, but the overriding theme was consistent—medical school was going to be a lot of work, very difficult, and the students were going to need family support as much as ever. And the school, for its part, would do whatever it took to make sure each student succeeded.

As the evening wore on, Matthew became more and more anxious. He had read the Hippocratic oath many times and he knew that the overriding principle was that a doctor should first "do no harm." Matthew knew from his research that Hippocrates, a Greek physician who lived 2500 years ago, is considered the father of modern medicine. He is thought to have penned the most widely known of the Greek medical texts. The oath requires new doctors to swear to uphold a number of moral and ethical standards. The classical oath, written before the birth of Christ, dictated that the oath be affirmed by Apollo and other Greek gods. The modern version calls for each doctor to fulfill the special relationship covenant that he or she has with each patient, and above all else, not play God. Would he feel like a fraud swearing allegiance to that pillar of medical practice, when his sole purpose in becoming a doctor was to kill another human? Would it be better to remain silent during the oath? He tried to steel himself for the moment.

"Will the class please rise," said Dean Masterson. "Now raise your right hand and repeat after me."

The dean read the first sentence of the oath and waited for the class to echo his words. Matthew joined in. As the end of the oath drew near, Matthew felt weak and his voice softened. But then he glanced over at his beaming mother. He thought of what she had been through. He thought of his dad lying in a pool of blood. He thought of his fatherless childhood. Most of all, he thought of Ted Nash living, breathing, and eating three meals a day courtesy of the State. By the end of the oath, Matthew's voice was loud and clear. "I will practice my profession with conscience and dignity. The health of my patient will be my first priority. I will not use my medical knowledge to violate human rights and civil liberties. I will maintain the utmost respect for human life. I will not play God." He looked again at his mother and made eye contact. Matthew smiled and gave her a big thumbs-up.

Chapter Seven

Along with most of the other aspiring physicians, Matthew secured a room in the graduate student housing on campus. A few of the students chose to live off-campus in nicer apartments, but Matthew did not mind the spartan accommodations. He thought the convenience of being within walking distance of the medical school was well worth it. Move-in day was hectic for everyone but around dinnertime someone ordered pizza for Matthew's entire floor, which was informally served in the third-floor lounge. Matthew recognized several of the faces from the White Coat Ceremony, but he knew few names. One face and name he remembered for sure was that of Torrey Jamison.

She looked cute in short cut-off jeans and a plain white tank top. She walked right up to Matthew.

"I never expected that the big-deal baseball star was medical school material. I grew up not far from here and saw almost all of your games last year. That double you got against UCLA in the bottom of the ninth to win the league championship was clutch."

"Well thanks, I got lucky there," said Matthew making a dismissive gesture with his hand. "How did you come be such a big baseball fan?"

"When I was little, my father used to take my younger sister and me to a lot of Stanford games. The games were cheap entertainment and the Sunken Diamond is so cool. You were lucky to play there. After I transferred to Stanford from the local community college, I figured I would check out the team. You guys were fun to watch."

"We had our moments. Are you going to have some pizza?"

"I'm just going to take a couple of slices with me." She gave him a toothy grin. "See you tomorrow in class I guess." Matthew watched her walk away. He liked what he saw, but he had no time for a girlfriend.

The first day of class was scary. Matthew did not know what to expect from his professors or his fellow students. There are no traditional grades during the first two years at most elite medical schools. It is strictly pass/fail. This sounds good in theory, but Matthew was more than a little worried about the potential of failing. He wanted to find a study group of extremely bright students to give him an extra boost in understanding the material. And he had heard that there is so much material to digest that he wanted as much help as possible to ensure success.

The first quarter of the first year was dedicated to the Foundations of Medicine, which meant sections on biochemistry, cell tissues, genetics, development of disease, and human anatomy. The rest of the first year and most of the second was devoted to advanced courses in immunology, principles of disease, and the nervous, cardiovascular, and reproductive systems. This preclinical curriculum required the students to memorize mountains of material and then apply that knowledge to the treatment of patients. Additionally, both years required that all students participate in and pass clinical workshops during which they are trained in how to take medical histories, how to deal with uncooperative patients, and generally how to maximize bedside manner interactions with patients. It only got more difficult after that. But right now, Matthew needed to get through the first two years of intense classroom learning and testing in order to get to clinical rotations in year three and independent clerkships in year four.

Most of the professors were medical doctors who devoted time away from their clinical practices in exchange for the prestige and the lifestyle of academia. Naturally, some were more devoted than others to the nuts and bolts of actual teaching. The large lectures were given by experienced and entertaining instructors. But the class was also divided into small groups for laboratory work and discussion. In these groups the quality of the group leaders varied. Most saw the molding of young doctors as a solemn duty, but some saw it as a menial task not worthy of their vast talents. Unfortunately, Matthew's first small group was headed by Dr. Britsky, who swaggered in late, yawned while looking at his phone, and made it clear in the initial meeting that he had better things to do and the students were going to be on their own to learn the material.

"Once around the room to introduce yourselves," Dr. Britsky instructed.

The seven students sat at small desks in a semicircle. Besides Matthew, there was a guy who looked like he had just arrived from India, but he had actually grown up in Virginia and had done his undergraduate studies at Harvard. There was a preppy African American fellow from Columbia, a pretty Chinese girl from Yale, and an Asian man who looked forty years old dressed in a suit and tie—he said he had gone to college in England. Of the remaining two, one was a braces-wearing white girl who had a master's degree from Caltech, even though she looked like she should still be in junior high school. Matthew was unsure of the last woman's race, but she claimed to have a PhD and six published research papers having something to do with sea slugs.

Dr. Britsky explained that this group seminar on ethics would meet twice a week. At the first session each week, the students would be given a case study of a patient with a particular set of symptoms. They would discuss the possible causes and treatments. In between the first and second meetings, the students were to research each theory and then email their findings to the group. The final session each week would be devoted to dissecting the merits of each student's conclusions. Dr. Britsky made it clear that he was there only to guide the discourse, not to provide answers. And if he did not make it to some of the classes, they were to go ahead without him.

As the students looked at each other blankly, in walked Torrey Jamison. "Sorry I'm late. Did I miss anything?" Dr. Britsky stared at her.

"This should be interesting," thought Matthew.

"Your fellow students can catch you up after class," Dr. Britsky replied coldly. Matthew looked around at the unsympathetic faces. He figured he would have to be the one doing the catching up.

Chapter Eight

The first case study was intended to introduce the ethical, moral and legal issues that confront modern physicians.

"Under what circumstances, if any, can you treat a patient against his will?" Dr. Britsky asked. No one spoke. Hearing no eager responses, he continued.

"Suppose the patient is mentally ill? Suppose the patient claims to have a religious objection to the proposed treatment? Suppose a mother comes to you and says her five-year-old daughter is terminally ill with a diseased liver. The young girl has an older teenage sister who is a good donor match. The mother wants you to harvest a portion of the older sister's liver and give it to the sick daughter. Is the teenager competent to consent? Can the liver slice be taken without the teenager's consent? What if she doesn't want to give up part of her liver? Can the mother force her do it for the benefit of the sibling?

"Or suppose a patient comes to you and says, 'I have a pancreatic cancer and have only three months to live. I am in terrible pain and I am told it will only get worse as the end nears. I don't want to live like that, and I don't want my family to have to deal with it. Please give me something to end my life now.'"

Dr. Britsky paused. "Let's start with that one. You all took the Hippocratic oath the other day. As you know, a key tenant of doctoring is 'thou shall not kill.' So, is euthanasia ever ethically permissible? Ever legal? Is it ever morally justified?"

The Indian guy was the first to speak.

"No, no and no. Killing another human intentionally is always morally and ethically wrong. We don't even have to reach the legal element in this discussion. We know that the more evolved societies have done away with the death penalty even in capital murder cases. Of course, we are compassionate towards the dying woman but we, as doctors, have sworn to not assume the role of God."

The girl with braces seemed to concur as she lisped, "Suicide is a sin and euthanasia is assisted suicide. It is punishable as murder in most states. Oregon is one of the few exceptions, but those people up there are godless hippies." She did not smile at her own last comment. She was dead serious. And there was of lot of nodding accord in the room. Matthew, never having given thought to the matter, neither nodded in agreement nor spoke in opposition.

Out of the blue, Torrey jumped in.

"Passive euthanasia has been around for centuries and happens every day in hospitals and homes throughout the world. If a doctor withholds or withdraws life-prolonging measures to a patient on artificial life support at the request of the family, no one blinks an eye. But for some reason, if the doctor engages in some affirmative conduct which results in an earlier death, then you want to crucify him or her. There is no moral distinction between a deliberate act or a knowing omission which causes a death. The patient is going to die anyway, but with less pain and more dignity."

The Indian guy sniggered and tried to interrupt with a condescending tone.

"Miss, you do not seem to understand that we are bound—"

Torrey did not let him complete his sentence. She flipped him away with a wave of her hand.

44

"I'm not finished, sir."

Matthew and everyone else, including Dr. Britsky, gaped at her. Apparently, in Torrey's book, the unwritten rule that one does not publicly disagree with a fellow student in front of the teacher did not apply to medical school classes. She obviously did not care what the Indian guy or anyone else thought about her. As she continued, Torrey's eyes hardened, and her voice raised.

"I thought we were supposed to act in the patient's best interests. I thought we were supposed to respect a patient's wishes. If passive euthanasia is accepted, how can it be illegal, immoral, or unethical to follow a patient's instructions?" She looked right at the Indian guy. "You're arguing form over substance if you claim that the affirmative act is wrong but that the decision to passively allow the death is okay. Who are we to say that an elderly man with an incurable disease should suffer a few more days or weeks? Similarly, who are we to say that a terminal little girl should have to cry out in pain for even an extra hour when it can be avoided?" She pointed an accusatory finger at Indian guy. "You cite the moral code to do no harm. What about the directive to end suffering?" Torrey suddenly stopped. "That's all I have to say."

Dr. Britsky, somewhat taken aback, said in a reproachful tone, "Well, that gives us all something to think about." He glowered at Torrey.

"Class dismissed."

Chapter Nine

After the students filed out the classroom, most of them crowded around the primary victim of Torrey's diatribe. The pretty Chinese girl stated, "Hey, you were so right. Where does she get off talking to you like that?" The older-looking Asian man chimed in, "She's ridiculous. Just ignore her." The Indian guy quickly composed himself and asked rhetorically to the group, "How did she ever get admitted into medical school?"

Torrey quickly walked off in the opposite direction. Matthew followed. "Hey, wait up Torrey!" Torrey slowed and turned around. Matthew said, "You were great in there. I wish I were that eloquent on my feet. Are you okay?"

Torrey smiled. "Yes, I suppose I got a little too riled up in there."

"Do you want to grab a cup of coffee?" asked Matthew. "I know a place around the corner, and I can fill you in on what you missed if you want."

They started to bond over their shared affection for coffee shops, although they had contrary penchants. Matthew ordered plain black coffee whereas Torrey selected a vanilla latte—extra pump and added whip. They agreed on freshly baked croissants but disagreed on the method of consumption. Matthew pulled his croissant apart into bite-sized pieces and made liberal use of his handful of napkins. Torrey devoured hers like she hadn't eaten in a week. In five or six large bites her pastry was gone, except for a small piece that fell onto the table. "Five second rule!" she laughed as she pinched up the wayward bit and popped it into her mouth. She tongued off most of the crumbs on her lips and disposed of the rest with her sleeve. Matthew raised his eyebrows and stared. Torrey stared back with playful eyes and said, with a half-full mouth, "I really like croissants."

As for the flakes on the front of her baseball jersey shirt, she simply stood up and hand brushed the scattered baked goods off her shirt and pants onto the floor. She wetted a tip of a napkin with her water bottle for the final clean up around her mouth.

When the coffee cups were almost empty, Matthew grinned and broached the subject of the Britsky class. "I hate to tell you this, but I don't think you are in line to be teacher's pet."

Torrey smiled. "I'm okay with that."

"But seriously, I really admired how you took on the class. What you said made a lot of sense. How do you know so much about mercy killing? What was it that got you so upset?"

"Oh, I just didn't like the way that they were trivializing the issue. Let's talk about something else. What brought you to Stanford?"

In a flash, she had deftly parried by changing the subject from herself to Matthew. Matthew had himself become an expert at doing the same thing whenever the subject of his father was brought up by well-meaning relatives or friends. Matthew knew about harboring secrets. He had learned how to avoid any subject that might shed a light on his hidden world. He wondered what inner demons Torrey was battling.

The conversation was pleasant enough but mostly superficial. Matthew tried to dig into her past but was getting nowhere. Matthew felt like he was sparring with someone much smarter than he was, and it turned out that his intuition was correct when he asked about her acceptance into Stanford University and the medical school.

"School has always been easy for me because I have what you would call a photographic memory," Torrey admitted. "Most scientists doubt that the ability to recall every sight, sound, and event actually exists. I only know that if I see something in print, I can recall it verbatim during tests, so I always get near perfect grades. I prepared for the MCAT by reading a bunch of practice tests and official study materials. I found that the answer to almost every question on the MCAT was a repeat of something that I had read. Being a female, with grades and tests scores in the top 1%, and coming from a low-income family, I had my choice of medical schools. And, of course, I picked Stanford to be near my parents."

"There must be more to it than that," replied Matthew. "Even if you have a great memory, you have to be able to apply what you know to a set of facts."

"Well, my first-grade teacher convinced my parents to have me tested and they said my IQ is pretty high."

"How high?"

"They wouldn't tell me, but after the test my parents were being pressured to have me join Mensa. They refused and that was the last time it was mentioned in my presence."

Matthew was perplexed.

"Mensa is the high IQ society, right? I'm not sure how to phrase this, but I thought you said you went to community college after high school. If grades were not an issue, why did you do that? Why not come to Stanford as a freshman?"

"Stanford did offer me admission out of high school but not a full scholarship. My parents did not want me to take on financial aid loans. Plus, I wanted to live at home for those two years. My parents needed me."

"What do you mean?" asked Matthew.

There was a long pause. Torrey's eyes started to mist and her voiced dropped.

"My little sister died when I was fifteen. Ever since then my parents have wanted me to stay close and I have been happy to do so. I needed them too. After the two years of community college, my mother insisted that I get out of the house and live at college to get the full university experience. Fortunately, Stanford offered me a full need-based scholarship for the last two years of college. Then I earned a scholarship to the medical school."

Matthew was impressed with her achievements but felt Torrey's pain about her sister. "What happened with your sister? How did she die? Can you tell me?"

"Leia—we called her 'Princess' after Princess Leia of Star Wars fame—was diagnosed with an incurable and inoperable brain tumor called glioblastoma. It was very aggressive. She withered away before our eyes within months. Her last few days were excruciatingly painful for her—unbearable headaches—and the doctors said there was nothing they could do. California had yet to adopt any End of Life legislation like they had in states like Oregon. Her doctors refused to give Princess an injection or a lethal medication so that she could die in peace with all of us holding her hands. It was terrible because by the end she couldn't even swallow pain medication because her throat wouldn't stay open. There was no medication that could relieve her suffering." As she talked, she rolled up her sleeve to reveal the tattoo he had seen briefly at the White Coat Ceremony. It simply read '*Princess.*' "That's when I decided to become a physician."

"I'm so sorry!" said Matthew. They sat in silence for a few minutes.

In an attempt to lighten the mood, Matthew asked, "Didn't it hurt? The tattoo?"

"I'm not some delicate flower!" Torrey had turned her face away from

Matthew, but he could tell that she was rubbing tears from her eyes. Before he knew it, Matthew said in a voice so low that Torrey could barely hear, "My father was murdered when I was eight years old."

"Oh my God! Matthew! How terrible!" Now Torrey made no attempt to hide her tears. "Can you talk about it?"

Matthew surprised himself with his answer. "Actually, I've avoided talking about it with anyone for years. I think about it all the time, but I've never wanted to confide in anyone until right now. I feel you would actually understand the unbearable pain."

Torrey did not say another word. She just looked at Matthew and nodded for him to continue.

"It was a neighbor's son who lived up the street from us. I didn't know him. He was in his twenties. Wealthy family. From what we were told, he was a pothead. No job. Just lived off his parents. One day he broke into our house. He thought no one was home, but my dad walked in on him as he was rifling through the drawers in my parents' bedroom. The guy admitted in open court that he shot my father."

Torrey hugged Matthew and whispered, "I don't know what to say. I can't believe it." After another moment of silence, she added, "What happened to the jerk? I assume he was executed."

"Nope. My mother decided not to ask the DA to seek the death penalty. So, the guy pleaded guilty and was sentenced to life without parole."

Torrey was at a loss for words, so she simply uttered as her voice trailed off, "I hope he rots in prison."

Matthew thought it prudent to get both their minds on something else, something productive.

"I have an idea. I'm looking to put together a study group. You probably don't need it, but would you like to join?"

"As you saw in class today, I'm not very good with people. And I don't think I would be welcome in any group that involved that Indian guy."

"I was never going to ask that condescending idiot. But I do need to assemble a study group. I know I'm weak in the sciences and I need help."

Torrey looked at Matthew for several seconds. Then she looked up at the ceiling as she slowly spoke.

"What about this? You say you need help with the academics and I'm nervous about passing the hands-on aspects of the curriculum. I tend to lose my patience too quickly and, as my mom has always said, I don't play well with others in the sandbox. I can see how polished you are, and I suspect that your bedside manner will be perfect. Perhaps we can have our own private study group. I'll help you with the academic workload and you can help me with the social skills and the more practical aspects of patient interaction. I understand that they will bring in actors to play sick or obnoxious patients, and we will have to take their histories and diagnose them. My advisor says that the actors will try to shake us up, or mislead us, or just be obnoxious. I'm worried that I won't deal with that stuff very well."

Torrey lowered her voice and stared directly at Matthew. "Look, as Dirty Harry famously said, 'A person has got to know his limitations.' And I know mine. What do you think?"

"Do you really think you can help me with the academics?" asked Matthew. Torrey nodded.

"Okay, it's a deal," declared Matthew as they exchanged a high five.

Chapter Ten

Matthew and Torrey started a Saturday night ritual of take-out pizza and studying in the empty third floor of the medical school library in Lane Hall. They divided up the preparation in a most logical way—Matthew picked up (and paid for) the extra-large pepperoni and mushroom pizza and Torrey went ahead to the library and reserved 'their' table by the window overlooking the quad. Matthew ate his share of the pizza in small bites over a thirty-minute period. Torrey scarfed hers down before the books were open. She also planned the study agenda so that the evening would be the most productive. She usually started with identification and treatment of diseases because that required memorizing which drugs affected which organ systems. Torrey could tell that Matthew needed more help on this than any other subject.

They started with the most basic diseases like diabetes. To a layman, if you have diabetes, you take insulin. No such superficial analysis in medical school.

"Matthew, we have to come up with a way to remember the different classes of drugs for diabetes. There are several classes of type 2 diabetes medications and each works in a different way to control blood sugar levels." As she spoke, Torrey was penciling out a crude chart to organize the medications in a way that would be easy for Matthew to remember. "One class of medications might achieve the desired result by stimulating the pancreas to release more insulin. Let's write down the primary drugs in that class." Torrey did the writing while Matthew watched.

"Another class may work by blocking the action of enzymes in the stomach that breakdown carbohydrates. Another may inhibit the reabsorption of glucose in the kidneys. Some are taken by injection, others orally."

After they figured out a mnemonic to recall all of the medications on the two-page chart, Torrey then said, "Ok, now we need to go over the advantages and disadvantages of each diabetes medication depending on the age, sex, and condition of the patient." Matthew groaned.

While Torrey took charge of the book-learning part of their study sessions, Matthew controlled the meetings when it was time to prepare for the patient interaction and clinical phases of their education. Matthew had learned from his uncle that clinicians often have to care for patients who evoke feelings of frustration, irritation, and even anger. These patients are labeled as "difficult" and their negative behavior can interfere with the ideal doctor/patient relationship. Physicians have to not just cope with these people, they need to be proactive to avoid a cycle of poor communication which leads to poor medical results. Matthew knew he did not have the highest IQ in the world, but he had gathered something about bedside manner from his uncle. And his mother had made sure that Matthew grew up learning the social niceties and how to behave like a gentleman.

Torrey was as smart as a whip but obviously did not go to finishing school. To soften her behavior with mock patients and her insolence with actual clinical doctors, Matthew utilized role-playing to practice the different scenarios which they might encounter. Not only did he know it would help Torrey, but he actually enjoyed it.

"Let's pretend I'm a middle-aged man who presents with chronic pain in his lower back. I've been to many doctors and no one has been able to diagnose or treat the problem. I'm very upset with doctors in general and you in particular because you are saying there are no objective findings to support my subjective complaints. So here I am in your office and you walk in after reading my chart." Matthew pointed to his back at his belt line as he spoke. "Please doc, I don't need any more tests! Just give me something for the pain!"

Torrey thought for a moment and said, "Now sir, I can't prescribe pain medication without first knowing what is causing the pain. All of your tests are negative. There isn't much I can do under the circumstances. Maybe a psychiatrist could help."

Matthew raised his voice, "You think this pain is a figment of my imagination? I'm going to file a report on you!"

Torrey could not help herself. "I have a good idea where you could file that report. In fact—"

Matthew did not let her finish the sentence. "No, no, no. First of all, you've got to start by making a first good impression. Smile! Offer your hand to shake! Look the patient in the eye. You were looking out the window when the patient was talking."

"Second, rather than becoming defensive or rude, try to reflect his feelings. 'Gee Mr. So-and-so, you sound upset. You come to me complaining of physical pain and I'm suggesting a mental examination. I can see why that might make you angry. How about if I explain my thinking to you and you let me know if it makes any sense to you. Would that be okay?'" Torrey looked skeptical.

Matthew continued. "And finally, you've got to at least pretend that you support the patient and you want to help him with his pain. Say something like, 'I think you deserve a lot of credit for how well you have been coping with this pain. I would really like to help you going forward. Can we work together to solve this?'"

Torrey tried to protest. "C'mon Matthew, no real patient needs to be treated like a two- year-old."

"You wish. Just ask my uncle about that sometime. Besides, I hear they will try to trip us up in our clinical exams with really bizarre patient behavior. You have to be ready for anything."

Torrey sighed and said, "Okay, let me try it again." They tried it again, and by the third time Torrey sounded sort of compassionate, somewhat empathetic, and even a bit like she wanted to actually help the patient.

Torrey and Matthew spent many hours together during the school week discussing the assignments and substantive material. But their Saturday evening sessions were the longest and most grueling. One Saturday night in late September, Matthew's brain was fried after just a couple of hours. He felt too tired to continue so he asked Torrey if they could pick it up again the next day.

"You know I can't do that. I always go see my parents on Sunday."

"No problem. It was just a thought. Maybe when you return, we could get together."

"Well, I won't be home until late tomorrow. It's my Dad's birthday and I'll want to stay there after dinner until he goes to bed." After a brief silence, Torrey said with a slight smile,

"Hey, want to come with me? I've told my parents all about my study partner and my father would love to meet you!"

"Gee, I don't know. He wouldn't want a stranger there on his birthday."

"Believe me, he would. And you two could talk about baseball. He knows you played at Stanford. And he loves the San Francisco Giants. What do you say? It would mean a lot to him and I'd really appreciate it."

Matthew shrugged and forced a grin.

"If you truly think he wouldn't mind—that he would really like more company—then I'd be happy to come. Especially if it will make you happy. One condition—you let me see your bedroom."

"That sounds weird, but it's a deal. One other thing. I know you grew up in Southern California, but don't mention the despised and cheating Dodgers."

Chapter Eleven

The next afternoon, Matthew and Torrey hopped in Matthew's car for the 20-minute drive to the Jamison residence on the other side of Palo Alto. Matthew had stashed in the trunk a small florist bouquet of daisies for Torrey's mom and a birthday-themed envelope for her father.

Torrey turned to Matthew, "I want to warn you about my dad. He says what he thinks on everything from who was the greatest hitter of all time to which politicians should be run out of office. And by *which,* I mean *all.*"

"What a shock. I knew you had to come from somewhere!" quipped Matthew.

The farther they traveled from the beautiful Stanford campus and the closer they got to Torrey's East Palo Alto family home, the sketchier the neighborhoods became. It was hard to believe that the two areas were just a few miles from each other. Older homeless men and women aimlessly pushed shopping carts filled with meager possessions on cracked and buckled sidewalks. Cars in driveways were up on cement blocks, rusty axles protruding. On the potholed street just before the final turn onto Torrey's block, Matthew was somewhat startled to see groups of young toughs congregated in front of boarded-up storefronts. He glanced over at Torrey, who couldn't have looked more at ease, and wondered to himself what it must have been like growing up so close to potential danger and mayhem.

As advertised, Torrey's childhood house was an old, but well-kept, three-bedroom one-bath, clinker brick ranch house on a street with similar homes. The door was painted light yellow and the windows were framed with white trim. Torrey said that the neighborhood tract was built in the late 1940s. Despite the lack of wealth, there was pride of ownership on the entire block as seen by the brown but mowed lawns and tended flower gardens. The Jamison garden in front of the wooden porch had a nice variety of drought-resistant succulents. Matthew parked on the street and ran around the back of his 1965 partially restored, classic Mustang to open Torrey's door. She was already out and walking up the sidewalk before he got there. He didn't know why, but he was a little disappointed that she didn't allow him to act the gentleman. He watched her bound up the steps without so much as a glance back at him.

"Why should she wait? We're just friends," he muttered to himself. Matthew grabbed the presents out of the trunk and followed.

Torrey's parents welcomed Matthew warmly.

"We've heard all about you, Matthew," said Mrs. Jamison. "Torrey tells us you are her favorite study partner. Thank you for helping her so much!"

He gently handed the flowers to Mrs. Jamison. "These are for you." Matthew added, "Believe me. I'm getting far more help from her than she is from me. I'm very fortunate to know your daughter." After heartily shaking Matthew's hand, Mr. Jamison bellowed in a friendly way, "You two go amuse yourselves for 30 minutes. Dinner is at 4:30 sharp and then Sunday Night Baseball is at 5:30. Matthew, I have a seat reserved for you right next to me in the living room. You a fan of the Giants?"

"Well, I understand you are the biggest Giants fan in history."

"I'd like to think so. Ever since Bobby Thompson's homer!"

"Excuse me?" said Matthew with a blank look on his face.

Mr. Jamison looked perplexed. "You know. The 1951 World Series. The shot heard around the world!"

"Sorry," said Matthew, in a matter-of-fact tone.

"You're killing me man!" exclaimed Mr. Jamison with outstretched hands.

Mrs. Jamison jumped in.

"Dear, leave the young man alone. Not everyone knows about all things Giants."

"But this is Bobby Thompson!" he cried.

Matthew pulled the envelope out of his pocket and pressed it into Mr. Jamison's hand. "Happy birthday sir. I hope you can use these."

Mr. Jamison ripped open the envelope. "Giants tickets! For tomorrow's playoff game against those scum-sucking Dodgers! Are you kidding me!" He gave Matthew a Herculean thank-you bear hug.

Mrs. Jamison echoed her husband's earlier sentiment. "Yes Torrey, you and Matthew run along while I finish getting things ready. And no, I don't need your help. I can make your father's favorite dinner in my sleep."

Torrey grabbed Matthew's hand in a playful way and took him on the thirty-second tour of the house. Matthew couldn't help but notice the evangelical artifacts throughout that documented, in an understated but clear way, the religious beliefs of the family. A bust of Jesus by the fireplace. A praying hands sculpture on the coffee table. A Last Supper plaque over the dining room table.

After seeing the small backyard, Torrey then tried to lead him back to the living room. "Not so fast!" he declared. "Now would be a good time to see your room as promised."

"C'mon, it's just a room. Do you really want to invade my privacy?"

"Of course, I do," said Matthew with a mischievous look and a shrug of the shoulders. "Lead the way."

Off the hallway there was a single bathroom and three open bedroom doors. Matthew looked into the first bedroom and saw a little girl's room done all in pink with mountains of stuffed animals on the quilted bed.

"That was Leia's room," said Torrey. She gestured. "Mine is the one at the end."

Once inside, Matthew had to stop to take it all in. Although this was Torrey's room, every square inch was plastered with photos of and artwork by Leia. A shrine to her Princess. As Matthew walked around the small room, Torrey sat on the bed and whispered more to herself than Matthew, "I never want to forget anything about her."

Matthew didn't know what to say so he sat down on the bed next to her, put his arm around her, and gently pressed her head into his strong right shoulder. They didn't speak for several minutes. As they sat in silence, Matthew studied the décor. A hand-carved wooden sign quoted John 13:7, a saying that Matthew knew well from years of Sunday School—"Jesus replied, *you don't understand what I am doing. But someday you will.*" Matthew thought to himself, "To think that I used to believe that too."

Both had retreated into their own world of unbearable loss. Matthew looked down and saw tears gently rolling down her cheek. He tilted his head down just enough to kiss her on the forehead.

Chapter Twelve

The next few weeks at school were hectic. There were mid-year tests coming in December as well as a full-scale clinical exam on diagnosing a patient's condition based on a medical history. There was a five-day-long dead week after the last class until the battery of eight-hour tests, so Torrey and Matthew stepped up their study sessions. They started in the library at 8:00 a.m. and studied until noon, going through each discipline in excruciating detail. After a short lunch break, they quizzed each other on the substantive details that they had studied in the morning. The evening sessions were devoted to practicing for the clinical interactions with pretend patients.

Despite spending most waking moments together during the week before finals, Matthew and Torrey both seemed to understand that the shared tender moment at Torrey's house was best not repeated. They had work to do and they did it. By the time of the first examination, Matthew felt smarter than he ever had in his life. Of course, this was in large part to Torrey's attention to detail and her amazing memory. He was chock-full of obscure medical facts and data. And Torrey felt confident that she could handle whatever her mock patient threw at her. She just hoped that she would get an adult patient rather than a child with some dreadful or fatal disease.

When the exams were concluded, both felt that they had done as well as they possibly could. Matthew insisted on taking Torrey out for champagne and dinner to celebrate. They started with a toast to each other and by the time the bottle was empty, they had toasted to everything from 'three weeks of vacation!' to 'electing a young woman president!' After a meal of lobster and grilled vegetables, Matthew ordered coffee and a chocolate parfait to split.

Over his second cup of coffee, Matthew broached the idea of a visit to his house over Christmas break.

"Hey Torrey, you know how I met your folks? I would like to invite you to come visit me and my family over the holiday break. I've already asked my mom and she said she would be thrilled to have you as a houseguest. I know you'll want to spend Christmas with your folks but what about coming for a few days after that?"

"I don't know. Your mother wants you to herself I'm sure. And do you think it's a good idea for us to spend more time together than we already have?"

Matthew reached across the table and grabbed her hand.

"After spending all these months with you, I really can't imagine not seeing you for three weeks. Please, won't you come?"

Torrey gave a tiny nod of her head. "Okay. But you have to give me some information about your family. Tell me more about your mother. How did your parents meet?"

"Well, they met as sophomores at UCLA. As my mother tells it, they fell madly in love at a St. Patrick's Day party that they both had crashed. After that, they were inseparable. They got married right after graduation and lived in a small apartment while my father was busy trying to build a start-up company."

"I remember that I had to drag it out of you that you were raised in a rich neighborhood in LA. So, I presume your father was wildly successful?"

"Well he did eventually sell the company for a lot of money, but he used much of it to help other entrepreneurs and non-profit groups. After he sold the business, he did his volunteer work out of the house. That's how he happened to be home when he was murdered." Matthew paused for a moment to catch his breath. He then quickly changed the subject. "My mother actually inherited the house from her grandmother."

"How did that happen?" asked Torrey.

"Back in the day, regular working-class families could afford to live in Pacific Palisades. My great-grandmother grew up there and lived there her entire life. Her daughter Patricia, my grandmother, got divorced after a few years of marriage when my uncle TJ was six and my mother was just a toddler. So, the three of them went back home to live in the house. When TJ was away at college and my mom was a teenager, Patricia was killed in a car accident. So, my mother continued to live with her grandmother until she married my father. Later, when her grandmother was getting frail with age, my mother convinced my father to move back into the house so that they could take care of her grandmother. Despite his initial reluctance, my father took great joy in caring for my great-grandmother. After I was born, I know my father felt blessed to be in the house because he liked the big yard where he could play with me. My great-grandmother passed away at age 82 when I was a just a baby. But I feel like I know her through all the stories and pictures that my parents shared with me."

Torrey did not need to prod Matthew to continue. He spent most of the next hour regaling Torrey about the fun adventures he had with his father in the backyard. One of his favorite memories was when he was in the fort that he and his father had built.

"I was out there by myself one warm afternoon and suddenly my father, along with Uncle TJ, started pelting the fort with water balloons." Matthew was smiling as he continued. "The balloons started coming in through the windows and the door. I was getting soaked, so I made a run for it to the backdoor. I remember my father laughing hard as he and TJ chased me across the yard hitting me with balloon after balloon. Right before I got to the door, my mother locked the door barring me from entering. Through the window I saw the huge grin on her face. "I've never been so wet." Matthew's voiced trailed off. "And I've never had so much fun."

Torrey reached across the table and placed her hand over his.

Chapter Thirteen

Although it was only 6 pm, it was dark when Matthew arrived at Los Angeles International Airport on December 27 to pick up Torrey. He parked across from Southwest Airlines and went to the baggage carousel to wait for her to come claim her luggage. He stood off to the side to watch for her to descend on the escalator into the lower level of the terminal. Torrey was stuck on the moving stairs behind an older woman with a cane who was in no hurry to get to the bottom. Torrey was halfway down and scanning the room for Matthew when he called out.

"Torrey, over here!" She spotted him and waved.

When she finally was able to take a step, Torrey ran over to Matthew and gave him a big hug. "Matthew, how are you? It's only been about ten days, but it seems like forever since we finished our mid-term finals and started Christmas break!"

"I know. I hope you had a wonderful Christmas. Tell me, how are your folks? What did you do? Did you get any fun presents? Tell me all about it."

"I will, but later. First, what did you tell your mother about me? Will she be waiting at your home for us?"

"Of course. And don't forget, my uncle will be at the house tonight too.

65

They both are shocked that I invited someone to the house, especially because you are a *girl*," Matthew declared with a smile and air quotes. "I'm so glad that you agreed to come down here for a few days. Your parents got you for Christmas and now I get you through New Year's Day. I can't wait to show you around LA, and I have a fun surprise for us to do tomorrow."

Having left his trusty Mustang at school for the holidays, Matthew drove them home in his mother's Audi 8. He had taken the immense vehicle to make sure that there was enough trunk space for whatever luggage Torrey might bring. As it turned out, he could have used his dad's small MGB, which was still sitting in the garage. Torrey had brought just two small carry-on bags.

As they made the trip from LAX to Pacific Palisades along Pacific Coast Highway, Matthew acted as tour guide. "Just down there on the left is the famous Venice Beach. We have to come back this way and walk along the boardwalk while you're here. If we get lucky, your brain won't be able to process what your eyes are seeing. Once I was there during the summer and there was a guy juggling a chainsaw, while a girl in a micro-bikini stood on his shoulders."

"I'm not sure I want to be that lucky," said Torrey.

As soon as they entered Santa Monica, Matthew dropped down to Ocean Avenue so that Torrey could see the Ferris wheel on the pier. "We should go down there too," said Matthew. "I'll show you where my uncle and I like to eat lunch."

After a few more minutes of congested beach traffic, Matthew turned up the hill on Chautauqua and then right on Sunset Blvd. Torrey thought the area beautiful, but everything was turned up a notch after they turned left on Almafi Drive into the exclusive neighborhood where Matthew had grown up. Torrey imagined that this area was similar to the ritziest areas of Palo Alto. The irony did not escape her that most of these homeowners were probably the Hollywood rich and famous who shout about the need for income equality, but when the

TV cameras are off, they shield themselves from the riffraff behind iron fences, tall green hedges, and massive driveway gates. For some reason, she was glad that Matthew's family had lived in the area before it was so exclusive. After a few blocks and a left towards the mountains, Matthew finally slowed and pointed. The house was one of the few on the block that was entirely open to view from the street.

"Matthew, it's exquisite!" exclaimed Torrey as he stopped before turning into the driveway.

"Yes, I'm glad my mother decided to stay here after my father was killed. Uncle TJ thought she should sell the house and move out of town. My mother refused, saying that she was not going to be chased out of her family home. And she wanted me to be able to grow up here. The decision was made easier because the Nash family moved away right after the murder."

"Where did they live?"

Matthew pointed up the street. "See that house up there on the left? The one with the ten-foot high old-brick wall? That's the one."

"Where did they go?"

"Don't know or care. So long as they never come back."

"Well, I'm glad your mother didn't move you out of this house. I just love your property," she said as they pulled into the long, open, tree-lined driveway. The white, two story exterior of the house and some of the tall trees in the front yard were lit up with security lights. All four matching gables and the roof line were trimmed with miniature white Christmas lights. A pair of second-story Juliet balconies were filled with large potted poinsettias. Santa's sleigh and reindeer were spotlighted on the roof between two massive chimneys.

"Now that I'm here, I'm a bit nervous about meeting your mother and uncle." Even though the evening temperature was in the 50s, it felt like spring to Torrey compared to the cold weather in the Bay Area. Torrey was dressed in khaki shorts, gladiator sandals with leather straps around her ankles, and a long-sleeved cotton top.

"Do I look alright? Should I have dressed up more?"

"You look great as always," said Matthew. He unloaded Torrey's two small bags from the huge trunk. Matthew carried one in each hand as they walked up the stone steps towards the double front door. Mary Preston met them inside the entrance hall dressed in a holiday red dress and black pumps. "Torrey, so glad to finally meet you," she said while hugging Torrey.

"Good evening, Mrs. Preston," said Torrey.

"None of that. Call me Mary, won't you? Matthew has talked about you nonstop! Thank you so much for coming."

Uncle TJ, wearing a blue dress shirt and beige slacks, stood behind Mary with a wide grin on his face. "Hi Torrey, I'm Matt's uncle. You can call me TJ."

"Please, Torrey," said Mary as she motioned. "Let's go sit down in here."

Mary led them into a huge tastefully decorated living room where Torrey saw the biggest live Christmas tree that she had ever seen that was not in a shopping mall. Above the fireplace was a huge photo of Mr. Preston. There were burning candles on the mantle and a silver tea set and china cups on a side table. Vases filled with pink roses were scattered around the room. "May I pour you a cup of tea, Torrey?" Mary asked. "Dinner should be ready in an hour."

"Tea would be wonderful. Thank you." Torrey gestured around the living area and said, "Mary, I love all of these flowers. Wherever did you get them in the middle of winter?"

"Pink roses have always been my favorite. When Grant and I were first married, he struck a deal with a local florist to have them delivered to us every month. Where the florist gets them, I don't know." Mary had a faraway look in her eyes and added, "I have kept up the tradition."

They all chatted over tea until they sat down at the 14-foot-long mahogany dining table set with Wedgwood china and Lenox crystal. Mary didn't try to pretend that she had personally prepared the grilled halibut and vegetable salad. In fact, she insisted that the hired chef join them for chocolate crème brûlée and coffee at the end of the meal.

TJ questioned Matthew and Torrey about their studies and future plans. Matthew explained how he and Torrey helped each other prepare for the tests and clinical interactions with patients, but he always added that he was getting the better of the deal. Of course, Torrey disagreed and they both tried to one-up each other with examples of how the other was the more valuable partner. Having been through the rigors of medical school himself, TJ could see how combining their distinct strengths would make them both stronger students. They had passed every exam and clinic with flying colors.

Matthew was intentionally vague about his plans after medical school, but Torrey was totally focused.

"I intend to be a pediatric brain surgeon," said Torrey. "I want to have a practice where I can help families who can't afford the normal costs of complicated surgery. And if surgery is ineffective or not a viable option, I want to work with the family to provide whatever palliative care they want, including a dignified death."

TJ responded, "Thankfully the California legislature has emerged from the Dark Ages and recently passed the End of Life Option Act which makes it easier for terminal patients to choose when and where they will die. But there are still many people who can't get over the misconception that this is simply physician-assisted suicide—and that suicide is a sin. I have even heard the argument that the right to die would be abused. That people would seek this option prematurely if they are in distress. And some say physician-assisted death is contrary to the Hippocratic oath that doctors swear to uphold."

Torrey was not satisfied with the current law.

"The California statute doesn't go nearly far enough. There are all kinds of administrative hoops that patients and willing doctors have to jump through. Many hospitals and physicians refuse to participate for fear of missing a mindless bureaucratic step and exposing their practice to liability and fines. And Seconal, the drug that is used to cause the death, is extremely expensive and therefore out of reach for many families. I'm going to do what the patient and family want, regardless of what the politicians decree. Do you think the California legislature really cares about anything other than reelection? As far as the Hippocratic oath is concerned, yes doctors can extend lives with all the technology available but sometimes all they are doing is extending the suffering. That's not what I signed up for and I won't do it. Terminal patients want what we all want—a choice. They want the ability to choose a peaceful dignified death rather than a painful, miserable one. They want to be in control of their destiny."

Matthew interjected, "I have heard that the Catholic Archdiocese has lobbied heavily against any assisted dying legislation in California. They are concerned that such a bill might lead to death panels and impact the poor who may not get the care they need in the name of cost cutting. And they say that such bills change the way suicide is viewed across society in general, not just by the terminally ill."

Torrey's jaw clenched, and she was quick to respond.

"Baloney. There is no evidence that the poor would suffer any cutback in service. In fact, California is more than generous with its healthcare system to not only poor American citizens, but also to poor undocumented immigrants."

Torrey found the opposition to a dignified death preposterous. "The California law simply allows mentally competent, terminally ill patients to obtain a specific dose of a medication to end their suffering. Many groups are still opposing it and have filed appeals to have the law overturned. The

70

California Supreme Court will eventually rule on whether it can remain in effect.

"Think about this if you need another reason to expand the right to die. There was a case not long ago in California of a newlywed woman who had terminal brain cancer. She could not get the dose of medicine she needed in California, so she and her husband moved to Oregon to take advantage of that state's law allowing physician-assisted suicide. Does it make any sense that person would have to leave their home and family support system in order to escape a painful and degrading death?"

As the conversation and night wore on, the group retired to the patio. The outdoor propane heaters took the chill out of the night air. They didn't talk just about medicine. The four of them discussed everything from world tensions to sports. It became evident to Mary and TJ—what was already known to Matthew—that Torrey wasn't afraid to voice her opinion on any subject, even normally taboo issues such as politics and religion. And even though outspoken, she was articulate and well-versed no matter the discipline.

Mary was quite curious about Torrey and her relationship with Matthew. Matthew had never brought a girl home for dinner, much less for an extended stay. Even though some young women might have been overwhelmed by the Preston home and grounds, Torrey appeared confident and at ease. Matthew had told his mother about Torrey's childhood on the poorer side of Palo Alto and about Princess Leia. Mary thought Torrey might be a good match for Matthew despite their opposite backgrounds and personalities. And Matthew could not stop gushing about how smart she was. Was she too good to be true?

By midnight, TJ had gone home, and Mary had gone to bed. "I guess we should turn in," said Torrey. "I'm pretty tired."

"Okay," said Matthew. "You know where your room is, but I'll walk up with you." At the top of the stairs, Torrey looked at her bedroom door and then gave Matthew a quick kiss on the cheek. "Thank you again for inviting me. You have a wonderful family."

Torrey went into her room and closed the door behind her. She plopped down on the four-poster bed, wrapped herself in the puffy down comforter, and whispered to herself, "Seriously Torrey? You know this is impossible."

Chapter Fourteen

Early the next morning, Matthew led Torrey down a maze of wooden plank walkways at the Marina Del Rey harbor marina to Uncle TJ's boat. They passed fantastic vessels of all sizes and shapes. Torrey was astounded at the opulence of some of the largest yachts.

"Who owns these?" she asked.

"Not sure, but I have heard that very few of these mega-yachts ever get used. Most stay docked just like this all year round. Some of the smaller vessels go over to Catalina Island once or twice a summer. And you will notice that some young people actually live aboard their boats right here in the marina. I suppose it beats living in their parents' basement."

"So, TJ has a yacht?" asked Torrey.

"I'm not sure it's a yacht." Matthew stopped and pointed at a big white cabin cruiser with polished wood railings. "This is *The Preston Endeavor*. My uncle named it for my mom's foundation, but she has only been on it once. She and my father had always dreamed of taking a long boat trip and I guess this just is a painful reminder."

As they boarded, Matthew gestured to the dinghy hanging over the rear of the boat. "The cruiser is a nice 60-footer, but we're just going to take out this small motorboat that TJ has in case of emergencies. He has let me use it before."

With a chuckle, Matthew added, "And you know what they say—the only thing better than owning a boat is using someone else's."

"Are you sure about this?" asked Torrey as Matthew helped her into the narrow 10-foot aluminum craft. "When you said we were going whale watching, I thought you meant on one of those big ships that hold 100 people. It seems pretty rough out there for this little boat."

"Those commercial tours are for wimps. And by federal law, those tour boats aren't allowed to get too close or to chase the whales. I want you to see some whales close up. One time I saw a whale surface about twenty feet away. I've done this before and it's unbelievable."

They travelled in silence for a few moments while Torrey watched Matthew's serious expression while he steered the boat. "Hey Matthew, you said you hope we see whales. Here's a quiz question for you. What do you call a group of whales?"

Matthew laughed. "A pod, of course."

"Okay Mr. Smarty. What do you call a group of hippos?"

"Uh, is there really a name for that?"

"There most certainly is. The correct terminology is a 'bloat' of hippos."

"Seriously? Give me another one."

"Okay. What is a group of zebras called?"

After several ridiculous guesses, Matthew agreed that he was stumped. "I give up."

"A 'dazzle' of zebras."

"How do you know this stuff?"

Torrey just sweetly smiled as she explained, "I read an animal picture book when I was four years old."

"Well aren't you a clever girl. No more questions. Please just keep your eyes peeled for whales!"

"How do you know we'll even see any whales?"

"Well, there is no guarantee but every year the Gray whales in the Gulf of Alaska migrate to the waters off of Baja California. They pass by Los Angeles starting in December. They mate and give birth in warm shallow lagoons in the first part of the year. Then they begin the nearly 6000 mile north bound trip back to the arctic. And it's rare but we sometimes also get huge Blue whales, Fin whales, and Orcas coming through here."

Through the early morning marine layer, they slowly motored out of the harbor until they were clear of the breakwater. Torrey sat on the bench seat near the middle of the boat while Matthew sat in the rear in order to use the tiller. Matt had to almost yell to hear himself over the noise of the outboard engine. They headed south towards Long Beach staying only a few hundred yards offshore. "You know what those big whale watch boats are good for? When you see one slow down, you know that they have spotted some whales. But I don't see any out here yet. Let's see what this thing will do." Matt opened the throttle. The boat jumped up out of the water and within seconds they were bumping through the choppy water at top speed. It wasn't exactly warm yet and cold water sprayed every time the boat hit a wave. Matthew had told her that it was going to be a hot day due to the Santa Ana winds from a high- pressure system over the inland deserts, but so far it was only 65 degrees. Torrey wished she were wearing more than cut-offs and a Stanford tank top. She looked under the seats for life preservers, hoping to put one on for extra wind protection. There weren't any. However, the marine layer soon dissipated, the sun came out, and Torrey started to enjoy the open water and the view of the coastline. She marveled at the pristine sand beaches of Manhattan Beach, Hermosa Beach, and Redondo Beach. They saw lots of surfers and a small pod of dolphins playing in the waves. As they passed the Palos Verdes Peninsula jutting out into the bay, they saw small figures playing golf on the Trump course.

"Do you play golf?" yelled Torrey.

"Nope. Never had the time before, and I really don't have the desire to learn now."

Torrey smiled and replied, "Maybe you can pick it up when you are a big-shot doctor in Beverly Hills." They both laughed at that one. They went as far south as San Pedro and then Matthew said, "Well I guess we won't see any whales today. Let's head back." He made a tight U-turn and headed north back toward the harbor.

"This was still fun. And think how great it would be to do this on a beautiful summer day."

Matthew responded, "Except that there are no whales here in the summer. By then they are all back in Alaska."

Torrey suddenly let out a muffled cry and pointed ahead of the boat. "What was that?" In the far distance a geyser of water shot up into the air directly in front of the boat. They immediately saw two more spouts. "Oh boy!" shouted Matthew. "They're coming right at us!" He shut off the engine.

"Where are they? They're not spouting anymore!", whispered Torrey.

"Don't worry. Just keep watching. They have to come up for air every few minutes. They will surface soon and then we'll see them again."

"I'm not worried about not seeing them. I'm worried about them getting too close to us."

"Don't worry about that. They know we're here. I just hope they come up before they pass us by."

The two sat in silence, both scanning the water for any sign of the whales. The boat was drifting slowly farther away from the shore. Suddenly the spouts reappeared about fifty yards away, along with three giant dorsal fins. "Uh oh," said Matthew. "Those aren't gray whales!"

"What are they?" Torrey asked.

Before Matthew could reply, and without any warning or sound, a 25-foot mature Orca whale breached on the right side of the small boat. Matthew guessed that at least half of its body cleared the surface of the water. The sound when the whale belly-flopped two feet from the bow was like a tremendous explosion. Before he could brace himself, the boat violently tipped, and Matthew was thrown into the water. All he had time to do was to yell, "Hold on Torrey!"

Torrey didn't have to be told twice. She grabbed either side of her bench seat with both hands. As the boat lurched back and forth, she had a clear view of the other two massive black bodies with distinctive white patches as they passed directly under the boat. The orca that had breached was now between Matthew and the boat. And the huge mammal for some reason decided to stick around and investigate the overboard human. Its tall dorsal fin jutted out of the water like a tower and its right pectoral fin slapped the water repeatedly. For all his athletic talent, Matthew had never mastered swimming and he was now beginning to panic in the seasonably cold water. He could not make his way around the lolling whale and he knew he could not tread water forever. The spray from the blowhole was getting in his eyes and the sound was almost deafening.

"Matthew, what should I do?" yelled Torrey. "I don't see a life preserver in here! And there are no oars!"

"I know. Just stay there! I'm going to try to go around this guy!" Matthew had an epiphany and changed his mind when he saw the monstrous mammal opening and closing its jaws—he prudently decided to dog-paddle in the other direction.

As Matthew slowly and awkwardly began to make his way around the flukes of the whale, Torrey saw that the other orcas had turned, and two great white shark-like fins were heading toward Matthew. One's dorsal fin was curved and bent over while the other one was smaller but straight up.

Matthew could not get to the boat and so Torrey decided that the boat would have to go to him. Without saying a word, she lowered herself into the ocean, put her hands near the propeller of the outboard engine, and began to kick her feet. She guided the lightweight aluminum boat over the submerged back of the whale near the tail where there were a few feet of clearance. As soon as the boat was within reach of Matthew, they both climbed in. They stared at each other for a few seconds as the orcas circled. Matthew had a stunned look on his face.

A big smile crossed Torrey's face as she said, "Wow, that was fun. When can we do this again?"

✒

Although they were shivering from the wet and the cold, Matthew and Torrey were giggling like two fifth graders at recess as they headed back to the marina. They found humor in everything from the sputtering engine to three awkward-looking stand-up paddle boarders who kept falling into the surf. And Matthew didn't mind that Torrey's tank top was wet and clinging.

As they dried off on the deck of TJ's cabin cruiser, Matthew couldn't stop thanking her for her bravery and quick thinking. Torrey would have none of it.

"To paraphrase JFK, *a person does what she must*. And besides," she said with calculated coolness, "don't you know? That's just how I roll with killer whales." Wanting to deflect the conversation away from herself, Torrey asked in a mocking way, "How can it be that you don't know how to swim?"

All of a sudden Matthew's demeanor changed from light-hearted to somber.

"My dad told me a few days before he died that he was going to teach me to swim. We actually had a plan to go to the public swim at the Boys Club for five Saturdays in a row. He told me that once I got good enough, he would take me to the beach to try bodysurfing. After he was killed, I never got around to it. In the back of my mind I always thought that swimming was something we were supposed to do together."

"Oh Matthew, I'm sorry for bringing that up."

"You didn't know. And believe me, when I was next to that whale, it crossed my mind that I should have gotten around to it."

All the way back to Santa Monica in the car Matthew spoke with tears in his eyes about the loss of his father. Torrey was moved to hear him talk so passionately. She knew she was with someone who could understand how she felt about the loss of her sister. She tried to keep from sobbing, but she couldn't.

The rest of Torrey's stay with the Prestons was enlightening. She accumulated all manner of stories and tidbits about Matthew's boyhood and the strong bond between mother and son.

They had casual lunches around the pool and deep but enjoyable conversations at the evening dinner table. In between, Matthew showed Torrey some of his favorite haunts. They spent a full day at the Getty Museum, just a short drive from Matthew's home. Torrey had fun making use of her high school and college art history classes, and did her best to explain to Matthew the deeper meaning behind some of the famous works of art.

The two of them met Uncle TJ at Big Dean's on the Santa Monica pier one afternoon for beer and people watching. She could see what Matthew meant by his declaration that a good table during good weather would guarantee seeing more *look at me* costumes per capita than even in Hollywood. There were full-body tattoos and piercings everywhere. There was no shortage of white guys who were rapper or bad-ass gang-member wannabes; twenty-something girls who wanted to create the impression they were teenage hookers; and skinheads dressed in skinny jeans and stilettos.

TJ asked for more details about their medical training than he could get during a dinner at his sister's house. The three of them talked less about the substantive education than about the dynamics of learning and the culture of doctoring. It was clear to Torrey that Dr. Wilson not only treasured his own practice, but he also loved the fact that Matthew was going to become a member of the medical brethren. The mutual adoration between Matthew and TJ was obviously beyond a typical uncle-nephew relationship. Torrey had a feeling that the two of them would do anything for each other.

The more Torrey got to know Matthew and his family, the fonder she became of them. Now that Matthew had confided in her about the magnitude of his loss, she understood that many of his prior comments about life and living were made through the filter of traumatic loss. She recalled a conversation in the dorm lounge about the news that a fourth-year medical student had been killed by a drunk driver who had crossed the center line. Some of the dorm residents were in the kitchen discussing the news. Matthew and Frank Miller had gotten into an argument about punishment.

"Can you imagine the suffering of the family of the deceased student?" Matthew asked in a rhetorical way.

Frank replied in a patronizing tone, "Don't be so judgmental Matthew. People make mistakes."

Matthew had gone off on Frank. "The drunk driver committed murder and should be punished as one."

"You need to lighten up man! The guy's going to lose his license and his life will be ruined. Isn't that enough? Besides, the prisons are already overcrowded. We don't have room for drunk drivers."

Matthew began his reply in a steady but firm voice. "I'm certain you have never suffered the loss of a loved one at the hands of another. How else is it possible that you're so callous toward the victims of these criminals? Do you realize that our classmate has a family? That they had dreams for their son? That instead of watching him become a doctor and a man, they had to watch him lying brain dead in the hospital room while he was kept alive with machines? That they had to eventually make the decision to remove life support? You say this felon made a *mistake*. His blood alcohol level was .271 which is four times the legal limit. It was not a *mistake* that he got himself drunk knowing he was going to have to drive himself home from the bar. MADD says that victims of drunk driving crashes often receive a death sentence or a life sentence in a wheelchair, but the offenders rarely do. I'm so sick of this do-gooder mantra that the perpetrators of crimes deserve our sympathy more than the victims of the crimes." By this time Matthew was glaring and almost shouting. "And vehicular manslaughter by a drunk driver is a crime the same as pre-meditated murder. The death sentence should be imposed, and I would happily be the one to pull the switch."

With that, Matthew had stormed out of the lounge.

Torrey had been taken aback at the time. But now she understood.

Although she was only a guest in the Preston home for a few days, Torrey also got to interact with Matthew's mother in a way that is only possible by being in the same house day and night. Mary was warm and hospitable, but Torrey recognized a protective layer surrounding her due to the loss of her husband. Matthew had that same veneer. At times she thought his shell was getting thinner but at other times she was certain that he kept dark secrets, just as she did.

Chapter Fifteen

After the holiday break, it was back to the grinding existence of students at an elite medical school. One of the most challenging courses for Matthew was anatomy. It wasn't just the impossibility of learning the magical integration of the human organs and systems from a book, it was also the gruesomeness of the laboratory dissection of cadavers. As Matthew quickly realized, viewing a photo or diagram of a kidney in a book is much different than seeing and handling one in person.

In addition to the elderly folks who generously agreed to donate their bodies to science, another source of bodies in the Center for Clinical Sciences Research basement was from what the professor in charge of the anatomy lab called *donor cycles*. Dr. Travis Pom explained to the anxious students in the depths of the medical building that many of the donated organs and bodies come from motorcycle riders. As Dr. Pom put it, "A motorcycle crash is the most likely way to relocate a rider's organs into someone else's body. In fact, studies show that in those states that pass strict helmet laws, the number of available donor organs goes down. A Michigan State University study quantified the data which showed that while helmet laws save lives of motorcyclists, helmet-less riders prevent the deaths of many individuals on organ transplant waiting lists." As Dr.

Pom gestured to the bodies on the 22 slabs in front of the students, he added, "So here is a way that young reckless motorcyclists are helping others to live. Only a few lucky people ever get to see what you will see in this hallowed room. Fewer still ever get to do what you will do here. So, take advantage of the good will, and bad luck, of these unfortunate souls and soak up the knowledge."

Torrey could barely concentrate on what Dr. Pom was droning on about as she looked around the windowless room. "No wonder they call this *the dungeon*," she thought. Despite the bright lights and contemporary furnishings, it seemed cold and dank.

The small group from Dr. Britsky's class was assigned to rotate together through the various laboratory classes. When the group was asked to divide up into working dissection pairs, Torrey and Matthew found each other without a word—which was probably fortunate because the others in the group were still shunning Torrey for her euthanasia diatribe as if she had a scarlet *Dr. Death* emblazoned on the breast pocket of her scrubs. That was fine with Torrey. She would have done fine without any lab partner at all if Matthew were not in her group.

The lab smelled of preservative, which was off-putting. A few of the students had to regularly leave the room for fresh air until they got used to the assault on their senses. Matthew did not want to appear weak in front of Torrey, so he determined that he was going to stay in the room no matter what. He just hoped that he didn't faint when they actually opened the body bags to begin their work. "This is a tradition by which physicians have been trained for hundreds of years," he thought to himself as he put on his surgical gloves. "If they did it, so can I."

The body sprawled out in front of them on the stainless-steel table was a twenty-three- year-old white male whose skull was cracked open from an impact with a cement freeway divider at high speed. The rest of the corpse was in perfect shape. Matthew stared at the head and thought about what a bullet must have done to his father's skull. Torrey sensed Matthew's unease and sought to refocus his attention.

"Matthew, how do you want to divide this up? We have a list of all these muscles, nerves, and blood vessels that we're supposed to find and identify. What do you want to do first?" Both of them stood still staring down at the corpse.

Dr. Pom walked over and saw the hesitation at their table. "Mr. Preston and Ms. Jamison, what seems to be the problem?"

"No problem sir," said Torrey. "We were just trying to decide how to change the position of the body so that we could start on the back."

"Very good, Ms. Jamison. Your intuition is spot on. I imagine your strong friend can manage to turn the body. Is that right, Mr. Preston?"

Matthew steeled himself, reached down, and flipped the dead motorcyclist. He looked up for the professor's approval, but Dr. Pom was already on his way to the next table.

Once the cadaver was face down, Torrey watched with curiosity as Matthew picked up a scalpel and examined it under the light. He lowered the scalpel to the body and bent over so that his face was inches away from the knife. Torrey's eyebrows raised, her eyes widened, and she leaned in to improve her line of sight. Just before he was going to cut into the body, Matthew jerked his head up and held out the scalpel to Torrey. He said, "Where are my manners! Ladies first! After all, you're the one who is going to be a surgeon."

Torrey snorted but did not flinch.

"You can wipe that smirk off your face. Be prepared to be amazed," she replied dryly. Matthew stood back; his hands stuck deep in his pockets.

She took several shallow breaths, placed the scalpel just above the shoulder blade, and pressed down. Torrey got used to the scalpel by making tiny cuts down the back to the waistline. It wasn't as easy as it might seem to cut through the skin. Once she got the hang of exerting significant downward force, the scalpel easily cut into the bright yellow subcutaneous fat and then into muscle. She said to Matthew, "Hey, I'm doing some actual doctor stuff!"

Once she grasped the excitement of wielding a scalpel, Torrey was loath to let Matthew take a turn. She used the scalpel as a pointer and identified for Matthew the various layers of the skin and the organs that were beginning to show themselves. Matthew tried to playfully push her aside, feigning an interest in giving it a go, but Torrey was now entranced with the open skull and the brain matter that was visible.

"Matthew, take a look at this! Notice how you can see the three parts of the brain. Here is the stem; here is the cerebellum; and this must be the cerebrum because you can see it is divided into these four lobes." She then gently turned the body's head so that the left side of the neck was in plain view. She drew an imaginary line up the neck to the brain as she spoke. "This is the carotid artery that supplies oxygenated blood to the brain! Isn't that unbelievable?"

"How do you know all of this?"

"We were assigned an anatomy book. Here's an idea. Read it!"

Torrey finally stepped aside, and Matthew reluctantly took his turn. While he was cutting, it struck Matthew that he was excited to be educated on the inner workings of the body. Maybe he could learn something that could help with the care and treatment of Ted Nash.

Matthew had mixed feelings as the end of his first year of medical school drew near. He was happy that he was passing his courses, with flying colors no less, and that he was a step closer to getting himself into the medical clinic at

San Quentin. Another positive was that he had become quite fond of Torrey. He was certain that he was getting the better end of the deal by studying with her. In fact, he doubted that he could have made it through the first year without her. A few of his classmates had dropped out and Matthew was grateful that he was not one of the casualties.

On the other hand, although he knew that his ultimate goal of killing Ted Nash was righteous and morally correct, he was disturbed by the mounting feeling that his life as a doctor in training was a fraud. All of the other students talked incessantly about what kind of physicians they wanted to be and how they were going to save the world's sick with their healing hands. Even Torrey bordered on annoying when she babbled on about her future life as a brain surgeon. She could not understand how Matthew was not able to articulate what he wanted to do with his medical career. Obviously, he could not tell her that his interest in medicine was finished the minute that the body of Ted Nash was buried in the cold earth.

Despite his double life, Matthew was a realist. He knew in his heart that his childhood fantasies of shooting Nash in the head were not going to work in real life. It would devastate his mother if he were caught and convicted of murder. And Uncle TJ would be heartbroken to learn that Matthew's interest in medicine was feigned from the beginning. He had to figure out a way to kill Nash without raising undue suspicion. Fortunately, the simplest answer is usually the best one.

Over time it dawned on Matthew that doctoring would not only be an entrée to the prison, it would give Dr. Matthew Preston the opportunity to treat Nash in the infirmary with whatever drug Matthew wanted to administer. If a drug caused Nash's death, who would know? Who would care?

So, in addition to his required first year courses, Matthew jumped ahead to study physiology, pathology, and pharmacology. He spent surreptitious hours in the medical library searching for information concerning drug interactions and contraindications. Most of the books and materials focused on which medicines might help cure which diseases or conditions. But Matthew was more interested in what medicines, if administered in the wrong dose, or to the wrong patient with the wrong disease, could cause death. He was making a list that he kept in the bottom drawer in his dorm room desk. He expected to make use of the list one day, then he could end the charade and get on with his life.

"So, Matthew, what are you going to do this summer?" Torrey asked one evening as they were preparing for final exams.

"Nothing. I'm going to sit around and rest my brain," said Matthew. "What about you?"

"I imposed upon one of the school's neurosurgeon professors to let me shadow him so that I can watch him do his rounds at the hospital. He says that I might even be able to observe him do a brain surgery operation on one of his patients. Won't that be cool?"

"Oh yes. You're the lucky one."

"C'mon Matthew. This is exciting stuff. Don't you want to do something this summer to get some practical experience?"

"I need a break. We only have a few short weeks off before second year and I need to recharge my batteries. And don't forget, we have to take the Step 1 board exams at the end of second year so next year is going to be super long."

"I know, I know. I'm not going to be a pest about it, but I wish you had a practice specialty in mind so that you could get as excited as I am about acquiring a medical license and saving lives."

"Don't worry about me. I'll do my part to make the world a better place."

Torrey did not want to argue. "Will I see you at all this summer?"

"I would really enjoy that. Do you think you could come back down to LA for a few days?"

"I was actually thinking you could come stay at my house for a week or two. My parents liked you and I want to stay close to them this summer. What do you think?"

Matthew grinned. "Did they really like me? What did they say?" He pushed her shoulder playfully. "What did they like about me? Details! Details!"

Torrey started to laugh. "They thought you were okay. Nothing special. So, do you want to come or not?"

"I would love to come see them." He gently touched her hair. "And you too."

Chapter Sixteen

Fresh off their short summer break, the second-year students at Stanford Medical School were ready to get back to the business of learning. The second-year classes were even more daunting than those of the first year. In addition to mind-numbing courses in neuroscience, respiratory medicine, endocrine and reproductive medicine, as well as advanced classes in immunology and pharmacology, there was the ever-present stress of unit exams which would determine whether they could continue as medical students. Torrey and Matthew coordinated their required and elective courses. They wanted to continue the successful partnership that had culminated with them both receiving nearly the highest first-year scores in the entire class.

Although most clinical rotations did not start until the third year of medical school, the second year did offer some opportunities for extra training in certain areas of interest. Torrey wanted to do anything she could to give her a leg up on her competition for a third-year rotation in surgery, and she needed help.

Hand-eye coordination is essential for a baseball player. It also comes in pretty handy if you want to be a surgeon. Matthew had the gift, Torrey did not. That presented a problem because it was Torrey who wanted to be a brain surgeon.

"Matthew! Are you in there?" Torrey yelled as she banged on Matthew's dorm room door. "Matthew!"

"Yes! It's open!" Matthew yelled back through the closed door.

Matthew was sitting at his desk looking through his *Neuroscience* textbook. When Torrey was safely inside, she shut the door behind her. She made no effort to conceal her excitement. "Look at this," she commanded as she shoved a flier in front of Matthew. It was a list of elective one-day courses that were available to second-year students. "There are two great classes we could take to improve our surgery skills. Then when we do our surgery rotation, we will be more experienced, and we'll stand out."

"But Torrey, you're the one who wants to be a surgeon. I never said that's what I wanted to do."

"I know, but you're an athlete. And you said you played lots of video games as a teenager. You can give me pointers on how to work with my hands."

"Look!", she said again as she pointed to the course description. "The first one teaches us how to suture. Every doctor has to have that skill. Even laymen should know the basics. Suppose we are out in the woods and I fall on a rock and cut my leg wide open. Wouldn't you want to know how to sew me up to stop the bleeding?" Matthew just looked at her. "And we get to practice on pigs' feet!"

"Oh boy," deadpanned Matthew.

"And see in this other course we get to try out the Da Vinci. I read about it a couple of years ago. It's a surgical system with four robotic arms. The surgeon never touches the patient. Instead, the surgeon sits at a console, sort of like a video game, and controls the robot's hands to make the incisions. The surgeon has a 3D high-definition view of the surgical site for enhanced surgical precision. It's supposed be less invasive than traditional surgery because the robot can make smaller and more precise movements than can a human hand. And the range of motion is far greater than a human wrist." Torrey straightened her right arm and rotated her wrist as far as it would go as she spoke. "We would get the opportunity to use the robot on a simulated human body."

After a short pause, Torrey almost shouted, "This is the future of surgery and we would get to practice with it!"

Matthew knew by now there was no sense in further protest.

"Okay, okay. I don't know how much help I'll be, but I'll go with you to the suturing class if you want. But I'm not doing the robot class. Let me know how that goes."

Torrey gave him a light hug. "Thank you! The suturing will be fun, you'll see!"

Before they were allowed the privilege of suturing pigs' feet, Torrey, Matthew, and the other aspiring surgeons were asked to gather around a table full of bananas. The instructor, a fourth-year medical student who looked like she would rather be anywhere else in the world, picked up a ripe banana and partially peeled it, exposing one side of the flesh. Without speaking, she then held the banana upside down so that the loose flaps of peel fell back into their original positions. Within sixty seconds, she sutured up the peel along the seam so that the peel stayed in place. It looked pretty straightforward.

It wasn't. Matthew and Torrey took a couple of bananas back to their table which was stocked with two suturing kits, each containing a curved needle that looked like a fish hook, some medical-grade nylon thread, a needle driver to hold and push the needle, and some diagrams of several types of knots.

"Now how did she do that?" Torrey said aloud to herself as they looked at their supplies.

"Well the first thing we have to do is tie one end of the thread to the needle,"

Matthew said. "And this drawing says we are supposed to use a square knot. Can you do that?"

Torrey looked unsure. Matthew was amused. "Didn't you do Girl Scouts or Brownies or something like that?"

"Are you kidding? I won't even eat a Camp Fire mint on principle."

Together they tied the knot, and then Torrey picked up the needle with the needle driver and tried to push the needle through the banana skin. After some effort, she got the needle to pierce the skin but was not able to smoothly bring the needle up through the adjoining piece of peel. Matthew placed his right hand over hers and rotated her wrist so that the tip of the needle popped up on the other side of the seam. "Hey we did it!" exclaimed Torrey. As she spoke, she jerked up the needle driver so that the needle and the entire suture pulled loose. The hook of the needle jabbed into the back of Matthew's hand.

"Are you serious?" Matthew stated impassively as the blood started to flow.

"Don't be such a baby. I told you this was going to be an adventure. Let's finish the rest of this banana so we can start on the pigs' feet. They say that pig and human skin is very similar!"

"Oh joy," said Matthew.

The dead skin on the anatomy lab cadavers is impassive compared to warm, living human flesh. But before medical students are allowed to suture actual injured humans, working on pigs' feet is the next best thing. Pigs and humans have many similar genetic characteristics and, fortunately for future patients, medical students can practice on pig skin which behaves much like the skin on a human forearm or leg.

Each pair of students in the suturing course were given an array of scalpels, in addition to the suturing equipment. The course instructor demonstrated that different wounds required different kinds of stitching. The eager medicos were shown a number of suturing techniques in addition to the most common running stitch and the simple interrupted stitch. Torrey and Matthew took turns with the scalpels making different kinds of cuts and gashes into the several pigs' feet on their table. Then they practiced. The prior work on the banana peels was of some help but the feel of the needle as it penetrated the pig skin was fundamentally dissimilar. With Matthew's encouragement, Torrey got the idea that the trick was to use both hands to firmly grasp the needle holder, then to gently insert the hooked needle into the correct position. Then she simply had to rotate her wrist fully to complete the stitch. Matthew thought she was proficient after an hour, but Torrey wanted to use the entire three-hour course to suture as many feet as possible. She used her scalpel to make short shallow incisions to practice a running stitch. She made long deep incisions to practice continuous interlocking sutures. She even stabbed her scalpel into the soft flesh and then dragged along the bone to simulate a knife fight wound in order to work on her interrupted suture technique. Matthew marveled at her dedication, but also cringed at her aggressive use of the scalpel.

When all of the other teams had gone home, and the course instructor was ready to turn out the lights, Torrey reluctantly put away her surgical tools and cleaned up her space. "Matthew, thank you so much for coming to this with me. I know surgery isn't really your thing, but you're a natural! I could practice for years and probably not be as good as you are already."

"You will be a wonderful surgeon. Your patients will be very lucky to have you."

Torrey did not let Matthew off the hook. "Matthew, you've completed more than a year of medical school and you're doing great. You have all kinds of natural skills that would serve you well in almost any specialty. You must have given thought to what kind of medical practice you want to have. You must know what kind of patients you want to serve. There must be something driving you to become a doctor! What is it?"

93

Matthew glanced at the instructor who was anxious to leave but also interested in overhearing Matthew's answer. Matthew whispered, "Let's walk and talk."

After they were outside and out of earshot of the nosy instructor, Matthew slowed his pace and took a deep breath. He thought to himself that he was going to have to tell Torrey sometime about his post-medical school employment plans. He didn't want his eyes to give anything away so, while he looked up at the night sky, Matthew nonchalantly declared, "I'm thinking of working as a prison doctor."

Torrey whipped her head around and looked at him with big eyes. "A what doctor?"

Matthew tried to sound as casual as possible. "You know. A doctor who works at a prison and treats the inmates."

"You're joking, right?"

"No, not at all," Matt protested. "I've looked into it. Great pay, banker's hours, and unbelievable benefits. Plus," said Matthew as he tried to look sincere, "don't you think that everyone deserves good medical care?"

"Seriously? Where is this coming from? I've never once heard you mention your desire to help the prison population. And honestly, I'm a little shocked to hear that you have such an interest in light of," she began to stammer, "well I mean, due to the fact that, well, your father!"

"I know it sounds a little strange. And I may not do it forever. But I expect that I can have a real impact, in a relatively short period of time, on making the world a better place."

Much to his surprise, Matthew found that he had a different, more engaged attitude during the first months of the second year of medical school. Torrey's elation about learning new things was infectious. By the middle of the second quarter he was thinking that doctoring might, eventually, be a worthwhile career, not just a means to an end. He was taking a deeper interest in the teachings. And he was thinking of Torrey as much more than a study partner. He was having some fun.

That all came to an end on October 30.

Uncle TJ texted Matthew with an urgent message to call him ASAP. Matthew could not imagine what could be so important. He had spoken to his mom just a few days ago and she sounded okay. Matthew called back between classes. He felt the blood rush from his face as TJ spoke.

"Matt, I am so sorry to tell you this. Ted Nash's family has just filed a petition to get him released from prison."

"Wait ... *what?*"

PART III

Chapter Seventeen

"Your mother just called me. She heard from the district attorney who handled the Ted Nash case. Apparently, Nash's lawyer, Greg Murtaugh, has just filed papers with the State asking that Nash's sentence be commuted on the grounds that he is rehabilitated and is no longer a danger to society. They are also suggesting that he has some kind of illness that requires he be released to the care of his own doctor."

"That's impossible! He was sentenced to life in prison without parole! How can they change that now?" shouted Matthew.

"I know, I know. The district attorney is appalled too and wants to meet with your mother about this as soon as possible. I am going to go with her, and I assume you want to go also."

"Of course. How's my mom taking this?"

"She's in shock. I'm headed over there right now to be with her. See you when you get down here."

Matthew texted Torrey and said he unexpectedly had to go to Los Angeles for a few days and would she please tell his professors that there was an emergency at home to which he had to attend. He included with his message that he would tell her all about it when he returned.

He then jumped in a cab to get to the San Jose airport so that he could get the next flight to Los Angeles. On the way to the airport and in the terminal while waiting for his flight, he got online and researched the absurdity of a murderer requesting an early release from prison. He was shocked to learn that there had been dozens of vicious killers whose sentences had been commuted or shortened by governors with questionable agendas or favors to repay. He noticed that often the governors signed the release orders on their last day in office, so they would never have to answer to victims' rights groups or to the families of the murder victims.

He read about a case in Michigan about a man who was convicted of first-degree, premeditated murder. He was sentenced to life without parole. Years later, the governor signed his release papers over the vigorous opposition of the murder victim's family.

He read about a robber who shot a bank guard in Illinois. The robber was sentenced to life without parole. The governor signed a clemency order despite robust resistance from the guard's family. The guard's youngest son was quoted as saying, "This petition came out of the blue. Our 28-year ordeal continues to this day."

There were many others and Matthew came to understand that a sentence of 'life in prison without the possibility of parole' is no guarantee that the murderer will never be let free. He wished someone had told his mother this when she was deciding whether to seek the death penalty.

Matthew found his mother and Uncle TJ in the living room. Mary's eyes were red from crying. She was shivering as if she were freezing to death. Matthew ran to her and embraced her. They held each other without speaking just as they had sixteen years ago right after the murder. In fact, to Matthew it seemed like the murder was happening all over again. His mother again was sad. Matthew again was angry. As he hugged his mother, he felt the old rage, stronger than ever, roiling inside.

The three of them sat together while Mary recounted for Matthew and TJ the gist of the conversation she had with District Attorney Livingstone.

"Livingstone said that the Nash family had contributed a ton of money to our new governor's campaign and, now that he was elected, they want something in return for all that cash—the release of their son." Mary continued. "I asked, 'how is that possible?' She said that the State is under a lot of pressure to alleviate prison overpopulation, so parole boards are more lenient, and the governor is commuting more sentences."

Matthew interrupted.

"I can see the argument for early release of marijuana possession inmates, but murderers? What did she say about that?"

"She'll have to explain it in our meeting. Frankly, I couldn't concentrate on anything after she said that Nash could be getting out."

They discussed until midnight the broken criminal justice system and how victims' rights have become secondary to criminals' rights in today's society. Before Mary was helped up the stairs to bed, they decided on one thing only— they would meet the next day with the district attorney to tell her that they would do whatever was necessary to oppose the petition for release, including attendance and formal opposition at any parole board hearing.

District Attorney Marcie Livingstone tapped her pencil on a yellow legal pad as she sat in her oversized government office waiting for the Preston family to arrive. She could not believe it had been sixteen years since Ted Nash murdered Grant Preston. Since then, she had risen through the ranks of the DA's office and had won a hard-fought election for the number one job just a year ago. In that time, her own two sons had graduated high school after which she had been willing to grant their father an uncontested divorce—she had spent too much time at her work desk, and not enough time at the dinner table. Her ex was now married to a perky blond real estate agent who only spent two afternoons a week in her realty office.

As much as Marcie acknowledged that she and her ex-husband had grown apart and a divorce made sense, she could not imagine losing him to a senseless violent crime. And even more abhorrent was the thought that her kids would have grown up without a father. As a lowly assistant district attorney all those years ago, she had cried for Mrs. Preston and young Matthew. Although she had naturally hardened from her many murder cases over the years, her stomach started to hurt as she thought again about the loss suffered by the Preston family.

The district attorney rose from behind her desk and warmly greeted Mrs. Preston, Matthew, and Dr. Wilson. She gave Mary a heartfelt hug and asked them to sit down.

"I am so sorry that we have to meet again under these circumstances. But I wanted you to know right away what the Nash family is planning. Assuming you want to oppose the early release, my office will do everything it can to help you. Have you had a chance to talk it over?"

Matthew jumped in before his mother could answer. "We aren't lawyers, so would you please explain to all of us how this could be happening?"

"Of course," said Ms. Livingstone. "The law provides for a couple of ways that a felon can be released before his complete sentence has been served. The most frequent avenue is to argue that the prisoner is rehabilitated and no longer a threat to society. Usually this approach is taken if the prisoner was young at the time of the crime or if the prisoner killed his abuser, something like that. And if he has been a model prisoner over a long period of time."

Matthew interrupted.

"But Nash was not a minor, or a victim of abuse. He was a 26-year-old privileged slacker at the time he shot my father. Older than I am now. How could that argument fly?"

"You're right, and I would ordinarily think Nash has no chance simply by contending that he is now a different, more mature person who would never hurt a fly. But there are several other things going on here. First, the U.S. Supreme Court has ordered that California relieve prison overcrowding. The prisons have to do something to comply with that order. More and more 'lifers' are being paroled under this guideline. Second, the Nash family was our governor's single biggest campaign contributor and the governor can make things happen. They are paying their scumbag lawyer, Greg Murtaugh, to come up with some fanciful arguments so that the governor can pay them back without causing too much of a public outcry. And third, Nash has not limited his petition to the claim he is now a good guy deserving of another chance. He has also filed a separate petition for what is called Medical Parole. In 2014 a federal panel ordered an expansion of the Medical Parole program as part of the effort to reduce overcrowding. The standards are being relaxed to allow more prisoners to take advantage of the program. Initially the prisoner had to be on his deathbed to qualify. Now prisoners who are not necessarily medically incapacitated are trying to get out."

"It can't be that easy," said Mary.

Ms. Livingstone only partly agreed.

"Well, the way medical parole is set up, the prisoner's family makes a special request to have the inmate's primary care provider evaluate the prisoner for medical parole purposes. I suspect, that with pressure from the governor's office, the prison doctor will agree to conduct the evaluation and, knowing where his bread is buttered, will likely find that Nash meets the medical parole criteria. Then, after more administrative review, the Nash case would be referred to the Board of Parole Hearings which would decide whether to grant medical parole and, if so, under what conditions."

The Preston family was at a loss for words. Ms. Livingstone continued, "So Murtaugh is trying to take advantage of the overcrowding problem in two ways. First, he says Nash has found Jesus and is fully rehabilitated. He does not pose an unreasonable risk of danger to society or a threat to public safety. Second, he says Nash is entitled to early release based upon his medical condition which can best be treated by outside specialty doctors. According to the petition, the Nash family intends to take Ted and move to Europe so that Ted can be treated by some doctor who is allegedly a leading expert in the field of Ted's disease." Ms. Livingstone's face darkened. "I personally think they just want to get him out of the country where they can disappear and be far away from the fallout when the news breaks about his release."

Uncle TJ, being a doctor himself, asked the obvious question.

"So, what dreaded disease does Nash claim to have that qualifies him for early release?"

"According to the papers that were served on us," said Ms. Livingstone as she thumbed through the lengthy petition, "Nash says he is suffering from something called 'Lambert-Eaton Myasthenic Syndrome' whatever the heck that is.' She paraphrased as she continued reading. "Apparently it is a rare autoimmune disease which affects muscles and nerves. Evidently, he is one of those prisoners who regularly comes to the infirmary complaining about anything and everything, so no one took him seriously when, a couple of years ago, he started saying he was fatigued, he had weakness in his legs, and he had difficulty hearing and seeing. When his symptoms worsened, testing revealed that Nash also had a small cell carcinoma of the lung, likely due to his long history of smoking. It says here that he started smoking several packs a day when he was fourteen and he smoked even more after he was sent to prison. His mother sent him lots of money each month for goodies and he apparently used his money to secretly buy cigarettes from guards and other prisoners."

Matthew interrupted with a slap on the table and a bitter snort. "I read somewhere that tobacco products were banned from California prisons. So how could he smoke there?"

"Despite the rules banning tobacco products, there is a thriving underground market for cigarettes in San Quentin and in every other state prison."

Dr. Wilson broke in. "Who cares how he got the cigarettes. Does the report say how far advanced the disease and cancer are?"

"Here," she said handing the paperwork to Dr. Wilson. "I really don't understand the details. Only that Nash is suffering from muscle weakness, fatigue, and speech problems. And then on top of that there is the cancer itself. What it says about the progression of the symptoms is beyond me."

The room was silent as Dr. Wilson scanned the petition and the attached medical reports. After a few minutes, he announced that he needed more time to research the condition, but it appeared to him that Nash's circumstances were the result of his own making. "It's true that Lambert-Eaton is a rare disorder. I remember reading that less than one person in a million is diagnosed with the condition each year. But the autoimmune aspect is thought to be merely a reaction by the body caused by antibodies produced in response to the lung cancer. So, Nash's choice to smoke heavily his entire life is the cause of the cancer *and* the autoimmune response. Why should he be allowed out of prison when he has a condition which he himself caused?"

Matthew and his mother looked at the district attorney for a response.

"I'm no expert, but I don't think the cause of the disease matters too much. Based upon my limited experience with this issue, I suspect that the parole board will only look at what disease is involved and what treatment is necessary."

Matthew was angry.

"So, you are saying that Nash can murder my father; he can end the life of a great man, of a wonderful husband, and of an extraordinary father; he can take something from us that we can never get back; and yet because he engaged in voluntary activity that has made him sick, he gets his freedom? Gets his life back. Is that it?"

Ms. Livingstone lowered her eyes and then looked right at Matthew.

"I'm afraid that is a possibility."

Silent tears ran down Mary Preston's face. Matthew put his hand on her shoulder. "Don't worry Mom. Nash is never going to get out."

Chapter Eighteen

After two days without hearing anything from Matthew, Torrey was getting worried. She thought she might have rated at least a voicemail explaining what was going on. She resisted the urge to call him, figuring he must be dealing with an important family matter. He would get back to her as soon as he could.

The next day, Matthew texted that he was on the way back to Stanford and asked if she could join him for dinner. She texted her agreement right away.

Torrey did not normally did not dress up for Matthew, but for some reason she felt the need to brush her hair, to put on some makeup, and to wear a light blue wrap skirt with a pretty white cotton top. She nervously waited for Matthew to arrive. She had a gut feeling that something was terribly wrong.

Torrey could tell that her gut was correct as soon as she opened the door and saw his face. Matthew looked like he had not slept in days. His face was drawn and unshaven. She couldn't wait for Matthew to start talking.

"Matthew, what's wrong? What's going on?"

Matthew just plopped down on the bed, put his head in his hands, and sighed. After several seconds of silence, he started to speak in a deliberate, almost unemotional voice.

"My father's murderer has filed a petition to be released from prison. His release would devastate my mother. I have to make sure he never gets out."

"But you told me that he pleaded guilty and that a part of the negotiated deal was that he was going to be put away forever!"

"I know. But the district attorney says nothing is forever anymore. Laws change, politicians change, and criminals' rights now trump victims' rights. And Nash is claiming to have some sort of disease. Apparently, we're supposed to feel sorry for him and let him out."

Matthew explained how prison overcrowding has spawned a whole new generation of activists and lawyers who, for some reason, have dedicated their lives to freeing as many criminals as humanly possible. When Matthew added the wrinkle that the governor may be beholden to the Nash family because of campaign contributions, Torrey started to lose it.

"I'm so sorry!" she yelled in exasperation. "My father always said that this governor was a jerk, *but this*? How does he have the authority to override the entire criminal justice system? Who cares if a murderer is sick? Why shouldn't he die in prison? He killed your father! He should've been executed way back when! He has had all these years of life that he took from your father! He should never get out!"

"He shouldn't. And he won't," said Matthew in his most strident tone.

"Matthew, I just wish there was something I could do to help."

"There's nothing you can do. I'll take care of it myself," grumbled Matthew.

"But there's nothing you can do either." Matthew did not reply. So, Torrey added, "Is there?"

"I'm working on a plan," said Matthew. "Nash will never leave that prison."

"What do you mean? How can you prevent his release?"

"I haven't figured out all the details, but the first step is to oppose the petition. My mom is hiring a lawyer to help us. Hopefully the lawyer has some ideas because the district attorney was not optimistic about our chances. I told the DA that we have to at least delay things by throwing up roadblocks. The DA said that the governor would likely not sign any papers until after his reelection, so we should have almost three years from now before Nash could walk out of there into the warm and loving arms of his wonderful parents."

"Maybe the jerk won't be reelected!" remarked Torrey.

"Are you forgetting we have the bluest governor and the bluest legislature in the bluest state? Our governor could be a serial killer himself and would still be reelected. Besides, we can't take the chance that the governor may decide to act immediately."

Torrey and Matthew talked until Matthew dozed off and awkwardly fell over into the middle of Torrey's bed. She watched him sleep. Naturally he was exhausted with what he had gone through the last few days, but could that explain his comments that Nash was never getting out of prison? It wasn't like him to make unsupported declarations. Something more was going on with him. There just had to be. And she was determined to find out what it was.

Eventually her mind began to wander away from Ted Nash and the criminal justice system. She wondered if Matthew had any feelings for her beyond genuine friendship. She tried to wrap her mind around how she really felt about him. She liked him of course. They spent most of their time together. They were best friends. But would he ever want more with her? They came from two different worlds. Sometimes she caught him looking at her in more than a friendly manner. At least she thought that's what he was doing. But maybe she was reading him all wrong.

Even if she were right, would *she* want more with *him*? As usual, the memories then came flooding back. About high school. About the trusted counselor and what he had done to her. All of her repressed feelings bubbled up. And she acknowledged to herself, once again, why she had rebuffed any romantic overtures since then. Why she had built a protective shield against male advances. Why she knew that anything more than friendship, even with Matthew, was out of the question.

Chapter Nineteen

When he woke up a few hours later, Matthew lifted his head and saw Torrey working at her desk. At first, he forgot how he came to be in Torrey's room. She didn't notice that he was awake, so he continued to watch her clicking away on her laptop as the details of the last few days came back into focus. As he became less groggy, he noticed that she looked all dressed up, like she was going on a date. She looked cute. He knew he must look as bad as he felt, which was pretty terrible.

He stared as long as he dared before speaking.

"Torrey, I'm embarrassed that I conked out in your room," he said in a hoarse whisper. "I have to grab a hot shower and some food. I don't remember much about what we were saying before I dozed off, but I would really like to get your take on what to do about Ted Nash. Would you mind?"

"While you were sleeping, I researched some legal maneuvers you might ask your lawyer about. Why don't you get cleaned up and come back here when you are ready to talk?"

Matthew dragged himself off the bed and trudged to the door. After he left, Torrey looked at what she had found so far. If the district attorney was right about the overcrowding and the Nash family's influence over the governor, it didn't look too good. She found many instances where the pleas from victims' families fell on deaf ears. Felons, even convicted murderers who were sentenced to life without parole, were being released more frequently in every state. And that was before the federal court order to relieve California prison overcrowding by any means necessary. Matthew was adamant about preventing the release. Of course, he and his mother should not have to stomach the Nash animal getting paroled on any grounds, much less because of political corruption. But Matthew seemed certain that he could stop Ted Nash from ever seeing the sky outside the walls of San Quentin prison. How could he be so sure?

A couple of hours after he left, Matthew returned looking like a new man. He was clean, shaved, and dressed in pressed khakis and a golf shirt. Best of all, he was carrying a large pepperoni pizza and a six-pack of Kirin beer. After they ate and drank their fill, both Matthew and Torrey were ready to talk about the parole hearing. Or at least that is what Torrey thought was going to happen.

Matthew motioned to Torrey and patted the dorm bed next to him.

"Come here, would you?"

Although she thought the request to be out of character, Torrey walked over to the bed. After she sat down, Matthew avoided her direct stare and instead looked at his feet.

"I knew before I started medical school that I'd have to devote 100% of my energies to my studies. And I have. I knew that I couldn't afford any distractions or anything that would get me off track from becoming a doctor. You've helped me more than I can say to become a better student and, more importantly, a better person. For so long I have avoided getting close to anyone. I never thought I would have the type of feelings that I have for you." Matthew looked up and met her gaze. "I have no idea if you think of me as just a study partner, but you have become much more than that to me. And you look so beautiful right now. I would really like to kiss you, but I don't know if you'll kiss me back or slug me."

Torrey was somewhat taken aback by this sudden confession, but she replied with the honest truth.

"I don't know either. Why don't you try it and see what happens?"

Matthew was not sure whether he should be emboldened or frightened by her challenge. But he took a chance. Their first kiss was tentative, but the next ones were not. At first Torrey seemed as engaged as Matthew but he quickly divined that something was off. She began to pull away. "What's wrong?" he asked.

"Matthew, I want to. I really do. I like you a lot. I think I might even love you. But I haven't let anyone touch me for so long, I don't think I can do it."

"What do you mean? You are everything a guy could want. Surely you had boyfriends in high school and college!"

"No, I didn't." He silently waited for her to explain. Her voice lowered so that Matthew could barely hear her. "I've never told anyone this, but I was raped when I was a sophomore in high school."

"Oh no! I am so sorry! By some jerk senior? Please tell me they got him, and he went to jail."

"No. Actually it was by a counselor at the school. And I never told anyone. Not the school, not even my parents."

"Why not?"

"I was just a smart-alec girl, and he was a long-time respected teacher and counselor. And he was married with two kids. Who was going to believe me? And my sister had just died so I could not burden my parents with any more grief."

Matthew was struggling to decide what to say. He resolved to just let her talk about it as much as she could manage. "Can you tell me about it?"

"I'll try." After several false starts, Torrey let it all out at breakneck pace. "I remember like it happened yesterday. I had been out of school for several weeks during the last stages of Leia's illness. After she finally passed away, my folks thought it best if I returned to school and got back into my normal routine. They arranged for me to see the school counselor, George Rincon, thinking he would help me readjust. When I went in to see him at lunchtime on my first day back, he seemed sympathetic about my sister. He suggested that we meet several times a week and pretty quickly he wanted to meet every day. He was in his mid-forties, wore a suit and tie, and seemed nice. I said 'sure.' After five or six weeks, he started giving me hugs, and bringing me Starbucks and other little gifts. He made me feel special. Of course, now I know he was grooming me, but back then I didn't even know that concept.

Anyway, one day I went to his office after gym class. I was still dressed in my gym clothes. Most of the other administrator offices were empty. I guess they had left for the day. He invited me to sit down on his couch. Then he took off his suit jacket and his tie and closed the door. I didn't know it at the time, but he also locked it with a deadbolt. He sat down next to me and we talked about Leia for 15 or 20 minutes. I started to cry, and he was comforting me. He put his arm around me and said my shoulders were very tense. He said he could help me relax."

As Matthew listened, he was getting more and more agitated. He noticed his right hand was now balled into a fist. He wanted to protect Torrey from what he knew was coming but he was helpless to do anything but listen.

"Mr. Rincon suggested that I lie face down on the floor of his office so that he could massage my shoulders. He said it would make me feel better. He even gave me a pillow from the couch for my head. I feel so stupid now, but it never occurred to me then that he was a pervert."

Matthew placed her hand into his as she continued.

"So, I was lying there dressed in my T-shirt and shorts and he knelt beside me and rubbed my shoulders through my shirt for a few minutes. Then I felt him pull my shirt up so that it was bunched up around my neck. He began rubbing my bare back above my bra strap. He said he could loosen up my muscles better without the shirt in place. I was a little nervous by then, but it still didn't dawn on me that anything bad would happen. Then his hands started to move lower until they were at my waistline. The next thing I knew, he had changed position so that he was sitting on the back of my thighs, so I couldn't move or turn over. He kept calling me 'Honey.' He kept saying, 'C'mon, Honey. I know how to make you feel good.' In an instant, I felt him pull down my gym shorts and panties and he was started to grope me. I was yelling 'Stop!' and 'Get off me!' but I don't think he even heard me. It was like he was in some sort of trance or something. As he shoved a finger inside me, he kept talking nonstop in a low monotone voice about how I just needed to relax and how he was going to make me feel better. While I was struggling to get free, I heard him unbuckling his belt. I jabbed my right elbow backwards and must have caught him in the face because he started to cry out that I was going to be sorry. When he shifted his weight to unzip his pants, I was somehow able to kick up from the floor and push him off me. I pulled up my shorts and ran to the door, but it would not open. I looked back and there was blood gushing from his nose. He looked right at me and said in a low menacing voice, 'If you tell anyone about this, I'm going to kill your mother.' I finally saw the deadbolt, opened the door, and ran out of there."

Matthew muttered, "Oh my God, Torrey. I am so sorry." He thought for a second and then asked, "Did you ever see him again?"

"Oh yes. I would see him in the halls, and he would act like nothing had happened. Once he even smirked and spoke to me as I passed by." She mimicked his oily voice. 'Well, how are you today, Honey?'

"I basically withdrew for the rest of high school. I stayed away from boys and any social activities. Spent all of my free time with my parents. It took years for me to get back to being myself, if that's ever possible."

"I can understand how you as a 16-year-old decided that you couldn't report him to the school or to the police. But what about later? What about after you graduated from high school? Did you think about reporting him then?"

"Of course. I still think about it today. Sometimes I fantasize about leaving an anonymous note for his wife. She should know what a snake her husband is. But what bothers me most of all is that he is still teaching, and it makes me sick to think that he might be doing the same thing to other girls. But if no one was going to believe me then, no one is going to believe me now."

"I doubt that you were his only victim. He probably used his position of trust and authority to prey on other vulnerable girls." Matthew's mind was working hard. "So he works at your old high school still?"

"I'm pretty sure."

For the first time in days, Matthew's focus was not on parole hearings or Ted Nash. His focus was on a new monster. He announced in a steady voice, "I know how to get a gun. I am going to take care of the smug bastard that did this to you."

Chapter Twenty

"No! You are not going to do anything of the sort," protested Torrey. "I admit that I used to dream about tying him up and torturing him, but those days are gone. I have lived with this secret for so long. It feels like a weight off my chest just to have told someone about it. But we can't take the law into our own hands. That would make us as bad as him."

Matthew would not let it go. "No way. Not even close. He brought on himself what happens to him now. And you just acknowledged that he would have lied his way out of it if you had gone to the police. The guy does not deserve to be walking around free as a bird. And he definitely shouldn't be around underage school kids. We have to do something."

"Matthew, listen to me. You're right that we have to do something. And I should've done something before now. But you have to let me handle this in my own way. I assume that it's too late to take legal action against him, but I could report him to the teachers union."

"Seriously? You can't believe that the teachers union is going to voluntarily discipline one of their own. We had a teacher in my school district who was accused of sexual misconduct with first graders! The teachers union fought tooth and nail against revocation of his license. You know how it was finally handled? He was transferred to another district! So, then he had access to an entirely new group of unsuspecting students and parents."

Torrey was horrified at that but still thought there had to be some grownups out there who would put the interests of student victims ahead of teacher predators. "There must be an agency that oversees the public-school teachers so that the evil ones can be weeded out."

"The parents of the molested children looked into that when we had the incident in our district. Yes, in California there is something called the Commission on Teacher Credentialing. I will tell you how much they care about protecting students. They will only revoke a teacher's license if he is 'convicted' of a heinous crime. So, unless there is an actual trial and a conviction, the teacher can continue to teach. I'm telling you, sometimes you just have to take care of things yourself."

"So, what are you saying? That we should all turn into vigilantes to get justice?"

Matthew thought *vigilante* too strong a word because it implied over-the-top behavior.

"You can use that term if you want to, but obviously I'm not in favor of shooting people for jaywalking. It is easy to dismiss an activity by using a far-fetched ridiculous example. I'm talking about simple justice. When the government is unable or unwilling to enforce existing laws, isn't it our duty as citizens to do it ourselves? And vigilantism doesn't have to mean *killing* bad guys. In many cases we can shine the light on evildoers by less drastic measures. Regarding Rincon, if he can't be touched by the law and you don't want me to maim him, we might have to resort to public shaming. But to let monsters get away with no consequences is morally wrong. Think of all the folks in Hollywood who knew Harvey Weinstein was abusing young actresses. It went on for years and no one said a word. I am sure you have heard the saying, 'The only thing necessary for the triumph of evil is for good men to do nothing.' We cannot do nothing."

Torrey was afraid of the revenge aspect of vigilantism.

"I don't doubt the wisdom of punishing people like Rincon. It is good for his victims and for society. But the idea of vigilantism seems like a Hollywood invention which automatically casts suspicion on its reasonableness."

"What if I told you that vigilantes have been around and lauded since biblical times—check out Genesis 34. And in medieval times there was Robin Hood. If you want recent examples, what about Richard Goetz who shot four men on the subway who were trying to rob him? Crime was rampant on the NY subways, but the law-abiding citizens were not being protected. After the Goetz shooting, subway crime decreased, and a lot of New Yorkers were grateful. And what about the Guardian Angels organization which was formed in New York in the late 1970s to protect citizens?"

"Well, New York is New York."

"You think New York is an anomaly? I remember reading about a case where a local resident in a small town in Missouri shot and killed a repeat criminal because the authorities wouldn't punish him. Many of the other residents witnessed the shooting. These other townspeople were not only happy about it; they protected the identity of the shooter. So, what you call vigilantism, I call natural justice. Besides, no matter what you call it, don't you agree that evildoers deserve punishment?"

Torrey was a bit taken aback by Matthew's passion for retribution. And she knew that taking revenge was not going to make her whole. But she could see that nothing was going to be resolved at that moment concerning Rincon. She wanted to handle her rapist in her own way. She had to think. Besides, her immediate priority was to get Matthew back on track so that he could focus on the opposition to the parole request. After a long pause, she said, "How about this? I promise that I will think about what I should do about Rincon. And I promise that I will do something. But for right now, let's concentrate on how we're going to keep Ted Nash in prison. And don't forget, we have classes to prepare for and tests coming up. It won't do either of us any good to flunk out of medical school."

Torrey's mention of schoolwork brought Matthew back to the reality of their medical school requirements. She was right—if he flunked out of school or if he even failed a class, then his chances of getting to treat Ted Nash in prison would be out the window. He had to stay on track so as not become a victim of the voluminous workload. And every student knew that if they made it through the second year of classes, they would then be faced with the standardized licensing exam, Step 1, which is a comprehensive test of all material learned in the first two years of school. This test is given to all medical students across the country. Not only must this rigorous exam be passed in order to move on to the third year of school, but anything less than a quality score would limit residency choices upon graduation.

While Matthew was most concerned about doing well in the substantive courses, Torrey, as usual, was more obsessed with the clinical skills seminars and workshops. One of the clinical requirements was that each student would shadow a real doctor who was seeing real patients with real medical problems. Torrey had heard that some of the doctors have the medical students prescreen the patients and write comments in their official medical charts. That made her nervous. And she wouldn't have Matthew there to hold her hand. They both knew that their first-year division of labor was a successful model, but they also knew that much of Matthew's attention this year was going to be diverted to helping his mother oppose the early parole of a killer.

Chapter Twenty-One

The course on reproductive medicine was difficult for Matthew in several ways. First, although a cliché, he had to admit he knew virtually nothing about the female reproductive system. He had certainly admired the female form and the sexual aspects of female anatomy, but he was woefully ignorant about how the parts worked together to lead to the birth of a baby.

Second, even though he was going to be a doctor, and a doctor is supposed to be above base urges and the embarrassment of sex education, he felt sheepish about learning about the female organs with Torrey. The long suppressed, but possible, prospect of *having* sex in the future was far more appealing than *learning* about the gory details with her.

Additionally, according to past graduates, the professor, Dr. Ruth Winston, was an outspoken women's rights advocate who was very tough on male students. Matthew decided he was going to keep a low profile in her class. As it turned out, flying under the radar was not in the cards.

In the first week of class Dr. Winston echoed every known platitude about women in politics, women in the workplace, and in particular, women in medicine. Apparently, men were not just unnecessary, they were counterproductive to the world order.

"As we all know, there is a war against women in this country. The sexual assaults addressed by the #MeToo movement are just one element of the power that men seek to impose over women. The glass ceiling exists. The highest paid jobs are reserved for men. Even the more traditional female careers in medicine are being usurped by interloping males. At the very least, these professions should be the exclusive domain of women. We cannot perpetuate the history of men telling women what to do with their bodies."

Matthew looked around the room. Nearly all of the female students and most of the males were nodding in agreement. Matthew wished that the class could get on with the material in chapter three of the textbook but, as he might have guessed, Torrey could not let the professor's remarks go unchallenged.

Torrey politely raised her hand and Dr. Winston pointed at her. Torrey looked at Dr. Winston and stated in an even voice, "I disagree with your premise. Men should be able to go into any field of medicine, just as women should have that opportunity. I'm not sure *why* a male would choose gynecology, for example, but he shouldn't be precluded from that path. Just as I would not want gender stereotyping to get in the way of my choice of specialty."

Dr. Winston's face reddened, and her voice raised. "The male-dominated health care system has historically been a tool of the patriarchy. The time has come for change. Young woman, you are embarrassing yourself."

Torrey did not back down. "Why? Just because I think men and women should have the same job opportunities? Besides, I believe diversity in *any* field improves the value of the experience. If you exclude 50% of people from a medical specialty, then the quality of care will decrease."

Dr. Winston's head looked like it would explode. She then did what many do on the ideological extreme—when you can't debate an argument on the merits, you just resort to calling your opponent stupid, evil, or both.

"I see what's going on. You are one of those anti-abortion fanatics who want to take away a woman's right to choose. You want to go back to the 1950s when women had no reproductive rights."

Torrey remained surprisingly calm. "With all due respect Professor, this is not a discussion about reproductive rights or abortion. It's about equal employment."

Dr. Winston would have none of it.

"Miss, you are not showing the requisite concern for women's issues that I would expect to see from a student admitted to this medical school."

Matthew was not a political creature, but he knew right from wrong. He hated bullies who used positions of power to chastise captive underlings. And he couldn't stand for Torrey to be subjected to verbal abuse. He wanted to support Torrey even if no one else in the class was willing to do, so he decided to lighten the mood. He waved his hand as he began to talk. "May I interject? Although gynecology is not for me," everyone except Dr. Winston started to laugh, "I can see how obstetrics would be extremely interesting. After all, as a doctor you would be treating two individuals at once. The mother and the baby both would be depending on your expertise. I can see how a career dedicated to *new life*, rather than to injury, sickness, and death, would be very fulfilling. I would like to be able to consider that specialty."

Matthew glanced over at Torrey. She was mouthing a silent "Thank you."

Dr. Winston was addled. She could hardly believe her ears. She took great pride in her ability to shape her students' world views. She organized students to shout down any campus speaker with whom she disagreed. And now she had *two* students spewing nonsense *in her own class*. She decided to end the discussion before others in the class began to question her mantra.

"Let's get back to the study of the uterus—the most amazing organ in the body."

Chapter Twenty-Two

Back in Los Angeles, Matthew's mother and uncle met with a private lawyer on how to handle the parole hearing. Attorney Harold Smithers started by simply explaining the unexplainable California parole system.

"Look," said Mr. Smithers, "the laws relating to parole procedures are in a constant state of flux because victims' rights groups have to fight tooth-and-nail to gain the most basic protections from those criminals that murdered their loved ones. If you can believe it, in the past the State was letting convicted felons out on parole without even notifying the families of the victims. In 2008, California Proposition 9 was put on the ballot to add new provisions to protect crime victims. The Proposition, called the Victims' Rights and Protection Act of 2008, required, among other things, notification to victims and an opportunity to be heard at the parole hearings. Can you imagine that the legislature would require voter consent in order to provide such a commonsense protection?"

"Another example of the inmates running the asylum," noted Dr. Wilson. Mary Preston gave a silent nod as she looked at her brother.

"In any event," continued Mr. Smithers, "the voters approved the measure and now victims get a voice—at least until a criminal-loving activist group finds a way to get some judge to rule that the victims' rights bill is unconstitutional for some reason."

"So, what can we do to oppose the early release of my husband's killer?" asked Mary, wanting to refocus the conversation.

"The hearing itself will be conducted in front of two parole board commissioners, and at least one of them will have been appointed by the governor so there are a lot of politics involved. Also present will be the prisoner and his attorney, the district attorney, you, and me. Typically, the DA talks first and tells the commissioners why the State is opposing the parole. And say what you want about Nash's attorney, Greg Murtaugh is a great lawyer and will be very tough to beat. He will go next and he will try to spin a tale about how poor Ted Nash is remorseful and rehabilitated. He will pour it on thick about how Nash has a complex medical condition which cannot be properly treated in prison. He will say that the release will save the taxpayers hundreds of thousands of dollars in medical expenses. And that his parents have agreed to care for him and hire private doctors. Murtaugh is a formidable opponent.

"Ted Nash himself will likely talk about how he is a new man and how sorry he is for his conduct when he was an immature 'kid.' He will probably detail how he cannot function in the prison due to his medical disabilities.

"You, of course, will have an opportunity to speak directly to the parole board. I recommend that you prepare in advance what we call an 'impact statement' that you can read at the hearing. You will speak from the heart about the impact your husband's death has had on you and your son, and the further negative impact that an early release would cause. Neither Nash nor his attorney has the right to question or cross-examine you."

Mr. Smithers then mentioned his important role. "Right before you speak, I will have a chance to comment. Another facet of Proposition 9 is that victims can assert their right to have an attorney representative at the hearing." Harold added with a smile, "The criminal defense lawyers hate that."

"Will you be able to question Mr. Nash?" Mary asked.

"No. But I will be able to review his entire medical history and his prison record before the hearing. I will be able to correct half-truths or flat out lies by either Nash or Murtaugh. I will in essence give a closing argument to the commissioners as to why an early release for Nash is not only legally and medically wrong, but why the idea is morally reprehensible."

Dr. Wilson hated the fact that his fragile sister would have to go through this ordeal. "What is the timetable with all of this? And is Mary obligated to attend and testify?"

"The hearing date is not yet set. Usually it is scheduled about six months from the date the petition is filed. So, we are likely looking at a spring date. Testimony is not mandatory of course. The impact statement could just be submitted into the record. But I have been to quite a few of these hearings over the years and it seems to me that the commissioners are swayed more by personal testimony than by written statements, however artfully drawn. Besides, with the Nash family having campaign contribution ties to the governor, and with that politically-connected asshole Greg Murtaugh involved, I think we need to utilize every possible advantage we can get."

Mary had to ask about the elephant in the room. "Tell us the truth. What are our chances?"

"50-50 at best."

After they left, Mary said to her brother, "TJ, I don't think Mr. Smithers is the right attorney for us. I want someone who is more confident about beating Murtaugh and who is willing to think out of the box. And I think I'd rather work with a woman lawyer."

Chapter Twenty-Three

Despite everything else that was going on, Torrey wanted to keep her promise to Matthew. She formulated a plan.

Torrey typically left her parents' house each Sunday evening after dinner and chitchat. But she had concluded that it was time to do what she could to get George Rincon out of the school system. The first step was to tell the principal of the high school what had happened. "Hey Mom, would it be okay it I stayed over tonight? I was thinking about going over the high school tomorrow morning to say 'hi' to Principal Bollinger. He contacted me recently and asked if I'd be willing to come by sometime to talk to the honor students about the college experience and medical school. I have no class Monday morning, so I thought I would stop by and schedule the talk."

"Oh sweetie, I think that's a wonderful idea. Mr. Bollinger was always so nice to you. Of course, you can stay the night. And pancakes for breakfast."

"Thanks Mom. That sounds perfect."

When Torrey arrived at East Palo Alto High on Monday morning at 8:30 am, she made a beeline for the administrative offices. She knew that she would have to pass by Rincon's office on her way to see the principal and she certainly didn't want Rincon to notice her as she walked by his doorway. Because the day was cool and drizzly, she donned a nondescript stocking hat and an old raincoat with the collar turned up.

As she neared the row of offices, she slowed her pace. She recalled that Rincon was in the second office on the right. She let out a sigh of relief when she could see that the office door was closed. She kept her eyes on the door and prayed he did not step out into the hallway as she was walking by. When she got to the door, she stopped dead in her tracks. Torrey stared at the nameplate on Rincon's office. It read: 'Sara Morehead, Counselor.'

Torrey's mind started to race. Was Rincon no longer there? Had he changed offices? Was he *dead*? As Torrey stood in the hallway staring at the unexpected nameplate on the closed door, a school secretary walked by. "May I help you Miss?"

"Why yes. I'm a former student and I came by to see Mr. Bollinger. Is he in today?"

"Yes, he is, but I'm not sure if he is in his office at the moment. Do you know the way?"

"Is he still in the office at the end of the hall?" Torrey said as she took off her hat and coat.

"Let's see if he is there," said the young secretary as they started to walk.

The secretary led Torrey to Mr. Bollinger's doorway. The office door was ajar and so Torrey stuck her head in while knocking. Mr. Bollinger was sitting behind his desk looking down at an endless pile of administrative paperwork. Before she could say a word, Mr. Bollinger leapt up from his chair with a huge grin and said, "Torrey! So good to see you. I was hoping you would come and visit us someday!"

"I've been meaning to swing by and see you. Medical school has been so busy. But you always said that you enjoy alumni visits, and I was at my parents' house last night, and I had no class this morning," Torrey realized she was rambling, "so I thought I would pop in and say hello!"

"Well I'm glad you did. Catch me up on everything since you left us!"

Torrey gave a historical account of her education since graduating high school. Mr. Bollinger knew most of it already because he had been following the accomplishments of one of East Palo Alto High's most successful graduates. There were not many former students who went off to Stanford University, much less Stanford Medical School. After the necessary small talk about her future and some of her classmates, Torrey asked about a few of her former teachers. Most had left as soon as they got enough seniority to move to another district. Some of her favorites had retired. Torrey then asked as casually as possible about Mr. Rincon. "I noticed that you have a new counselor, a Ms. Morehead. How long has she been here?"

"Oh, about two years now."

"What happened to Mr. Rincon?"

Torrey wasn't sure, but she thought she detected a change in Mr. Bollinger's expression, like he was more guarded all of a sudden. After clearing his throat, Mr. Bollinger hemmed and hawed, "He retired early with a serious medical condition. Some problem with his kidneys, or maybe his liver... well I guess I'm not sure. He moved to San Diego, so he could live out his retirement in warm weather and still get his public employee medical benefits. I understand that he gets regular treatment at some hospital in San Diego."

"Really? So, he is no longer teaching or counseling at all?"

"Correct. He didn't tell me much about his diagnosis or prognosis, but I gathered that his medical treatment was going to be a full-time job." Mr. Bollinger did not sound sympathetic.

Torrey processed this information. No other girls were in danger. She had time to decide what else she might do about Rincon. Just as she was getting up to leave, Torrey thought to add, "Would it be helpful to you if I came back soon to talk to your students about the value of higher education?"

Mr. Bollinger was delighted by her offer.

Chapter Twenty-Four

After a long day of class and studying, Matthew and Torrey retreated to Matthew's dorm room to relax. They usually went to Torrey's room for non-school activities, but Matthew said he wanted to share a nice bottle of wine and some goodies that he had been saving.

Torrey lounged on the bed while Matthew wrestled with the corkscrew. "What's the big occasion for your fancy wine?" asked Torrey.

"There are actually a couple of things," replied Matthew. "First of all, we finished Professor Winston's class without getting kicked out of school and, thanks to you, we did well on the unit test. I now know more about the uterus and the fallopian tubes than I ever wanted to know."

Torrey chuckled. "Now you could be a gynecologist if you wanted to utilize all that knowledge."

"Hmm, I think I'll pass on that."

"What else are we celebrating?" Torrey wanted to know.

Matthew said with a dash of hopefulness in his voice, "Well, I was thinking that if you had a few glasses of this great wine, you might consent to letting me kiss you again."

Torrey laughed. "Let's see what happens. Pour the wine." After a slight pause, she added, "And do you have any crackers and cheese to go with it?"

"As a matter of fact, I have a whole box of treats that my Mom sent," he said as he lifted an opened large cardboard box from the floor to the bed. "What do you want first?"

Torrey hesitated for a second and then blurted out, "I want you!" as she jumped up from the bed and into Matthew's arms. Unfortunately, the moment was lost because Matthew was caught off guard and off balance. The impact caused him to fall backwards, hitting the crown of his head on the nearby desk. Blood started to flow from his scalp. "I'm so sorry!" Torrey exclaimed. Matthew held his right hand to his head as he tried to get up from the floor. He was dizzy.

"I'm okay. I just need a second," said Matthew as Torrey helped him move over to the desk chair.

Torrey said, "Just sit here. Apply pressure to the wound. Where is your suturing kit?" Matthew looked at her without responding. "C'mon, where is your kit? They told us to keep it with our stethoscope. And where are your sterile wipes?"

"I probably put all that stuff in a desk drawer. Maybe in the second or third one down."

Torrey threw open each drawer looking for the medical supplies. She found the suturing kit in the third drawer along with miscellaneous office supplies and a tablet of college-ruled notebook paper filled with Matthew's handwriting.

"Now hold still while I sew you up." Torrey cleaned and sutured the gash just as she was trained to do in class.

"Ow that hurts!' Matthew cried out.

"Of course, it does. Now stop whining. I'm almost finished."

Torrey was quite proud of her stitch work. She held his arm as they walked over to the bed so that he could lie down. When he was comfortable, she went back to the desk to clean up and put away the medical supplies. She couldn't help but notice again the papers in the third drawer. She took a closer look as she was working. The top sheet was titled 'Contraindicated drugs that can cause death.' Torrey was confused. They had always shared their study tools, but they had never discussed these drugs.

Matthew lay on the bed with his head propped up by several pillows. The color had returned to his face and he even smiled when recounting the absurdity of his fall. "Did I hear right that you wanted to hug me?" asked Matthew.

"Let's not think about that right now. How's your head?"

"I'll be fine thanks to you." He gingerly felt the wound area and the stitches. "How many sutures did you put in?"

"Enough. And don't worry about the scar. Your hair will cover any sign of a bad job by me."

"I'm not worried about that. What was it like? Doing the procedure on an actual patient?"

"I must say that your scalp was remarkably similar to pig skin. So, it was easy," Torrey said with a laugh.

"Gee thanks."

"You need to rest quietly for an hour or two. So while we are confined to quarters so to speak, let me ask you something. I noticed when searching for your suturing kit that you have lots of notes in your desk drawer about drugs and their effects. But those are not drugs that we have studied yet. Why did you make that list?"

Matthew never intended to share his plan with anyone, not even with Torrey. He decided to stall so he could think how best to respond to her question. "Gee I would have to look at those notes and I am still feeling a little lightheaded right now. Do you mind bringing me a glass of water?"

Torrey complied but after he took a few sips, she walked over to the desk, grabbed the notes from the still open drawer, and brought them over to the bed.

She plopped them down on Matthew's stomach. "You look fine now. And I should know—I am almost a doctor. So, tell me about these notes regarding weird medicines and their effects."

Matthew was conflicted. On the one hand he felt really close to Torrey and he hated to keep such a secret from her. On the other hand, he had sworn to himself countless times over the years that he would never tell *anyone* about the driving force in his life and the true reason that he was going to medical school. Sidestepping was the only course—it was in her best interests to be ignorant of his plans. "Oh, those were just some notes I made early in our first year of medical school. I was going to quiz my uncle for the fun of it about some of the drugs he used during surgery and what would happen if the drugs were given to a patient with certain medical conditions. I actually never got around to doing that. In fact, I forgot those notes were in there. I should take them with me next time I go home." Matthew changed the subject. "So, speaking of going home, I am going to have to miss some more school soon so that I can go to the parole hearing. Our lawyer says a hearing date could be scheduled any day now. Do you mind holding down the fort again?"

"Well, I've been thinking about that. I'd like to come to the hearing with you. And before you say 'No,' I realize you and your family can handle it. I know you don't need me there. And I promise I will not get out of line and start yelling at Nash or at the hearing officers. What do you say? Do you mind if I come? I would like to help you with this burden, but I can't do that without being more involved."

"That is so sweet of you, but I couldn't ask you to do that. It will be a very difficult and stressful day. You don't need that."

"First, you're not asking me to come. I'm asking you. Second, I want to come. I want to be there for you. And finally, it would be more stressful for me to not be there and to not know what's happening. Please, may I come?"

Matthew was too choked up to speak. Shakily, he stood up, walked over to her, and gave her a long hard embrace. She hugged him back.

Chapter Twenty-Five

The parole board hearing was finally set for April 7. The two sides had just one month to gear up. Because Mary Preston was not inspired by Harold Smithers' apparent bromance with Nash's attorney, and because she wanted to retain a female lawyer to whom she might better relate, TJ had asked around and one name kept popping up—celebrated California attorney Carly St. Cere.

A former federal prosecutor now working as a prominent victims' rights advocate, Carly was known as 'The Saint' in certain legal circles for her angelic face and timeless beauty. She was touted as someone who would work well with District Attorney Livingstone and who was not afraid to take on The Sleazeball. In fact, though at 55 years old she looked like an ageless cover girl, Murtaugh and the rest of the criminal defense bar had a quite unprintable nickname for Ms. St. Cere based on her 'go for the jugular' and 'no compromise' style of practice.

But as The Saint looked through the Ted Nash files while she waited for Mary Preston and her brother to arrive at her Santa Monica office, she was concerned for her prospective clients. Carly had developed an acute sense of smell in her thirty years of practice and she smelled a very big rat. She doubted Greg Murtaugh would have taken this case without having under-the-table assurances that the governor of California was going to pull the appropriate strings at the appropriate time on behalf of his single biggest individual political donor. The Saint suspected that the upcoming parole board hearing might be a sham.

"Please come in and be seated," Carly said as Mary and TJ walked into her spacious and comfortable office. "I see you have already been furnished with coffee by my industrious secretary. If you need anything else this morning, just let me know."

Mary and TJ smiled politely. Mary was anxious to cut to the chase. "Ms. St. Cere, thank you for having us in this morning. As you can imagine, we are starving for information. You said on the phone that you had received the prison files on Ted Nash. What have you learned?"

"You must call me Carly. Of course, I will go over all of that with you. But first let's talk about some procedural issues and the big picture. You already know about how these things normally go. But this case is not normal—it is going to be high profile and a political hot potato. I hope the rules will be followed but I want to prepare you for the worst-case scenario."

TJ and Mary looked at each other and then back at Carly. TJ was the first to speak. "What are you talking about Carly?"

"Well, we know that the Nash family contributed heavily to the governor's election campaign. And I have heard from a confidential source that their lawyer, Greg Murtaugh, got an audience with someone in the governor's office to talk about this case. I suspect that a deal has already been made for the governor to sign off on the release. I would not be surprised if the governor's appointed parole board commissioner simply acts as the governor's puppet at this hearing."

Mary could hardly process what Carly was saying. "Are you saying that the decision has already been made and this hearing is just an academic exercise? And what about the other commissioner? We were told there would be two at the hearing."

"Yes, there will be two commissioners. But let's not be shocked if the civil servant appointee simply rubber stamps the decision of the chief commissioner appointed by the governor. Look, I'm not saying we can't successfully oppose this bogus petition. And maybe I'm totally wrong about the governor. Maybe there is no collusion to worry about. Maybe the case will be decided on the merits as it should be. We will certainly oppose an early release vigorously. And I will be here for you every step of the way. Now let me fill you in about Ted Nash's prison records and his claim of a debilitating medical condition."

At the conclusion of the meeting, Mary Preston stood, looked Carly in the eyes, and declared, "I like you. I trust you. I would love it if you would represent us." Mary extended her hand to seal the deal with a firm handshake. Carly brushed her hand aside and instead gave Mary a long heartfelt embrace.

In his downtown Los Angeles high-rise office, Greg Murtaugh smiled as he prepared for a meeting with Mr. and Mrs. Nash. He knew that he had already all but secured Ted's release in a secret meeting with the governor's chief of staff. Murtaugh had been told that the chief commissioner at the hearing would be under instructions from the governor to interpret the evidence in such a way that would justify the grant of early parole. In return, the commissioner would be reappointed with an increased salary and a healthy bonus. But there was no need to tell that to the Nashes. Murtaugh knew when he had clients with more money than common sense, and he always took advantage of it.

"Clara and Theodore, this is going to be a tough one. We are directing all of our resources to this case, but Ted is not really your typical candidate for early release. I have gone through your son's file and frankly he has not shown any real remorse. In fact, there are some incidents in prison that suggest he has not changed at all. And the medical condition issue is fuzzy. I have had one of the doctors I use take a look at the medical charts and I wonder how much sympathy there will be for someone who caused his own condition by his smoking and lifestyle choices."

Mr. Nash interrupted.

"Look Greg, we contributed nearly a million dollars to the governor, and we are paying you a fortune to take advantage of that bribe. We were told that you were the man for this job. Can you do it or not?"

"Let's put it this way. If I can't do it, no one can. My biggest concern at the hearing is that your son will have to speak. I met with him twice years ago and, no offense, but he is not very likeable. I am worried that he will not make a great presentation. Of course, I will work with him for as long as it takes before the hearing, but getting him to come across as sympathetic, and to follow my instructions, are our biggest challenges. Perhaps you can tell him at your next weekly visit that he has to listen to me and do as directed."

Mr. Nash knew exactly what Murtaugh was talking about. He had tried talking to his son all of his life and could never get through to him. It wasn't that Ted was dumb as a stump, although at times it sure seemed like it. The main issue was that Ted always imagined that he was the smartest guy in the room and he never was. Not even close.

Mrs. Nash, on the other hand, had no idea why Murtaugh was maligning her brilliant and handsome son. Yes, he had made one mistake, but everyone should get another chance. She made no attempt to hide her feelings.

"Mr. Murtaugh, I am sure that you are trying to help but you do not know our Teddy. He is a very nice boy who just forgot where he came from on that day way back when he was just a child. I will see to it that he does whatever you tell him to do and that he says whatever you tell him to say. He really is a good boy, and smart too."

135

Murtaugh used all of his willpower to avoid rolling his eyes. Her comments reminded him that right after Ted Nash was arrested for murder, Mrs. Nash referred to him as 'the perfect son.' Murtaugh knew that there was no purpose in debating with Mrs. Nash; she was effectively blind to the manifest character flaws in her only son. But as long as Ted stayed on script, Murtaugh knew that he was as good as back home. "As I was saying, I think we have a decent chance to get your son out of prison, whether he deserves it or not. But I am going to have to call in some additional favors at the governor's office and that might get expensive. And don't forget that realistically the governor can't sign the parole until after the election in another two years. He can't afford a scandal before his next election. If I know the governor, and I think I do, he won't risk provoking those pesky victims' rights groups to organize against him."

Mr. Nash knew where this was going. "Greg, how about this? If you can get the parole board to recommend early release, there is an extra $100 thousand bonus in it for you. Will that take care of any extra expenses?"

Murtaugh thought that sounded fair. Before the meeting was over, Murtaugh had Mr. Nash sign a written bonus agreement.

Chapter Twenty-Six

A week out from the parole hearing, Murtaugh made another visit to San Quentin. He despised this part of his job. It wasn't so much that he had to go to jails and prisons to see his clients. It was that his clients were typically so much like Ted Nash that he hated having to interact with them. And Nash was even worse because of the added layer of misplaced arrogance.

Murtaugh watched through the small plexiglass window as Ted was escorted into the interview room by the bored guard. Ted had that same smirk on his face that he had sixteen years ago when Murtaugh first met with him in the police station. Murtaugh might have expected that more than a decade of incarceration would have diminished Ted's sense of self-importance, but clearly that wasn't the case.

"Good morning Ted. How are you today?" Murtaugh politely asked.

"I'm doing pretty damn good. I hear from my mom that I will be getting out of this joint pretty soon. When will I be back home?"

"Not so fast. Nothing is guaranteed. There are a few more hoops we have to jump through. The main one is the parole hearing next week. I'm here today to prepare you for that proceeding."

"My mom says they're paying you a ton of money to get me out and so you better do it, and fast."

Murtaugh sometimes thought the money was not worth the aggravation. And this was one of those times. Part of him wanted to tell Ted off, walk out the door, and let him rot in prison. But then he remembered the big payday waiting for him, and he decided to put up with the depraved little delinquent until after the hearing.

"Ted, if we are going to get you out, you are going to have to listen to me and do exactly as I say. If you aren't willing to do that, there is no sense in me being here. Do you want to check the ungrateful attitude and have me help you or not?"

"Sure boss. Whatever you say."

"Okay then. At the hearing you will have the opportunity to speak to the commissioners who will decide whether you get out or not. Your fate will be sealed if you act like a jerk. You need to sound humble and contrite. It would be nice if you could shed a tear when talking about how sorry you are for the killing. Why don't you practice that between now and the hearing so you can cry on cue?"

Ted grinned at the thought of such a fun challenge.

"I bet I could do that," he said.

"You will have to cover three topics at the hearing. I'm going to give you a script which I want you to read at the hearing. Memorize some parts of it so that you sound more genuine. As you'll see, the three subjects are: how you have changed as a person since your crime, how you are not a threat to society, and, of course, your medical issues. When I address the commissioners, I will expand on these points and will emphasize that your medical conditions are too complex for prison doctors and too expensive for the taxpayers to bear. You will say nothing else unless I tell you to. Got it?"

"Sounds like a winner boss. By the way, I lost a bet to a guy named Big Whitey in my cellblock. His name doesn't do him justice—he is huge. If I don't pay him, he is going to take it out of my hide. Can you lend me a few bucks until I get out?"

Unfortunately for Matthew and Torrey, the week before the parole hearing was particularly busy at school. Not only were the students confused by a complicated and indecipherable neurology textbook, the immunology professor was incomprehensible. He was visiting from Ukraine and his accent was so thick that he might as well have been Charlie Brown's teacher. Some students were recording the lectures and sharing in the cost of having them transcribed by a Russian undergraduate. Matthew and Torrey decided that it was a waste of their time to go to either the neurology or the immunology classes. Instead they used a combination of on-line study materials and the class notes of a brilliant fourth-year student who had auctioned off his beautifully typed and understandable memoranda from his days as a second-year student. Matthew was the high bidder.

Torrey had to be the patient disciplinarian this week more than at any other time in order to keep Matthew's mind from straying to San Quentin, and more importantly, to his mom. While Matthew was ruminating with a ball of hate in his gut at the thought of coming face-to-face with Ted Nash, he was worried sick that the parole hearing was going to be very traumatic for his fragile mother. Every hour or so during their study sessions, Matthew would ask a rhetorical question about the parole procedure or the possible outcomes. Torrey was sympathetic but did her best to gently draw Matthew's attention back to the drudgery of memorizing obscure facts about diseases and treatments.

A primary topic in neurology was the danger of a misdiagnosis in an emergency room. To Torrey, one of the more shocking case files concerned a woman who was brought by ambulance to a hospital emergency room after her adult son found her sprawled out on their kitchen floor. The floor was wet with spilled wine. She was conscious but incoherent; her speech was heavily slurred. There was a bump on the back of her head. The son told the hospital staff that his mother drank every day and had probably consumed five glasses of wine that evening, but that her level of speech impairment and drowsiness was not typical of her normal intoxication. The hospital nurses and doctors considered her symptoms to be alcohol-induced and therefore did not perform a CT brain scan until her condition had so far deteriorated that the later discovered closed head injury with subdural bleed was fatal. The coroner determined that the hospital staff's failure to investigate the brain injury potential was a direct cause of the patient's death.

Torrey's and Matthew's assignment was to learn the protocol that should be followed to identify or rule out brain injury when a patient presents with signs that could be attributed to head trauma.

"Can you believe that the hospital completely ignored the son's account because it was inconsistent with their assessment of intoxication?" Torrey asked. "After all, the woman was found on the floor with a head contusion, so you would think they would run tests for brain injury before doing anything else."

Matthew agreed that, in hindsight, the hospital should have immediately done the CT scan.

"But let's face it, the personnel in the emergency room were likely dealing with gunshot wounds, car accident victims, and who knows what else. And then in comes this middle-aged lady with a wine-stained dress, with a history of alcohol abuse, who is slurring her words and acting drunk. Is it any wonder that she was not rushed in for very expensive medical tests? I bet the family sued and got a lot of money, but I question whether that's fair."

Torrey did not need much time to reply. "Fair or not, that's what we signed up for. Remember the oath we took when we started medical school? If we don't uphold our sworn duty to our patients, we deserve the consequences, don't you agree?"

"Well, let me put it this way. I agree that all people, not just doctors, must suffer the consequences that they deserve."

Torrey raised her eyebrows.

"If you're talking about Mr. Rincon again, I told you that I learned that he is no longer working. There is no danger that he will molest other girls. Now I have time to think about what else I should do about him."

Matthew was a bit ashamed that he had been thinking only of Ted Nash, not George Rincon, when he made his comment about consequences. Rincon had never entered his mind.

But Matthew took the opportunity to address Torrey's molester.

"I know he's retired. It's great that he no longer has access to high school girls. But didn't you say he had children of his own? And for all you know he now has grandchildren. If so, how old would they be? And who is to say he isn't so perverted that he also preys on little kids. And even if he has no kids or grandchildren, what about getting the punishment he deserves? What about suffering some consequences for what he did to you and probably to other girls?"

Torrey stared at the floor slack jawed. She hadn't considered that Rincon might be capable of molesting his own family members.

"I have for so long put that part of my life in a locked box. I didn't want to dwell on what he did to me, much less on what he might do to others."

Matthew walked over to Torrey and held out his hand. She grabbed it and he pulled her close.

"What else can I do?" she sobbed into his shoulder. "I don't even know where he lives or how to find out about him anymore."

"Don't worry. I know a private investigator that my family foundation has used over the years. I've met him a couple of times at the house. I'm sure he can find Rincon and can tell us everything about his life. Rincon will never know about it." Before Torrey could raise any objections, Matthew added, "I will have him send his bill to the family accountant. No one will ever question the amount or the nature of the invoice."

Despite everything else on his plate, the next day Matthew made a point to call gumshoe Joe Cook. A former UCLA football star until he blew out his knee, and then a 20-year veteran of the police force, Joe was boyishly handsome, with a quick smile and a charming veneer. Those attributes and the normal tricks of the trade usually allowed him to gain access to the information he needed to expose cheating husbands, trace hidden assets, and find missing persons. But Matthew knew from prior experience that Joe was willing to bend the rules and ethical canons, if necessary, to get the job done. And Matthew suspected that getting ahold of Rincon's confidential public-school discipline records and any criminal files would require more than a flirty grin or a good-old-boy pat on the back.

"Joe, hi, this is Matthew Preston. How are you doing?"

"Matthew, good to hear from you. What can I do you for?"

"I'd like you to find someone for me. Do you have some time?"

"I always have time for you and you mother. You know that. How big of a rush is this?"

"Well, finding the guy is the easy part. I need a few other things. First, this guy was a public-school teacher and I need any records showing whether he lost his teaching credential and the details of any discipline taken against him."

"Those records are privileged. They are not a matter of public record."

"I know. That's why I need you. Is there any way you can get them?"

"Matthew, my boy, you cut me to the quick. I will figure out a way. Don't worry. What are the other things you need?"

"I suspect that this guy may also have a sealed criminal record. May I presume that you will find a way to get a copy of those records too?"

"Affirmative. Just give me the name and any background that you already have on the guy."

"One more thing, I understand this guy has some sort of medical condition for which he is being treated somewhere in San Diego. I need you to find out what his condition is and where he is being treated."

"Should I send my bill to the foundation?"

"Actually, I was going to have you bill the foundation. But now that we have talked, why don't you just send the bill directly to me and I'll see that you are promptly paid. And let's communicate by phone. No written reports, emails, or texts without my consent."

"Got it. I'll give you a call on your cell when I have something for you."

"Thanks Joe. I really appreciate your help."

Chapter Twenty-Seven

After a successful career as an LAPD detective, 51-year-old Joe Cook had been ready to work on his own without the constraints of the bureaucracy and the politics of government service. Public employees had to answer to all layers of bosses and the public. Joe wanted to answer only to himself and his exclusive cadre of clients. The tricks and backdoors he used as a beat cop, a gang dispute mediator, a burglary detective, and finally as a homicide detective proved to be very helpful in his new line of work. And he wasn't above using his charm and athletic good looks, along with the occasional bribe, to obtain the information he wanted.

Joe had more than a few well-off clients, but he had a soft spot in his heart for Matthew and his mother. They had been through a lot after Matthew's father died and he was happy to do whatever he could for the family. Most of his work was mundane, but Matthew had hired him to do some interesting background investigations having to do with the family foundation. One in particular required Joe to threaten bodily harm in order to scare off some internet troll who was trying to take advantage of Matthew's good nature and naivety in business matters. Joe did not expect to have to use violence for his current assignment, but he had a sufficient armory if necessary.

After Matthew had supplied the basic identification information on George Rincon, Joe put everything else on hold and retreated to his basement home office filled with two powerful computers and three giant screens arranged like a wall around the perimeter of his six-foot-long old-school metal desk. He had two landline phones which he used in the basement where cell reception was spotty. He kept a supply of burner phones for when he wanted to ensure untraceable contacts. He reserved his iPhone for his best clients, like the Prestons. In a separate cabinet he kept the other tools of his trade—things like multiple specialty cameras and lenses, surveillance equipment, and night goggles. His guns and knives were kept in a vintage Wells Fargo bank vault that he had purchased from a Missouri collector of Old West artifacts.

On computer number one, he followed his standard operating procedure by listing each item of information he needed. He tilted his head as his thoughts churned. He muttered out loud to himself as he typed.

"Let's see here. I need to get this guy's employment records from the school district. I need any police records. I need court records. And, of course, I need personal information like residence, family, autos registered to him, and banking information. Oh, and I need his medical records from wherever he's being treated." He leaned back in his late mother's wooden rocker and closed his eyes. "It is a good thing that Matthew Preston is the client. This is going to be expensive."

He fired up computer two and logged into the professional-grade databases that he legally subscribed to as a licensed investigator. For locating people and obtaining personal information, he preferred TLOxp, which, although pricey, was fast and complete. Within minutes, he knew where Rincon lived, his social security number, and the names of his family members. He obtained DMV records listing the cars Rincon owned. So far, so good.

He used the Tracers Info database to access the criminal court records. Most are a matter of public record, but it was here that Joe encountered his first problem. The only records of Rincon's that existed were marked sealed and confidential. Joe raised his eyebrows, put his hands behind his head, and looked at the ceiling. He then looked back down at the screen and squinted. "What could this guy have done that merited sealing the records?"

Joe shifted gears. "Let's see if I can get into the police report records." His fingers flew across the keyboard. He found a report stating that someone who lived at Rincon's address had been the subject of a Peeping Tom complaint. A neighbor claimed that the Tom had been caught spying on the woman's teenage daughter through the bathroom window. For some reason, the identity of the Tom and the complainant were redacted.

"Now that's really odd," said Joe to himself. "I'm going to have to call my old sergeant down at the station to get to the bottom of that one."

Joe also came up empty on his search for Rincon's employment history. At first, all he could get through normal channels is that he had worked at East Palo Alto High, first as a teacher and then as a counselor, until a few years ago. There was nothing about whether he had left under a cloud. The rest of his school records couldn't be accessed without a court order. Joe distrusted secret files. They always raised his suspicions and got his juices flowing. Fortunately, Joe did not have to rely only on the available databases. Joe had arrested many hackers in his previous career, and he had learned some tricks of the trade. Maybe he wasn't a world-class computer geek, but he surely knew enough to bypass whatever half-assed controls had been put in place at the school district by some dinosaur who probably didn't change his own password more than once every five years. He was right. A few clicks and the entire Rincon file appeared on his screen.

"No wonder it was sealed," said Joe to nobody. A student named Vicki Post alleged she was raped by Rincon. Of course, he had denied it. A classic 'he said, she said,' with the teacher's union attorney jumping to the aid of Rincon.

146

Because Ms. Post could not prove her allegation, the district took no action against Rincon. Reading between the lines, Joe concluded that Rincon had been allowed to avoid jail or public shame, to retire early, and to keep his pension in exchange for his agreement to leave the district and never come back. "Sounds like the perp got a pretty sweet deal," spat Joe with disgust.

Although Matthew Preston hadn't said why he wanted all of this information about Rincon, Joe could see he was on the trail of a really bad guy. But even if Rincon was some true evildoer, why did Matthew care?

Joe had a bit more luck with his search for medical records. Rincon was definitely seeking regular treatments for Crohn's disease at Kaiser in San Diego. It was unclear what the treatments were exactly, but he was visiting the hospital every two or three months.

Joe knew what he had to do next. He had no political or money connections, but he had the best social capital that existed. He picked up a landline phone and called the number he knew by heart. Sergeant William 'The Bull' Rodland, a Sigma Alpha Epsilon fraternity brother from college, picked up on the second ring. "Rodland here."

Joe knew that William would recognize his voice if he used their secret affectionate, but manly, greeting. "Phi Alpha, Bull!"

"Not you again, Joe. You want to get me fired?"

"How come you never call me anymore? How come I always have to be the caller?"

"I actually still have a real job. I have bank robbers and murderers to catch. You have all day to play because you spend your nights spying on cheating husbands through bedroom windows. What a life!"

"Yeah, yeah. Just wait until you qualify for your pension. You'll be out of there the next day. And then you can work for me. I'll let you be the one hiding all night behind hotel dumpsters with a long-range lens and a cup to pee in."

"Okay. Cut the crap. Why're you really calling? I have work to do."

"Listen Bull. I do need a favor. I have a police report on a guy. Looks like he was ogling the girl next door. Both the alleged delinquent and the victim's names are blacked out on the report that I have access to. Why would that be?"

"Could be any number of reasons but none of them innocent. Most likely the guy lawyered up and then convinced someone at the station to bury the report for all intents and purposes. Let me look into it and I'll call you back. Just give me the report number."

"Sorry to be a pest but any chance you could do it today and get right back to me?"

Rodland moaned. "Man, you owe me big time! A pitcher of dark beer and two cheeseburgers at McGinty's on Friday. Deal?"

"Deal."

While he was waiting, Joe ground some Starbucks beans, heated up some water, and poured himself a nice big mug of dark coffee. Before he could take his first sip, Rodland called back. "Wow, that was fast! What did you find?"

"I have the original report right in front of me. The perp's name is George Rincon. Is that the guy you are interested in?"

"Yup. That's him alright. What about the lady next door?"

"Her name is Camila Vasquez. Her daughter is Sofia, who was sixteen at the time. Is that what you need?"

"Thanks Bull. See you Friday. Bring your appetite."

Now that he knew Camila's full name and last known address, he easily traced her to the Blue Mountain Paradise Estates in Phoenix. She picked up on the first ring. "Hello," she said nervously with nary a trace of accent.

"Ms. Vasquez, good afternoon. My name is Joe Cook." He didn't mind if she gained the impression that he was still with the police force. "I'm investigating a man by the name of George Rincon. I know you used to be his neighbor and you filed a complaint against him. Do you recall Mr. Rincon?"

"Oh my God! What did he do now? That man is a pedophile! Are you guys finally going to put him in jail? We moved to Arizona to get away from that creep!"

"Ma'am hold on a second. Let me ask you more about your complaint. According to the police report, you said he was spying on your daughter Sofia, is that right?"

"Yes! I saw him! I told them, but they didn't believe me!"

"Wait. How did you see him? Where was he? And where was your daughter?"

"Sofia was in the private bathroom off her bedroom on the first floor. There was a window that she had opened to let out the steam. I heard the water go off and a few seconds later she opened the door and called to me in a loud whisper. I came to her and she pointed to the window and said in a low voice that the man next door was looking in at her through the fence. I went to the window and I could see him standing behind the fence looking through a gap in the boards. I yelled at him and he ran inside." She took a quick breath and continued. "When the police came, he denied that he was spying on Sofia. He said he was just out in his yard minding his own business. But we found a pile of cigarette butts right where we saw him standing. He must have been lurking there, who knows how often, waiting for her to shower. The bastard even denied to the police that he had heard me yell at him. He said he just went back inside to make some tea. He's such a liar! But they believed him and not me because I'm Hispanic. But I'm an American citizen too!"

Joe had enough information, but he let her vent for another ten minutes about the unfairness of her encounter with the police. She was convinced that the police believed Rincon and not her because he was Caucasian, and she was not. Joe hoped Camila was mistaken, but he suspected that she was probably correct.

Joe Cook was nothing if not resourceful. Rincon was in his crosshairs and Joe wanted to finish off the investigation in style. He still needed the sealed criminal court records and the more complete medical records. "Looks like Mohammad will have to go to the mountain," Joe uttered.

He dressed in his 'professional' attire of a Brooks Brothers dark gray suit with a light blue dress shirt and a bold red tie. He put a crisp $100 bill in his pants pocket clipped to a 3-by-5 index card containing Rincon's criminal case number. His first stop was the downtown criminal courts building. He had been there a thousand times in his career, but it never ceased to amaze him that in the shade of the building where crimes are prosecuted was one of the most prominent homeless camps in the state. Walking from the parking lot Joe was accosted no less than five times for money, drugs, or both.

He made his way to the filing windows and checked each one to see where Barb was stationed today. She was at window 5. He dutifully stood in her line for thirty-five minutes before making his way to the front. She was looking down at paperwork when she heard Joe's familiar voice. "Hi beautiful. How's life treating you?" He gave her his charismatic smile. Barb looked up, glanced at Joe, and pretended she had never seen him before.

"Can I help you sir?"

"Yes, I believe you can." As he talked about some nonexistent case file that he wanted to see, he surreptitiously slid the folded index card to Barb. She didn't look down at it. She simply palmed it and left her seat. A few minutes later, she returned and handed a file to Joe. "Here you go sir. Have a good day."

He folded the two-page document length wise and stuck in in his inside suit pocket. "Thank you. You too."

He waited to look at the paperwork until he was in the parking garage and walking to his car. "Jeez. A restraining order from his own daughter. This guy is a real piece of work."

He drove out of the garage and jumped onto the 5 freeway for the ninety-minute drive to San Diego. He was not a fan of this route, but it was the fastest way to get there from downtown Los Angeles and he wanted to arrive in plenty of time. He thought he would treat himself later by driving back home along the coast. Maybe have an ocean view supper in Del Mar.

The Kaiser hospital was in the San Diego suburb known as Kearney Mesa. Joe had been there once when his aunt was having hip surgery. But there was no Barb down there who he could bribe with a C note. He knew from Rincon's online medical records that he was scheduled for a 2 pm appointment today but Joe doubted that a smile was going to give him the access to the complete file that he needed. He had a vague plan but would likely have to wing it. That was okay. Joe had no problem winging things.

Joe checked with the docent on the first floor and found out that the infusion center patients received scheduled treatments on the 5th floor. It was only one o'clock, so Joe set up across from the elevators with a newspaper and waited for Rincon to arrive. He figured that he could recognize Rincon from the ten-year-old photo in the school records.

There was no mistaking Rincon when he arrived and pushed the button for the 5th floor. He looked his age of fifty-five but was making a real effort to look twenty-five. His hair was dyed black, but the gray roots were visible. He wore the ridiculous millennial uniform of tight blue slacks and brown dress shoes. And an untucked dress shirt. Joe was surprised that Rincon was not walking a rescued *emotional support* dog and wearing a backwards baseball cap to complete the ensemble. Joe followed Rincon into the elevator and they both rode up to 5. Joe allowed Rincon to get out first then he followed at a comfortable distance to the nurses' station at the far end of the hall. He saw Rincon check in and take a seat on a bench in the hallway. He watched as Rincon sifted through the magazines on the side table. He picked up a Cosmo.

Joe approached the nurse behind the half circle desk. "Hi. I have a brother with Crohn's disease and I'm checking out some of the hospitals around here to find the right one for him. They told me downstairs that this is where Crohn's patients come for IV drip treatment. Can you tell me about how that works here?"

"Of course. The doctors and facilities here are second to none. The infusion treatments last about four hours and occur every eight weeks. How far advanced is your brother's disease?"

Joe noticed Rincon's chart sitting on top of the stack at the side of the desk closest to the exam rooms. "Actually, I don't know. He was just recently diagnosed, and I'm just starting to learn about it."

"No worries. Most people don't know much about the disease until they have it." As the nurse droned on about the various protocols and treatments, Joe nodded where appropriate while he waited for her attention to be diverted. It took several minutes but finally her phone rang. She excused herself, turned away from Joe, and began a discussion about employee schedules and vacations. Joe snatched Rincon's file, stuck it inside his jacket, and headed to the men's room. Inside a stall, he pulled out his micro camera and photographed the most current ten pages. When he returned to the nurse's station, she was still on the phone and Rincon was still waiting. He returned the chart to its place of honor and sauntered back towards the elevator.

Chapter Twenty-Eight

With the parole hearing only a few days away, preparations on both sides were in full swing. Murtaugh and the Nash clan were busy orchestrating their lies and coordinating their half-truths. Murtaugh met with Ted more often than he had with any other previous client. He hated every minute of the scheduled meetings with the creepy little moron, but he knew he had an uphill battle, if not an impossible task, to show Ted in a sympathetic light. Meanwhile, the Nash parents were busy planning a post-hearing fundraiser for the governor.

When Ted was escorted into the attorney room for his last visit with Murtaugh, he was grinning. It took a second for Ted's new look to register with Murtaugh. Then came the double- take. Ted was sporting a Hitler-type mustache and a new hair style. The mustache was bad enough but now his head was shaved on the sides and back. The top was still long and was slicked back in a North Korean dictator sort of way. He looked ridiculous. "What happened to you?"

Ted angled his head from side to side. "You like it?"

"No."

"Why not?"

"It makes you look like a punk."

"Agree to disagree. Plus, you always say I look like a punk."

153

"That's true, but now you look like a punk with genocide on his mind."

"What does that even mean, boss?"

"Ah, the public-school system at its finest. Where did you come up with that look?"

"All the guys are getting this style. Some of the old dudes too. Big Manny, he's in for armed robbery of an old lady bingo tournament, started it. Everyone just started copying it, but I think my hair is now even better than Manny's. One-Eyed Frank in the cell next to mine even asked me what kind of gel I use to get my hair to look so shiny."

"I know I asked, but this is too much information."

"Hey, I think it makes me look more mature. I thought you'd be happy!"

"Heaven help me," said Murtaugh with a grimace. "There is nothing to be done about the hair at this point but lose the mustache."

"What? You're not the boss of me."

Murtaugh sat stiffly in his seat. "Yes, actually I am. You heard me. Get rid of the mustache before the hearing."

"Ok, but you better know what you are doing. It took me three weeks to grow this beauty. If we lose this hearing, I'm going to tell my father that you made me shave."

Murtaugh murmured, "Were you dropped on your head as a baby?"

Ted wasn't sure if his lawyer was kidding or not. So, he just gave a wonky smile to cover all the bases and added, "Hey, look what Eddy-the-Giraffe taught me!" Ted proceeded to crack his knuckles to the tune of Mary Had A Little Lamb. Murtaugh waited patiently for Ted to finish then he politely clapped. Ted explained during the applause, "If you were wondering, Eddy is not really a giraffe. We just call him that because he has a long neck."

"Then isn't that nickname a little too *on the nose?*"

"Huh?"

"Never mind."

For this last meeting with Ted, Murtaugh brought with him Ted's prison file. Based on what Ted had originally told him, Murtaugh had anticipated that the file would reflect Ted's exemplary behavior behind bars. After he reviewed the file, he kicked himself for being a chump. Ted's record was replete with broken rules and boorish antics. Two were particularly discouraging. The first was that another inmate had shown Ted a picture of his wife. Ted stared at the photo for a minute or two and then announced, "I'd tap that!" The other inmate was not amused. The two of them were written up for fighting.

The second event was even more troubling to Murtaugh. A prison nurse claimed that Ted sexually attacked her. When he confronted Ted with the accusation, Ted remained true to form. "Hey man. She came on to me. She wanted it."

Murtaugh couldn't help himself. He actually let out an involuntary belly laugh. He was glad he was not drinking coffee. It would surely have come out of his nose and stained his silk tie. After he composed himself, Murtaugh read out loud the nurse's version verbatim. "Let's see. Here's what she says. 'I came into the examining room to take the inmate's temperature and blood pressure. I put the cuff on his arm, and he said I was hot. That I was the type of girl that he really goes for. I ignored him. He then reached down and started to lift up my skirt. I swatted away his hand and he called me a bitch and grabbed me. I pushed him away and ran out of the room. I called the guards and they came in and got him.' So, Ted, is that the way it happened?"

"Yeah, I guess so. My bad."

Things went downhill from there.

The mood was more somber with the Prestons. Mary and TJ were scheduled to meet again with their attorney in the afternoon. TJ showed up at Mary's house several hours early. Mary was surprised. She always wore her hair librarian style when she went out of the house, but she hadn't yet put it up. It fell softly around her face and down to her shoulders. She gave TJ a kiss on the cheek and exclaimed, "I didn't expect you so early." She looked at her watch. "Did I get the time wrong?"

"No," said TJ. "I came early because we have to talk."

Mary looked down and saw that TJ was carrying a small box. "What do you mean? Can't we just talk when we get to the lawyer's office?"

"Let's go sit down," said TJ.

She hoped she was wrong, but Mary had a feeling she knew what was on TJ's mind. And she knew what was in the box. She steeled herself as her brother began to talk. "Sis, I know we decided when Matthew was eight years old that we would not tell him about the video. And we agreed that we wouldn't give it to the police for fear it would end up on the evening news. And I believe that was the right decision at the time."

"It's still the right decision, TJ. There is still no need for Matthew to see the tape of his father being shot. We agreed it would scar him even more than the fact that his father was killed." Mary started to blink back tears.

TJ gave an apologetic nod but continued in a firm big brotherly tone.

"Look, things have changed. First, Matthew is a full-grown man now. He can handle it. Second, and more importantly, Nash is up for parole and we have to use every tool at our disposal to prevent his release. We have to tell Carly that there were video cameras hidden throughout your house and that the one in your bedroom captured the entire scene from the moment Ted Nash entered the bedroom until Grant was shot."

Mary's face darkened, and she shook her head back and forth. TJ continued.

"Remember, according to the DA, Nash will say that Grant's death was an accident in the course of an ill-conceived attempted burglary. The video shows it was no accident. We have to change the narrative, especially if Nash has the ear of the governor." Mary gave her brother a pleading look. TJ let his comments sink in, then added, "I don't like it either. I wish we had some other way to gain an advantage. But I can't think of one. Can you?"

"But Matthew will also see Nash going through and touching my underwear. I don't care for me so much but that will be so embarrassing for Matthew. And more importantly, *seeing* the brutality is much worse than only *hearing* about it."

"Believe me, I understand. It is not ideal. I just want to leave no stone unturned. Remember when we were little? Mom always told us to do our best. To never look back asking '*what if?*' We will always second-guess ourselves if the parole board recommends parole and we left something on the table."

TJ decided to give Mary some time to chew it over. "How about this? Let's tell Carly about the tape and let her decide whether to use it. As you see, I brought it with me. I'll take it with us so that Carly can take a look." Mary put her head in her hands. Her hair hung straight down so her face was totally obscured. Mary's shoulders and hair shook as she quietly sobbed. "What do you say?" asked TJ.

Without looking up, a resigned Mary said softly, "Okay."

By the time that Mary and TJ arrived at Carly's office, Mary's demeanor had changed. Her jaw was set, and she had a determined look in her eye. TJ knew that look. Mary was now primed to take a cannon to a knife fight. Ted Nash had better get ready for disappointment.

Carly was at first disturbed that they hadn't told her before about the video. She typically dealt with clients who hid *bad* information from her. This was the first time she could recall when clients had withheld helpful evidence. "You're telling me that this video shows the murder? Why on earth didn't you tell me about this until now?" Carly stared first at Mary, then at TJ. Both were waiting for the other to speak. TJ broke the silence. "I'll take the blame on that. I should've talked to Mary about this as soon as we heard that Nash was seeking parole. I dropped the ball."

Mary looked at her brother and smiled. She interjected, "Actually I'm the one who has resisted using the tape. I didn't want Matthew to see it. He doesn't know about the video. He was too young at the time and I never thought there was a good reason to tell him. Until now perhaps."

"Well, let's put the delay behind us and watch the tape." As Carly queued up the video, she added, "But don't forget that I represent you. I have to know everything that you know in order to protect and further your interests. Understood?"

Mary and TJ both gave faint nods.

The three of them watched the video together two times. Carly leaned back in her chair and gave a sigh. "I can only imagine how hard this is for you. But we're going to cram this tape down Nash's and Murtaugh's throats at the hearing. We will let them commit themselves to their story about an accidental shooting. Then I'll spring the video on them and hang them with it. We will ensure that Nash never gets out and, as a side benefit, we will knock that smug son of a bitch Murtaugh down a peg or two."

Mary could not have been more pleased to have Carly St. Cere as her attorney.

Chapter Twenty-Nine

"We have to tell Matthew," said Mary on the drive home. "He's coming home tomorrow."

"I know. Do you want me to be there?"

"Of course. This is going to be a big shock. Maybe we could just tell him the tape exists but not show it to him. What do you think?"

TJ replied, "Not sure how that would work. He'll see the tape during the parole board hearing even if we don't show it to him beforehand."

"Maybe we could tell him about the tape and instruct him to leave the hearing before the it is played?"

"Do you really think Matthew would agree to that? Do you suppose you can still tell him what to do as if he were a child?"

"Will he forgive us for keeping this a secret from him all these years?"

"Only one way to find out," said TJ.

They did not have to wait long to test the waters. Matthew came home that evening, unexpectedly early and without notice. Mary and TJ had just finished dinner and were plotting over coffee how best to break the news to Matthew. They hadn't gotten very far when the front door burst open and Matthew yelled out, "Anybody home?"

Mary and TJ looked at each other in silence. After a few seconds, TJ called to Matthew, "In here, Matt!" TJ stood to meet Matthew as he sauntered into the room, backpack still hanging on his shoulders. When Matthew broke free from his uncle's hug, Mary half ran to Matthew and embraced him. She didn't let go until Matthew chuckled and said, "Hey, what's going on? I can't remember when I've gotten such a greeting!"

Mary said, "You must be starving. Have you eaten? Why didn't you tell me you were coming tonight?"

Matthew replied, "Just wanted to get here as soon as I could to spend time with you before the hearing. How did the meeting go with the attorney? Anything new with the parole stuff?"

TJ jumped in. "The meeting with Ms. St. Cere went fine. She thinks our chances are good."

Matthew gave an uncertain gaze. "Really? That's great but last I heard she was not overly optimistic. What changed?"

"Let's all sit and have some coffee, shall we?" said Mary.

They retired to the living room where they arranged themselves into a small semicircle with Matthew in the middle. TJ gave a nod to Mary to see if she would begin the conversation. She didn't. Matthew looked at his mom and then at his uncle. "Ok, what's going on? Tell me about the meeting with the attorney."

TJ took up the mantle.

"Matt, I know you were a toddler when your great Nanna passed away. You were too young to remember but she was very frail the last few years. Once she tripped on a rug in her room and fell. She broke her hip. Your father was the only person at home and he, as usual, was in his study doing paperwork. Nanna yelled for help, but your father couldn't hear her. It turns out that she lay there for almost an hour before he came out of the study and heard her muffled cry. Nanna was in the hospital for days having hip replacement surgery.

"Your father was so upset about what happened that he had cameras placed in every upstairs room so that he could keep an eye on Nanna when he was in his study. He ensured that each camera was well hidden because he did not want Nanna to know he had gone to that trouble and expense. And he did not want Nanna to feel like her privacy was being invaded. Your father kept a bank of small monitors in the credenza next to his desk. Whenever he was in there and your mother was out of the house, he opened the doors of the credenza so that he would always know where Nanna was and how she was doing."

Matthew interrupted and said in a matter-of-fact way, "Yes, I knew dad had cameras installed to observe Nanna."

"What! What do you mean?" exclaimed Mary. TJ and Mary both stared at Matthew in dismay.

"Once when I was five or six, I was with dad in his study and I opened the credenza. I saw all the monitors and asked him about them. He told me about Nanna's accident and how he had the cameras installed after that. He said he had never gotten around to taking the cameras out after she passed away. He said, 'You never know, they might come in handy someday.'" There was silence for a few moments. "But what has that to do with the lawyer and the hearing?"

TJ again took the lead. "Well, although the system was quite crude by today's standards, one of the features of the surveillance system was that each camera recorded what it saw. Kind of like a first-generation nanny-cam. Neither your father nor I ever gave that much thought because we were told that the system incorporated auto-overwrite once storage capacity was reached. Apparently, it held seven days of recordings. Then the old recordings would be taped over." He glanced at Mary. "I don't think your mother ever knew about or focused on the recording aspect." Mary nodded.

"Anyway, a few days after your father's death I got to thinking about the cameras, so I slipped into the study while your mother was upstairs lying down. It took me a few minutes to figure out how to work the darn thing, but I eventually determined that the system had captured and recorded the shooting. I saved it. I shared it with your mother after Grant's funeral."

Now it was Matthew's turn to look shocked. "Are you saying that the murder of my father was recorded? And that you have the tape?"

"Yes, and today we gave the tape to Ms. St. Cere."

Matthew was part puzzled and part angry. "Why didn't you ever tell me?"

Now Mary spoke up. "You were too young at the time. And as the years went by, we felt there was no need to have you relive that emotional pain. I'm sorry if we made the wrong decision. But I still think it's best if you never watch the tape."

TJ jumped in. "The only reason the tape is back on the table is because our attorney thinks it will help seal the denial of the parole request. It will show that the shooting was intentional and cold-blooded."

Matthew said, "I want to see it. Now."

Mary replied, "Honey, we gave the tape to Ms. St. Cere. We don't have it here. And even if we did, I would ask you to avoid watching it. It's very disturbing, on many levels. In fact, Ms. St. Cere plans to show the tape at the hearing. May I suggest that you step out of the room while it is played?"

"Not a chance," Matthew said defiantly.

TJ smiled and put his hand on Matthew's shoulder.

"I thought you'd say that. And I don't blame you. Just prepare yourself."

"I have been speculating my whole life as to how the shooting happened. And now I'll finally know."

Each of them retreated to their own thoughts for several minutes. After reflection, Matthew's eyes locked onto his mother's and he said, "I'm so sorry you had to carry the weight of this secret for so long. I wish you had let me share the burden with you. But I understand why you and Uncle TJ made the choice you did."

No one had touched their coffee and it was now cold. TJ said, "Let me get another pot."

After TJ left the room, Mary asked about Torrey. "You said Torrey was going to come to the hearing. Are you sure you still want her to do that in light of the tape? That seems like a big ask."

"I'll call her later and see what she says. But she said she wants to come and she's a big girl. She'll probably handle the tape better than I will. By the way, I asked Torrey to meet us at noon at the coffee shop in Sausalito where we're meeting Ms. St. Cere. I figured we could all have some lunch and then drive together to the prison for the 2:30 hearing."

When TJ arrived with fresh coffee, and some apple pie he found in the refrigerator, Matthew was ready to hear more about the meeting with Ms. St. Cere. "So, is the tape the reason why the attorney now thinks we'll win at the hearing?"

"Yes," said TJ. "She thinks that blowhard Murtaugh fellow will suggest that the shooting was an unfortunate accident. The tape proves otherwise."

"What about District Attorney Livingstone? I understand she will be there as a representative of the People of California. What does she say about the tape?"

"Carly told us she will talk to Livingstone about it."

TJ said, "I've never been a fan of lawyers. But that Carly, she's one smart cookie. Not just book smart. Street smart too. If she is confident, then I am confident."

Chapter Thirty

On the morning of the hearing, Matthew, Mary, and TJ flew to San Francisco, rented a roomy Ford, and drove across the Golden Gate Bridge towards Sausalito. It was a good thing that no one was much interested in the view because the fog was so thick that they could barely see the car in front of them. When they pulled into the Sausalito Bakery & Cafe, the mist was heavy and gray. Just like they felt.

Matthew's spirits rose, however, when he saw Torrey standing in the doorway of the restaurant. She had arrived with time to spare in order to ensure she wasn't late. Pursuant to prison rules, she wore nothing the same blue color as the inmates' jumpsuits. Instead she wore a cream-colored business suit with a matching blouse. She looked great, and now Matthew didn't feel so out of place in his grey suit and tie.

Mary wasn't thrilled with the fact that Matthew hadn't shaved for a couple of days. She had never seen him with stubble but decided not to say anything about it. He had agreed to wear the suit and that was enough of a victory.

Ms. St. Cere was already inside and had secured a private round table in the back of the cafe. After pleasantries, they all sat down, and Carly asked that they join hands. She said a prayer for all the voiceless victims of violent crime. No one was hungry, but Carly suggested they eat something because it was going to be a long and difficult day. After placing their meager orders, Carly announced that they needed to go over some things.

"First some housekeeping matters. The hearing will be in a secure part of the prison but there is a slight chance that some event outside of our area will cause the entire facility to go on lock down. It happens about once a month. No need for alarm. Just a heads-up.

"Next, they are very strict about what you can and cannot bring into the facility. As pertains to this group, no purses, cameras or cell phones. I suggest you leave them in the car.

"The way this is going to work is that first we will be escorted by guards to a waiting room inside the prison. When everything is ready, we will be taken from the waiting room to the adjacent parole hearing room where we will be seated together. The Nash family may or may not already be in the hearing room. You will not be put next to them. Then Ted Nash and his attorney will be brought in by a correctional officer. The officer will stand guard during the entire proceeding."

TJ asked, "Who will actually make the decision about parole?"

"There is always a commissioner appointed by the governor, which means it is a political appointment by definition. Many criminal defense attorneys suspect that these appointees simply do the governor's bidding, and this is the biggest threat to justice being done today. And there is a deputy commissioner who is simply a civil service employee.

"The commissioner today is a man named Larry Nudick. Our research shows that Nudick is a 45-year-old career bureaucrat. He has been stuck in various low-level government jobs his entire working life. He is a walking example of the Peter Principle in that he never excelled at any position, but he kept being promoted when someone above him moved on. And there is a lot of turnover at the State. I am not sure how he got this job, but we have learned that his brother-in-law was a college teammate of the governor's new assistant chief of staff. I suspect some cronyism was involved.

"Our deputy commissioner is a complete unknown. If this isn't his first hearing, it's not far from it. He is a relatively young man with a background in social work. He seems to have no criminal law background whatsoever. My investigator talked to a few of his neighbors and they all said he was smart and 'a nice guy.' We will proceed under the assumption that he will try to do the right thing, although we have to wonder what personal agenda would drive his desire to be a parole board member.

"Any questions so far?" Carly looked around the table. Torrey had a confused look on her face. Carly was nothing if not observant. "Torrey, do you have a question?"

"I don't feel like I should say anything. It's not my place. I'm just here to support Matthew, and Mary too if she will let me."

Carly replied, "If you have a question, the others probably do too, whether they know it or not. What is it?"

"Well, this is more like a statement than a question. It sounds like the individuals who are going to decide whether a murderer gets parole are unqualified to make such a judgment, is that correct?"

Everyone nodded in agreement and looked at Carly. "Torrey, you are brilliant. I could not have said it better. Unfortunately, we have to work with what we have within the existing system."

Carly looked at her notes.

"Now let's talk about substance. Normally the order for speaking is that the People's representative goes first, and she basically outlines the elements of the crime and the sentencing parameters. She also typically recommends against the early release on the grounds of public safety. Now you all know the State's representative in our case is District Attorney Livingstone. I have spoken to her at length and I have asked her to make her appearance by video. She has recorded her remarks and we will play them on the TV screen that will be inside the hearing room."

Mary looked concerned. "Why don't you want her to appear in person? She has been very supportive to me. I would think we would want her to come."

"In any other situation, I would agree. But the tape of the shooting changes everything. I didn't even tell her about the tape."

TJ was the quickest to react. "Why not? Isn't she on our side? Why hide it from her?"

"Because she will not like the way I am going to use it. Ms. Livingstone is a courtroom lawyer who is used to playing nice and by archaic rules of evidence. This hearing is an entirely different animal. If I told her about the tape, she would have said that we needed to turn it over to Murtaugh before the hearing, and under criminal law rules she would have been right. But then we would lose the element of surprise. And even if I could have convinced her to withhold the tape, I was afraid she might mention it, intentionally or not, in her opening remarks to the commissioners. I couldn't afford to take that chance.

"The other wonderful consequence of her delivering her speech by videotape is that the video equipment and screen will already be in the room. If it had to be found and brought in, Murtaugh would have time to wonder what we were going to present. I don't want him to have any time to think."

Hearing no objections, Carly continued. "So, after Ms. Livingstone's recorded statement has finished, I expect that Murtaugh will make his pitch. Murtaugh has a very loose relationship with the truth so try not to get upset by how he describes his client and the crime. Then Nash himself will get to speak. I suspect that Murtaugh has Nash on a short leash, so his statement will likely be brief. Then I will use the tape to blast Murtaugh and Nash out of the water." Carly then nodded at Mary. "Finally, you will get a chance to speak. Have you prepared some thoughts?"

Mary said softly, "Yes, but I don't want to have to look at Nash. Can I just talk to the commissioners?"

"Of course. In fact, I would imagine Murtaugh has instructed Nash to avoid eye contact with any of you during the hearing. Not a bad strategy for us to follow also."

Carly opened her briefcase and pulled out a thick sheaf of papers. "I want to thank you for all of these declarations you have provided to me from Grant's friends and colleagues about what an extraordinary person, husband, and father Grant was. I have submitted the original documents to the board. Last we checked, Murtaugh had not submitted any character declarations on behalf of Nash. We'll see if he files any today before the hearing.

"And speaking of declarations, the only thing at all that Murtaugh has submitted is a flimsy affidavit from the quack researcher in Switzerland who claims he can treat Nash with some experimental drug that he has created. I have prepared and submitted three declarations from eminent doctors who conclude that Nash's disease is not fatal in the near-term and that he can be treated in prison as well as anywhere else. The medical issue is a red herring, but we have to address it."

Without reference to the medical parole issue or anything else, Matthew blurted out, "This whole thing is BS!"

Mary declared, "Matthew!"

Matthew pleaded with Carly "No. It really is. Why should my mom have to go through this charade? Why should she have to be in the same room with that killer? Why should our family have to relive this horror? It's outrageous!"

Before Mary could finish admonishing Matthew for his language, Carly interjected. "It's okay, Mary. Matthew is right. But I'll tell you what. I'm ready to go kick some San Quentin butt. Let's go."

While the Preston group was finishing up their meeting at the restaurant, Murtaugh was already at the prison. He wanted one more session with Ted just before the hearing. First though, he had to meet with Mr. and Mrs. Nash to temper their expectations and to secure the long-ago promised declarations from friends and family. Murtaugh wanted to create the impression that there were an infinite number of persons who would vouch for the character of Theodore Nash III.

"What do you mean you haven't got any support letters? You told me two weeks ago you just needed a little more time but would bring them with you today." Silence. "Let me guess," Murtaugh continued, "you couldn't get anyone to sign a letter of support in favor of Ted, right?" Silence. "No one?" Mrs. Nash tried to explain. "All of the other children have been jealous of Ted ever since he was little. Theodore, tell Mr. Murtaugh about when Ted was in first grade and the other kids pushed Ted in a mudpuddle because he had the nicest clothes. And remember when—"

Her husband cut her off. "Clara, stop! Give it a rest." He looked at Murtaugh and said, "Let's tell it like it is. Ted has never had any friends. And I even tried bribing some of *my* friends and clients. No one will sign. So, we will have to go forward without any support submittals."

Murtaugh scowled. "This is not going to play well with the commissioners." He had never had a client for whom they couldn't submit even one sympathetic voucher. But, of course, Ted was a once-in-a-lifetime client, fortunately.

Mr. Nash did have some good news. "I got that doctor in Switzerland to sign that supplemental letter you prepared about how his treatment protocol would help Ted. He made some revisions but, just like you predicted, he still refused to sign at first."

"How much did you have to pay him?"

"Let's just put it this way, his research will be fully funded for ten more years."

Murtaugh nodded as he read over the key text of the signed letter. "I can make this work."

169

After his meeting with Ted's parents, Murtaugh sat alone in the attorney conference room while waiting for Ted. This was his last chance to humanize the monster and he hoped against hope that his previous admonitions would pay off. In the first sixty seconds Murtaugh knew it was useless. Ted was led into the room by a thirty-something female correctional officer. She was sort of cute, seemed nice enough and had Little Orphan Annie freckles and red hair. She appeared to treat Ted with respect. But as soon as she left, and Ted sat down, he scoffed under his breath, "What a bitch."

Murtaugh was at the end of his rope. "Ted, that lady seemed perfectly professional. Why would you call her a bitch?"

"Didn't you see that? She was giving me the eye when she opened the door for me to enter the room. But when I gave her my 'come and get it' smile, she ignored me. What a bitch."

"Ted, I'm trying to like you. I really am. But you are making it difficult."

"Hey, I'm just keeping it real."

"I don't think that's a thing."

"Whatever you say boss. So how long is this going to take today? And when will I get released?"

Murtaugh just sighed and gave a silent shrug, "Let's not get ahead of ourselves. We've covered everything in our previous meetings but let's go over the highlights. Number one—Remember, I'll do most of the talking. When it's your turn, just say how sorry you are; how you were young and immature; and that you are a new man now. That you don't even recognize the boy that was involved in the crime. That the new man you are would never even think of hurting another person. This is the point where you could shed that tear we talked about."

"I have been practicing crying by picturing the horse head scene from The Godfather. I had a pony when I was a kid."

"Okay, whatever works for you."

After a long pause, and without prompting, Ted volunteered with a faraway look in his eyes, "My pony died."

"Oh, I'm sorry to hear that. What happened?"

"We kept the horse at a private stable and one day the pony got out. The stable owner said I left the gate open and I got in trouble." Ted's voice lowered. "The next day the pony was dead. Someone had bashed its head in."

Murtaugh looked shocked. "That's terrible!"

"I didn't do it."

Murtaugh was speechless. The silence was deafening. Ted started to squirm, and he continued his protest. "They all said I did it, but you can ask my mom. She believed me," said Ted as his lips curled into the slightest of smiles.

Murtaugh was sorry he had asked about the pony. He swallowed hard as he stared at Ted.

After a few seconds, he decided to get back to the business at hand. "Now as I was saying, Number one is that I will do the talking. Number two—with respect to your medical issues, don't worry about giving the disease or problems a name. Just describe your symptoms and complaints. It's okay to exaggerate a little. The commissioners might ask you some questions about how your medical problems impair your abilities to move, sleep, and so forth. If they do ask questions, just give short answers. Number three—don't mention anything about your prison record, especially the incident involving the nurse. Maybe the other side won't bring it up and even if they do, there is nothing particularly helpful to say about it. And Number four—do not fidget. Just sit still and keep your eyes forward. And whatever is done or said, do not engage the Prestons. Don't even look at them."

"Who are they?"

Murtaugh could barely hide his exasperation. "The Prestons. The family of the man you killed!"

"Oh right. Copy that. You can count on me."

Chapter Thirty-One

Never in her wildest dreams did Mary Preston imagine that she would be inside the gates of San Quentin prison, much less that she would be in the same room with Ted Nash. What a nightmare. And in her sheltered mind she assumed a prison that housed murderers, rapists, and general evildoers would be fashioned like a dark medieval dungeon where prisoners in leg irons were given microscopic rations of bread and water. Instead, she was greeted by open, park-like grounds and institutional buildings that could have housed any number of businesses and upstanding employees. She exclaimed, "Carly, this looks like a country club, not at all like Alcatraz. Look at all the trees and flowers in the courtyard. And look over there," she said while pointing to the left, "it's right on the beautiful Bay!"

Carly chuckled, "Yes it's wonderful, if you don't mind the high walls and the guards with machine guns."

"You know what I mean. I can't believe this place looks so," she hesitated while she searched for the right word, "*normal*."

Matthew had never told his Mom that he was already familiar with the grounds and amenities. He decided not to add insult to injury by telling her about the state-of-the-art athletic fields and equipment. Or the top-shelf free health care.

Carly replied to Mary, "Well, they do try to treat the inmates humanely these days. The original cellblocks date back to the 1850s. They say prisoners back then were routinely tortured." Matthew wasn't sure about anyone else, but he thought that sounded reasonable.

After the group signed in, it was on to security where the scrutiny was infinitely greater than at the airport. The guards running the metal detection devices made TSA agents look like cub scouts. But no one seemed to mind the tight security measures. Finally, they made it to their private waiting area outside the hearing room. There were enough chairs, but no one felt like sitting.

Carly tried to keep things as light as possible so that no one would start to freak out. She had seen it before. She had witnessed first-hand what being forced to relive traumatic memories could do. One of her clients was a mother who had lost her son when he was a customer in a 7-11 that was being robbed by an 18-year-old gang member. Apparently, the hold-up man was charged by his homeboys to rob the cashier and any customer who happened to come in. Four other gang members watched from their car. As the cashier was in the process of opening up the cash register, the mother's son walked in to buy a Slurpee. When the son's money was demanded, he panicked and tried to run. He was shot three times in the back. The cashier testified at the trial that the gang members in the car were cheering.

The shooter came up for parole after only five years. The mother was there to oppose the early release. Carly had left the waiting room to use the restroom. When she came back, the mother was standing by the door to the hearing room with her right hand tucked behind her back. When Carly asked her what was going on, the mother said she could no longer pretend to be all civilized about this. She raised her right hand to shoulder level at which time Carly saw the remains of a small hair comb. The mother had broken off the teeth on the hard-plastic comb so that the jagged edge of the spine could be used as a shiv. She started pulling on the locked door trying to get into the hearing room, crying out

173

that she was going to gouge out the eyes of the shooter. The comb idea was brilliant actually. In fact, it was so ingenious that, after that incident, plastic combs were put on the list of banned items at California penitentiaries.

So, Carly said airily to no one in particular, "Well, here we are in the belly of the beast. Probably the safest place to be within 100 miles. More officers per square foot than New York or Chicago." She looked over at Torrey.

Torrey said. "Don't look at me. I'm not scared."

Mary interjected, "Well, I'm worried, but not about my safety. It's just that, now that we are here, I don't know if I can do this. Be in the same room with Grant's killer." Carly admitted to herself that this was a very unnatural gathering—against human nature. But Carly didn't expect any outbursts from Mary. And she didn't have a comb. TJ put his arm around his sister and Matthew went to her, gently pushing her to sit in a chair.

"Don't worry Mom. It'll be worth it to see the look on his face when parole is denied. And I guarantee that he'll stay in here for the rest of his life."

Torrey gazed at Matthew as he spoke. The wheels began to turn.

Chapter Thirty-Two

Larry Nudick couldn't wait for the hearing to begin. This was going to be the best day of his professional life. He couldn't stop thinking, "The governor knows my name. He knows who I am, and he wants me to do him a favor." He only wished he could tell his father who always said he wouldn't amount to anything. Said his government jobs were dead ends. Said he was sucking off the tit of the taxpayers. "Just wait until he sees me getting an invitation to the Governor's Ball. Then we'll see what's what!"

Nudick had no idea how his life was going to change when his older sister married Franklin Williams, the best friend of a member of the governor's inner circle. Larry took an instant dislike to the guy when they were first introduced right before the wedding. His sister said, "This is my brother Larry." The husband-to-be snickered and said, "Oh, so you are Little Larry. Your sister told me all about you!" Little Larry had hated his nickname as a child and Larry hated even more when his family still used it at family gatherings. His father was the most frequent offender. Besides, at only 5'6" and two hundred and fifty pounds, Larry was more round than little.

But now that he was a beneficiary of the political machine, he was starting to like his brother-in-law. First Franklin put in a good word so that Larry got the commissioner job. Then, last week he got a call from the deputy chief of staff himself, Louis Barkley. Louis had said that the governor had heard good things about Nudick. That he had his eye on Nudick and was hoping to bring him onto the governor's staff in the next few months. Louis had asked, "Does that sound like something that might appeal to you?"

Naturally Larry didn't want to sound too anxious but then he heard himself burst out with, "Wow, that would be great!"

A day or two later he had a second call from Barkley.

"Hi Larry, this is Louis again over at the governor's office. Do you have a minute?" As a State employee, he had unlimited time, but he just replied, "Sure Louis, what do you need?"

Louis said, "Larry, we just learned that you have been assigned a parole hearing case over at San Quentin involving some poor schmuck named Theodore Nash III. Apparently, he accidentally shot a neighbor years ago when he was a troubled young man. He now has some sort of disease and he and his family want to move to Europe for treatment. This will save the taxpayers a lot of money, which we are all in favor of, right? And we know he won't be a threat to California's public safety because he won't be living here. The governor wonders if you could do him a personal favor and grant the parole."

Larry couldn't care less about whether some no-name criminal got released or rotted in prison. But he hemmed and hawed for a few moments as if he were considering the implications of the request. Before he could reply, Louis added, "Oh, by the way, the governor says a new position on his staff is going to open up even earlier than expected. It will pay twice what you are making now. Would you be able to start next month?"

"I think I could close things up around here by then."

"Great. I'll tell the governor. He will be pleased. So, what do you think about this Nash parole? You think you can get that done for the governor?"

"Of course. As you probably heard, I'm a team player."

"That's fantastic. You're going to have a newbie deputy commissioner on the Nash case. We cannot afford a split decision. You think you can get him to go along?"

"Leave it to me."

"Thanks Larry. We are counting on you." Louis hung up the phone, smiled to himself, and checked another item off his 'to do' list.

Larry was smiling too. Finally, the Golden Ticket.

Chapter Thirty-Three

Matthew could not believe how spartan and nondescript the industrial brownish-yellow hearing room was. A few old wooden tables and metal chairs that looked like war surplus were scattered on the linoleum floor. The largest table, with two chairs behind it, was at one end of the rectangular room. The two smaller tables at the other end were side-by-side, with about three feet in between. Matthew guessed these were going to pass as counsel tables. A large combination TV/VCR on a rolling metal stand was situated next to one of the tables. The only artwork was a hanging photo of California's esteemed governor. Fittingly, an almost dead fiscus tree was in the corner.

Matthew's group was the first in and they were led to a row of four chairs pushed against a side wall. Carly organized the tableau with Mary closest to Carly's table, then TJ, then Matthew, and Torrey at the end. While they waited for others to enter, Torrey squeezed Matthew's arm. As she did so, Matthew reached into his suit pocket and pulled out a pair of mirrored sunglasses and put them on. Matthew leaned over and whispered to Torrey, "The light is kind of bright in here." Torrey had never seen Matthew wear sunglasses indoors and she did not think the room was bright. In fact, she thought the old fluorescent ceiling lights were rather dull. But Matthew was playing it safe with his stubble and sunglasses. Carly had said that Nash wouldn't be looking over at them, but Matthew did not want to be recognizable during their next encounter if Nash snuck a glimpse.

Next into the room were the Nash parents. Mr. and Mrs. Nash were escorted to two chairs placed a few feet behind the Murtaugh counsel table. Matthew wondered why they had been granted special dispensation to be there. TJ leaned over to Matthew.

"I know what you are thinking. This is supposed to be for family members of the victim only. But Carly and Murtaugh made a deal, with your mom's blessing, that you could bring Torrey and Nash could bring his parents." Matthew knew that must have been a real sacrifice for his mother. He would thank her later. For now, he just said to TJ, "Oh, okay."

Murtaugh then entered, followed by Nash, dressed in a blue prison jumpsuit. Nash was not handcuffed but a burly-looking guard had hold of Nash's arm as he was marched to his chair. Nash was limping. The guard then took up a position just to the side of Nash. The guard wore a sidearm and a billy club. Matthew wished he could have five minutes alone with Nash and either weapon. Torrey poked Matthew in the side. "Is that him? That little twerp? And what's with that hairdo?"

"I guess that's him," Matthew said in his back-stage voice. "I've never seen him before." Matthew used his new sunglasses to good effect. He knew his eyes were not visible, so he could secretly stare at Nash.

Murtaugh stood next to Carly and tried to make small talk. Carly ignored him by sitting down to look at her files. He kept moving closer, trying to rattle Carly by infringing on her personal space. Carly huffed an exasperated sigh and waved her hand dismissively. He eventually got the message and pretended to adjust his already perfect tie while sitting down in his own chair. Murtaugh finally noticed that there were other people in the room. He ignored Nash's parents but looked over at the Prestons and gave his patented gleaming smile. Torrey was watching.

"Look at that guy," she said in a low voice to Matthew. "Can you imagine that he has the nerve to smile at us? He looks like a middle-aged Ken doll, except that that guy's teeth are whiter, and he's more suntanned." Torrey paused for effect. "And his hair is more perfect." Another pause. "And he has had more plastic surgery than Michael Jackson." Longer pause. "I bet his silk tie cost more than my entire outfit."

Matthew could see that Torrey was trying to get him to relax, but he could not manage even the slightest smile. All he could muster was a quick rub of her hand to acknowledge her efforts.

"Are you even listening to me?" asked Torrey with a jab and a crinkle of her nose.

"Sure," groaned Matthew as he continued to keep his eyes on Ted Nash. Yes, Murtaugh was a bad guy—a facilitator—but it was Nash who had pulled the trigger.

Finally, the two commissioners entered the room and sat at the head table. Nudick wasted no time in letting the participants, and his deputy, know who was in charge.

"Good afternoon everyone. I am Larry Nudick, Commissioner, and this is Assistant Commissioner, Anthony Mills. Here is what is going to happen. We will take the testimony of each side. Then when everyone has been heard, we will excuse you and the two of us will deliberate the testimony, the declarations, and the arguments. We will then call you back in and announce our decision."

Nudick did not want to give his sidekick an opportunity to say anything so Nudick nodded to Carly. "Ms. St. Cere, I understand that District Attorney Livingstone could not be here in person, but you have arranged for her remarks to be delivered by pre-recorded video, is that correct?"

"Yes, it is." Without another word, Carly got up, turned the TV monitor so that that everyone in the room could see, and pushed the 'play' button. Marcie Livingstone appeared. She was sitting behind her desk dressed in a black business suit. She opened the folder in front of her and began reciting the facts of the Nash crime. She made a particular point of stating that the Prestons and her office had agreed to not seek the death penalty in exchange for life in prison *without* the possibility of parole. She concluded strongly, "On behalf of the People of the State of California, I strenuously object to the grant of parole for this inmate. He has shown no remorse. There is no evidence that he is rehabilitated. And I fear for the public safety of our citizens. Parole must be denied."

Nudick was not impressed. Every district attorney at every parole hearing said the same thing. He was more interested in Murtaugh's presentation. Yes, everyone knew that Murtaugh was a sleazeball, but today, he was Nudick's sleazeball. He expected that he could use whatever Murtaugh said to convince his deputy to go along with parole. Nudick gestured to Murtaugh, who rose and gave his trademark smile. He bowed his head slightly to Mary Preston but thereafter focused his attention on Nudick, who he knew was supposed to do the governor's bidding. He glanced at Mills every so often to make it look good.

"Gentlemen, when Ted Nash was a confused and troubled youngster, he had an ill-conceived plan to steal some valuables from a neighbor's house when no one was home. On the morning in question, he watched everyone who lived in the house leave for the day. Ted went in the back door and made his way up into the master bedroom to search for cash or jewelry. Unfortunately for everyone, Grant Preston came home unexpectedly and surprised Ted. Being an immature kid, Ted had brought his mother's pistol with him to the house because that's what burglars did in the movies. He had no thought that he was ever going to use it. When Mr. Preston walked in and confronted Ted, Ted panicked. He drew the gun to scare Mr. Preston. It accidentally went off. Ted didn't even know the shots had hit Mr. Preston until the police arrested Ted and told him that Preston had been fatally injured. Ted is very sorry. He has grown up in the many years he has spent in prison. He is now rehabilitated and ready to reenter society."

Murtaugh looked back at Ted who was doing as instructed. He was keeping his head down and nodding. Murtaugh turned back toward Nudick.

"You could grant parole just based on the facts I have outlined, but there is much more to justify his release. First of all, Ted has been diagnosed with small cell carcinoma of the lung. But I would be the first to say that if that were his only medical issue, then medical parole would not be appropriate. As it turns out, the lung cancer is the least of his problems. Ted has also been stricken with an extremely rare disorder called Lambert-Eaton Myasthenic Syndrome. In this country, it is thought to be incurable. This is an autoimmune disease which affects nerves and muscles. It is very debilitating. Ted suffers from a variety of symptoms which are going to get progressively worse. He has weakness in his lower limbs which produces a waddling gait. The Chief of Medicine here at the prison says in her reports that Ted may be unable to walk at all in the near future. Furthermore, Ted has difficulty chewing and swallowing. His speech is affected and may soon deteriorate to garble."

Now Murtaugh was in the groove. He began walking towards the commissioners, chest puffed out, and gesturing as he spoke.

"Treating Ted for these diseases here in prison is impossible and the treatment is not working. He gets injections of immunoglobulin every three months and what is referred to as 3,4-DAP. Despite the cost and medical resources taken up to treat Ted here, the treatments have not even slowed the progression of the disease."

Murtaugh flung his open hand at Mr. and Mr. Nash. "But there is an alternative. Dr. Von Bergen in Switzerland is conducting experimental clinical research on treatments for Lambert-Eaton and the Nash family has agreed, as a condition of Ted's release, that they will move to Switzerland and pay for all of Ted's treatment for the rest of his life, however long that might be. Dr. Von Bergen wants to try plasma exchange and other cutting-edge therapies on Ted. That kind of attention and medicine is not available in the U.S. and certainly can never happen in prison. It requires round-the-clock medical resources and unlimited funds."

Turning his attention back to Nudick, Murtaugh put the finishing touches on his argument.

"You have the authority to grant early parole under Penal Code section 3550. And, as you well know, a federal court recently ordered California to expand the Medical Parole program due to overcrowding in our prisons. Granting early parole on a medical basis would not only comply with the spirit of the federal court ruling, it would also save the taxpayers of this great state millions of dollars over Ted's life span."

Murtaugh paused while he walked back to his table.

"Anything else, Mr. Murtaugh?" asked Nudick.

"Actually, yes." He stared directly at Nudick. "Your primary task is to ensure that the public safety is protected. That means the citizens of California. Setting aside everything else, there will be no threat to public safety when you grant parole because Ted will not be in California. As soon as he is released, he and his parents will be moving to Europe." He sat down with a contented sigh.

"Thank you, Mr. Murtaugh. I understand Mr. Nash would like to address the Board. Is that correct?"

"Yes. May he remain seated sir? It is difficult for him to stand for any length of time."

"Of course. Mr. Nash, the floor is yours."

Ted raised his head and looked at the commissioners. "I am so sorry. It was an accident. I didn't mean to shoot him." This was the point where he had planned to cry. He tried to summon a tear, but none would come. The horse head scene wasn't working because he couldn't think of the horse and what he was supposed to say next at the same time. He started to panic. He didn't know what to do. Should he proceed without crying? Should he ask Murtaugh for alternative instructions? He decided to cover his face with his hands and pretend he was crying. He put his forehead on the table. Ted was jiggling his foot so hard that the counsel table was shaking. After a few seconds, Murtaugh figured out what was happening, and he played along. "Ted, are you alright? Can you go on?" Ted didn't know if he should answer so he did nothing. Murtaugh put his hand on Ted's shoulder and addressed the commissioners. "I guess he is not going to be able to give the rest of his statement. He is too distraught. Please accept our apologies."

Nudick quickly replied. "We understand, Mr. Murtaugh. This proceeding must be very difficult for Mr. Nash."

Chapter Thirty-Four

Matthew gritted his teeth and balled his fists. He could hardly manage to avoid gagging over the performance he had just witnessed. It was a transparent joke. But Nudick seemed to buy it.

Matthew had been conflicted about seeing the video of the murder, but he was suddenly very grateful that Uncle TJ had saved the video and that Carly was going to use it to blow Nash out of the water. As Carly stood to begin her recitation of facts and argument, Matthew noticed that Ted had raised his head. His eyes were not red or wet. He looked remarkably calm.

"Gentlemen, I am Carly St. Cere, here on behalf of the wonderful Preston family." As she gestured to the group, Matthew kept his hidden eyes on Ted Nash. It probably took all of his willpower, but Ted did not look over at the Prestons. "The statements you have heard from Mr. Nash and Mr. Murtaugh were so full of misstatements, omissions, and falsehoods that it is difficult to know where to begin. So, let's focus on what was *not* said by them.

"First, Mr. Murtaugh stated that Penal Code section 3550 gives you the authority to grant early medical parole. But, as I am sure Mr. Murtaugh knows, that statute expressly states that it does *not* apply to inmates sentenced to life without the possibility of parole. So, it is irrelevant here.

"Second, Mr. Murtaugh stated that Nash was just a kid when this murder occurred. Actually, he was 26 years old. Hardly a child.

"Third, Mr. Murtaugh stated that Nash has been rehabilitated. In point of fact, his prison record is replete with rule violations, including a recent sexual assault of a staff nurse. Guards in the vicinity rescued the victim, otherwise who knows what Nash would have done."

Much to the dismay of Murtaugh, Ted whispered under his breath, but loud enough for all to hear, "She was asking for it!" Carly gave an *I told you so* look to the commissioners.

"Fourth, this entire medical parole issue is a farce. As you can see from the declarations I submitted from three expert doctors, Nash's medical problems have been caused by his own life choices. His lung cancer was indisputably caused by his smoking habit. The Lambert-Eaton disorder is nothing more than an autoimmune reaction to the lung cancer. Mr. Murtaugh left that out. And Nash gets state-of-the-art treatment here at the prison.

"The most glaring omission is that there was not one word about justice, about fairness, or about the victim's family. Nash has the audacity to take a life and then beg for his own. Shameful."

Carly got up slowly from her chair and walked over to the television monitor. She reached into her pocket and pulled out the videotape of the murder. She held it above her head as she spoke. "But do you know what is the most egregious aspect of this dog-and-pony show put on by Mr. Murtaugh and his client? Their entire argument is based on a false premise. They are lying to you about the facts of the shooting. This was no accident. It was cold-blooded murder."

Murtaugh jumped out of his seat. "Mr. Nudick, this is outrageous! I have been sitting here listening to these unsupported accusations and attacks on my character. Enough is enough!"

Torrey leaned forward in her chair, hanging on every word.

Nudick was caught off guard. This sort of back-and-forth was unheard of in these proceedings. While he was trying to decide what to say, Carly pivoted towards Murtaugh, pressed her fingers to her lips, and responded in a defiant but even tone, "Mr. Murtaugh, I did not interrupt you during your fantasy speech, I would appreciate the same courtesy so that I can finish my presentation."

Murtaugh did not back down. "Mr. Nudick, there is no evidence to support the claim of an intentional killing. There were no witnesses and Mr. Nash has testified that the shooting was a terrible accident. I object to Ms. St. Cere's entire argument and I ask that her comments be stricken from the record."

Nudick was surprised again, but this time it was because his assistant jumped into the fray without warning. Mills firmly stated to Murtaugh, "This isn't a court of law, Mr. Murtaugh. There is no court reporter or formal record in this administrative proceeding. The criminal rules of evidence don't apply here. Ms. St. Cere has an impeccable reputation for the truth and I, for one, would like to hear her out. So please sit down so she can finish."

Murtaugh reluctantly sat while Carly inserted the tape into the VCR. "Contrary to what Mr. Murtaugh just said, we all are going to be witnesses to the murder. This is a tape of Nash killing Mr. Preston."

Murtaugh wanted to jump up again but he was unable to move. Ted's mouth was gaping open. Both commissioners leaned forward in their chairs. Neither Mary nor TJ wanted to see the tape again. They looked down at their hands. Matthew was half in shock, but he knew he had to watch. Torrey figured she couldn't help Matthew if she did not know what happened. The tape started to play.

Torrey audibly gasped when she saw Ted pawing through Mary's underwear. She felt Matthew's entire body tense up where her arm was pressed against his. Although the tape played in real time, it seemed to Matthew to be in

187

slow-motion. Those few minutes seemed to take forever. Even without sound, the blast of the gun could be felt through the screen. There was no mistaking that Ted aimed the first shot into his father's face and the next two shots were simply for good measure.

When the tape went dark, Murtaugh loosened his tie and slumped in his seat. The room was silent. No one moved or spoke. Both commissioners glared at Ted and then at Murtaugh. Carly walked slowly over to Mary and rested her hand on Mary's bowed head. Carly said, "It's over, Mary. You can look up now." Mary couldn't. Her shoulders were shaking with grief as she rubbed her eyes with her fingertips. Carly said, "Take a few minutes. I am sure the commissioners would be willing to take a short break before you give your statement."

Matthew turned his attention back to a squirming Nash who blinked his eyes several times. Matthew was far away but he could see that now there was a tear in his right eye. From the expression on Nash's face, Matthew was pretty sure that the sorrowful look was not regret over the shooting, it was angst from being found out as a liar. But Matthew didn't really care which factor was the driving force.

He scoffed under his breath with a bitter, tight-lipped smile. "The chickens are finally coming home to roost, you bastard."

During the ten-minute break, Carly and TJ consoled Mary. Matthew saw Murtaugh standing with Mr. and Mrs. Nash having a heated discussion. Theodore Nash II looked like he was going to have a stroke, as he wiped sweat from his upper lip and pulled at his collar. Matthew could only imagine that Mr. Nash was giving Murtaugh the third-degree for not finding out about the murder scene tape. Ted Nash sat looking blank as if he had just seen a ghost. And he pretty much had.

Torrey watched Matthew staring at Ted. She didn't have to wonder what was going through his mind.

When the hearing reconvened, Mary did not turn in her chair to face the commissioners. She did not look at anyone. Instead, she stared straight ahead at the wall while giving her statement. Matthew noted that she was speaking in the same depersonalized tone that she had used in the months following his father's death. During that time, she would say to Matthew and TJ, "I feel like I am in the twilight zone. This can't be real."

As she addressed no one in particular, she could barely be heard—but no one dared to tell her to speak up. Everyone just strained their ears in order to not miss a word. "In the video you saw two extremes. On the one hand, you saw the face of a wonderful husband, a perfect father, and a man of honor and integrity. On the other hand, you saw the face of evil. All these years of grieving. All these years of imagining what our life together would have been like. All these years of struggling to cope. At least Matthew and I had some comfort in knowing that Mr. Nash would be in prison for the rest of his life. Now we are having to relive the old wounds and emotional pain—it is as if the murder were happening all over again. I thought we had closure. Yet here I am. Here we all are. But most of all, here is my only son, having to see a tape of his father's murder, simply to block an animal from being released from his well-deserved cage."

Mary then turned and looked at Matthew. Her hands were visibly trembling, but she suddenly had some life in her voice. "Grant was the best father in the world. He and Matthew had a special bond. Their love was palpable. My heart breaks to think of what Matthew missed out on by not having had his father since the age of eight. I weep at night thinking about the hole in Matthew's life, and the hole in my heart. Counsel for Mr. Nash is here asking you to show compassion for his client. I ask you for justice. Please keep my husband's killer behind bars."

After a respectful pause, Nudick said, "Thank you Mrs. Preston." He then offered the floor to other speakers. "Is there anyone else who would like to make a statement?"

Matthew's face clouded over. He stood and raised his voice.

"We should be talking about execution, not parole."

Nudick was quick to react.

"Young man, I can understand your feelings, but that kind of comment is not appropriate here. Please refrain from such remarks or we will have you removed from this proceeding."

Matthew continued to stand defiantly. Torrey started pulling on his forearm to get him to sit. He finally did. Nudick's face hardened and he said, "Now, do you want to put a statement into the record?"

"I said everything I had to say."

"Alright then. Everyone vacate the room please so we can deliberate. We will call you back in when we have made a decision."

Chapter Thirty-Five

"Carly, you were magnificent!" said TJ as they sat around the table in their private conference room.

"Yes," said Matthew. "Absolutely brilliant."

"Thank you so much for believing in us and our cause," added Mary faintly.

"I have never been prouder of any clients," replied Carly. "Mary, your statement was perfect in every way. And Matthew," she said as she grinned, "you have an uncanny way of cutting through the bull. A bit unorthodox, but I applaud you."

Carly had them do another hand-holding prayer for the voiceless crime victims in our society. Then they waited, each buried in his or her own thoughts. Torrey decided that silence was not healthy or productive. "So, that Nash really has a thing for women's underwear, right? What a pervert!"

Carly laughed out loud, giving the cue that levity was okay. TJ and Matthew followed suit. Even Mary, after some hesitation, gave a barely perceptible closed-lip grin. For the next hour, they rehashed the hearing, alternating between making fun of Murtaugh's looks and arguments, and talking seriously about the way the commissioners had reacted to the video. Everyone felt optimistic that parole would be denied but no one wanted to jinx it by predicting success.

Over in the Nash waiting room, the atmosphere was glum. Theodore and Clara could hardly look at Murtaugh, much less at Ted. After all they had done for Ted, he couldn't even tell *them* the truth. And Murtaugh, he was supposed to be a titan of the legal profession and the Preston attorney had made him look foolish.

Murtaugh knew there was no point in chastising Ted, but he couldn't help himself. He knew they were in big trouble and he wanted to shift blame away from himself in front of Ted's parents. "Ted, it looks like the story that this was an accidental shooting has backfired. And the commissioners probably won't believe that you have been rehabilitated in light of your prison record and your outburst in there about the nurse incident." The silence in the small room was deafening. "If parole is denied, we can try again in a few years," reflected a gloomy Murtaugh.

Clara cried, "We can't wait any longer. Ted is dying in here! And I need my baby back!"

Mr. Nash continued to berate Murtaugh. "I'm holding you responsible for this catastrophe. You had better come up with a better Plan B than trying again in a few years!"

Murtaugh swallowed hard. He was used to dishing out abuse, not receiving it. Before he could reply to Mr. Nash, there was a knock on the door. A guard announced, "They are ready for you back inside."

While the Nash and Preston groups were hashing over the hearing, Nudick and Mills had each gathered their thoughts and positions. Nudick was taken aback by the fireworks during the hearing, but he quickly got over any feelings of guilt or sympathy when he remembered his own self-interest in the outcome.

He searched through his booklet of *Parole Board Directives* and found what he was looking for. Mills looked ashen and was staring down at his notes. Nudick decided he should take the bull by the horns. He needed to work on Mills.

"So, Anthony, how about that for a wild hearing?"

"I'm new at this, so I'm still kind of shaking. Have you ever seen anything like that?"

Nudick wanted to sound like the voice of seasoned sage but he had to admit that this hearing was far more dramatic than any other over which he had presided. "Well I certainly have never seen a videotape of a shooting played at a parole hearing. Good thing for us that we have to disregard it in our decision."

Mills wrinkled up his nose and squinted. "What do you mean?"

"You know. Remember a few months ago we all got that written directive from the governor's office that emphasized that parole board commissioners are not to consider the severity of the crime that was committed." He opened the booklet to the section he had found. "See here," he said as he pointed. He gave Mills a moment to scan heading of the instruction—Directive #32: The Purpose of the Parole Board is not to retry the Case—without giving Mills an opportunity to read the small print exceptions that made the directive moot in this case. "Therefore, it doesn't matter if the shooting was first degree murder or not. We can't take that into account at this time. That was a matter for the criminal justice system."

"That doesn't seem right. And it doesn't seem fair to the Prestons."

"Perhaps, but we need to remain totally neutral. We can't let our personal feelings towards the perpetrator or the victim's family control our decision. In that regard, our hands are tied. So, let's talk about the other issues. It seems to me we have three things to consider, all of which weigh in favor of granting parole." Mills looked shell-shocked. Nudick could see that Mills was a malleable sort so he decided to hit him with everything but the kitchen sink before Mills could mount any opposition.

"First," explained Nudick, "the evidence is overwhelming that Nash's medical treatment hasn't improved his condition. In fact, even the prison doctors say he is getting progressively worse. It sounds like Nash will die a painful death if he is left here. I don't want his blood on my hands." Mills shrugged and nodded. "Second, the cost of treatment here is staggering even though it is ineffective. I have it on good authority that the governor would like to add millions to the budget for improvement of inmate care, but he can't do so when a few of the prisoners are using up the majority of the healthcare dollars. So paroling Nash will allow many others who are incarcerated get better care. Third, and perhaps most importantly, our primary charge is to protect the safety of our citizens. In this case, a condition of the parole is that Nash will move to Europe so there is no risk to any Californian."

Nudick gave an expectant look to Mills as if to say, "So are we on the same page?"

Mills knew in his gut that something was wrong, but he was intimidated by Nudick's experience. "I just don't know. That tape was compelling. It really shook me up," he said slowly.

Nudick had one last argument that he thought would resonate with Mills. "Think of it this way. We are just making a recommendation. The governor will make the final decision by whether he signs the parole papers. He knows all about the State's finances. He has access to every medical expert. He and his staff know what is required to comply with the prison overcrowding mandate. He is honorable and has available to him all the information in the world. The citizens of California voted him into office and trust that he will do the right thing." Mills had a painful expression on his face, but he couldn't think of how to articulate his opposition. Nudick looked at his watch and casually asked, "So are we in agreement? We need to get out of here if we're going to beat the rush hour traffic."

194

Chapter Thirty-Six

By the time everyone had reconvened in the hearing room, Murtaugh was sweating bullets. Not only would his reputation take a hit if parole were denied, he would also forfeit his bonus. In his mind he had already spent the money. Nudick had better come through.

The Preston group was loose and optimistic. Carly sat bolt upright in her chair, ready to leap up and hug Mary. TJ and Mary sat close together with locked arms. Torrey grabbed Matthew's hand and held tight. Matthew stared through his sunglasses at Nash with laser focus, even when Nudick started to speak.

Nudick cleared his throat and read from his handwritten order. "Ladies and Gentlemen, we want to thank everyone for coming today and participating in this serious and solemn proceeding. Both sides were persuasive and made convincing arguments. It has been difficult for all of us."

Matthew's shoulders tensed. He did not like where this was headed. Neither Murtaugh nor Nash had said anything remotely compelling. Both had been caught in outrageous lies. Matthew glanced towards the front of the room and noticed Mills was looking down at his lap. Matthew turned his penetrating glare back to Nash as Nudick continued reading. "The primary purpose of this hearing is to determine whether inmate Theodore Nash III can be safely returned to society. We have the added issue here of Nash's debilitating disease. The medical director of this prison states that the doctors here are unable to provide medical care that will halt, or even slow, the progression of the Eaton-Lambert symptoms." Matthew's jaw tightened, and his mouth went dry. "Nash has provided a declaration from a doctor in Switzerland who has agreed to try some experimental therapies on Nash. This will save the taxpayers of this State potentially millions of healthcare dollars and will help ease the prison overcrowding that the State has been ordered to rectify. It is irrelevant to this hearing that Nash may have caused or contributed to his medical problems."

Torrey felt the muscles in Matthew's arm flexing. She nudged his shoulder to look at her, but all of his attention was focused on Nash. Nudick finished his brief reading with the ultimate insult.

"As a condition of our recommendation that parole be granted, Nash must leave California immediately upon the governor's signing of the parole papers. This hearing is adjourned."

Nudick did not even mention the tape.

While the Prestons sat immobile in stunned silence, the rest of the room emptied as if someone had pulled the fire alarm. Nudick and Mills scuttled out the door behind them. Murtaugh exhaled, stifled a chortle, grabbed Ted by the arm and pulled him toward his parents and the exit behind them. The guard had to double-time it to keep up. Murtaugh knew he had dodged a bullet but, as soon as the door to the hearing room closed behind him, he was quick to put on his "*I knew it all the time*" expression. Though the door was shut, Matthew heard muffled sounds of glee and Ted's faint but distinctive, 'Woo hoo!'

The dazed Prestons were cemented to their chairs. Mary's eyes were blank. Her head began to throb. Matthew was enraged. No one spoke. Torrey, blinking back tears, was the first to break the silence.

"What the hell just happened?" she cried.

Carly said in a knowing tone, "I would say the fix was in."

The days after the hearing were filled with activity. Nudick wasted no time reporting his success to Louis Barkley. Of course, Barkley had already divined the result and had briefed his boss, the governor's chief of staff, Martin Barrows. Barkley had said, "Well, that half-wit Nudick got the deal done as promised. He's going to expect a job in the administration now. What shall we do?"

"Give him some make-work job with a made-up title. You personally supervise him, so you can keep an eye on him. Keep him busy until the governor is reelected. Then ease him out. Tell him it's nothing personal, just budget cuts." Barrows had added with a smirk, "After all, Nudick is a team player. He'll understand."

At his law office, Murtaugh sat at his huge oak desk and gawked at the $100,000 cashier's check that had just arrived from Mr. Nash. He was beaming with the expectation that he would never have to hear the Nash name again. His prediction was short-lived. The check was still in his hot little hands when he got a call from his clandestine contact in the governor's office. Murtaugh was reminded to instruct Mr. Nash that the parole papers wouldn't be signed until after the next election. And, oh by the way, the governor needed to replenish his campaign coffers. How much could the Nash family contribute?

At San Quentin, Nash reveled in his new fame after telling everyone in his cellblock that he was getting released. That it could be any day now. And knowing that he never had to see Murtaugh again, he celebrated by growing his Hitler mustache again.

Things weren't so bubbly in the Preston household. Torrey had driven straight back to school after the hearing while Matthew, Mary, and TJ had returned to Los Angeles together. Matthew knew he had to get back to his medical studies, but he wanted to spend one more night back at home with his mother. They spent the next 24 hours consoling each other and grappling with what had gone wrong. Carly made an unannounced visit to the house and explained their options. They were few and all were bad. Carly figured that if Nudick was somehow on the take, the trail would be well covered. And assuming the governor's office was behind the parole for political gain, there was no administrative action that was going to prevent the governor from signing the papers upon his reelection.

As Matthew took it all in, one thought was uppermost in his mind. The governor would be up for reelection in November—two and a half years away. Matthew was going to graduate from medical school the preceding June. That left a very small window of opportunity.

PART IV

Chapter Thirty-Seven

Matthew had a difficult time concentrating on his studies with the parole hearing still smoldering in his brain. But there was another month of class before the second-year finals, and he had to pass. In fact, he had to do better than pass. He had to solidify his standing near the top of the class in order to have his choice of clinical rotation electives during his third and fourth years of school. The first two years of medical school had been almost exclusively coursework with little exposure to actual patients. Matthew was ecstatic that the bookwork was almost at an end, and the hands-on treatment was about to begin.

Torrey was a strict taskmaster through the end of classes and finals. Torrey's goal was two-fold. First, she needed Matthew to focus on school in order to complete the academic year on a high note. Second, she needed Matthew to focus on school in order to divert his attention from the anguish in his heart to the memory banks in his head.

Through all the classwork, studying, and cramming for finals, there was little talk of personal matters. Nothing about family. Nothing about Nash. And nothing about Matthew and Torrey's feelings for each other. Matthew figured there would be plenty of time to talk about *things* come the end of the school year. Torrey wasn't so sure. She wondered if there would ever be a good time

200

to confront Matthew about his career plans, his Ted Nash comments, and *things*.

By the time their tests were over, both Matthew and Torrey were physically and mentally exhausted. They retreated to Matthew's room for a pizza and prosecco party. As was their ritual, when they toasted the end of the school year, Matthew sipped his champagne and Torrey gulped her glass in one giant swallow. Matthew cut his pizza with a knife and fork and Torrey gobbled her pieces in giant bites. And while Torrey was anxious to scheme out the summer, the only planning items on Matthew's docket were getting home to see his mother and then coming back to Palo Alto to see Torrey.

"I have to go home tomorrow," said Matthew.

"I know. How long will you be down there with your mom?"

"I'm not sure yet. Depends on how she's doing."

"May I come down and pay her a visit? I'd love to see her, unless you think having extra company would be intrusive or counterproductive to her recuperation."

"Torrey, I know for a fact that my mom thinks you are extraordinary. My uncle sent me a text saying she needs to get out of her funk, so I expect we'll want you to come down to help cheer her up. Let me call you tomorrow night after I get the lay of the land."

"Okay. I know you have an early flight, so I'm going to hit the road. I'm going to my parents' house." She added lightly, "And don't forget, you need to visit my family this summer too."

Torrey got up to leave and Matthew met her at the door. He gave her a longer than *just friends* hug and a meaningful kiss on the cheek. "Can I walk you to your car?"

Uncharacteristically, Torrey gently replied, "I would like that."

Chapter Thirty-Eight

In hushed tones, TJ tried to lay the groundwork as Matthew walked in the front door, but no amount of preparation would have been sufficient. Mary was gaunt. She had lost ten pounds that she could ill afford to shed off her tiny frame. TJ had told Matthew that Mary wasn't eating, but this was far more drastic than he had imagined. She looked ten years older than she had only a month ago. She was in a dressing gown in the middle of the day. Her hair had not been brushed. No makeup. There was a faraway look and no light in her sunken eyes. She was sitting on the living room sofa holding a cup of coffee that had gone cold. Matthew bit his lip as he worked hard not to cry. She looked so vulnerable. He ran to her. He leaned over his mother and touched his forehead to hers.

"Mom, I'm sorry that I haven't been here! How are you?"

Mary's only movement was to put her fingers underneath Matthew's chin to tilt his face up. She gazed in his eyes. There was a slight smile as she whispered, "Matthew!"

As Matthew held her hand, he looked over her shoulder and exchanged frowns and concerned glances with TJ. Matthew looked down at his mom's small hands, which were ice cold. The nails were chewed. Matthew had never seen her without manicured fingernails. "I'm here mom. I'm here," Matthew said as he shifted his position so that he could put his arm around her shoulders. He said softly in her ears, "Don't worry mom. Everything is going to be okay. I promise."

TJ gestured to the dining room indicating lunch was on the table.

"C'mon sis, let's get something to eat."

Mary looked away and said, "I'm not hungry."

"Me either but let's go sit at the table anyway." He helped her up from the couch and guided her to the dining room.

They sat at the table for almost an hour. Mary took a sip of water and nibbled on a cracker. She tried her best to make small talk with Matthew, but it was forced. Finally, she summoned her strength "Matthew honey, I want to hear more about your last few weeks of school. But I'm really tired right now. Do you mind if I take a nap?"

"Of course not." TJ and Matthew escorted her upstairs and helped her into bed. Matthew said, "I love you mom."

"I love you more," she replied with a soft kissing sound. She was asleep before they closed the door behind them.

Back in the living room, Matthew expressed his confusion and fear. "What is wrong with her? Shouldn't we get her to a hospital?"

"She won't permit it. She keeps saying she is just mournful about the parole and that she just needs some time to acclimatize to the news. I've pleaded with her. I've threatened her. I've tried everything, and she just says she will never leave this house again. I've even been sneaking in and taking her vital signs while she's asleep. Her blood pressure is low, and her heart rate is elevated. I wanted you here before I took the drastic step of taking her by force to an emergency room, for an IV if nothing else to get some nourishment in her."

"How long can we wait? I'm really worried."

"Me too. Naturally she was devastated after the parole hearing, but I thought she would bounce back. She hasn't. In fact, I would say she took a turn for the worse in the last week or so," he said gravely. "My biggest fear is that she has lost hope. One thing I know from my medical practice is that the mind is very powerful. If she has given up mentally, then her body will follow."

"So, what do we do?"

"I'm hoping your presence will give her the motivation to snap out of it. She needs to be around people. Around life."

"Torrey asked about coming down to see her. Would that help?"

"For sure. Your mom really likes her. And just so you know, she strongly hinted that she thinks Torrey is really good for you." TJ added with a furtive smile, "And I agree."

TJ and Matthew debated over the next several hours the treatment alternatives for Mary. They both agreed that she was severely depressed, but they disagreed on whether antidepressants should be prescribed. They also were not in accord regarding what physical ailments might be in play. In the end, they decided that doing nothing was no longer an option. They would take her to the hospital for a complete workup first thing in the morning.

While Matthew went outside to the backyard to call Torrey, TJ went to check on Mary. TJ entered Mary's bedroom with a light tap on the door. Mary was curled up in the fetal position, still peacefully sleeping. TJ bent down to give her a kiss on the cheek. He had been a doctor his entire adult life. He instantly knew. Mary was dead.

Chapter Thirty-Nine

The next morning was a blur. Matthew was exhausted from lack of sleep and anguish. The coroner listed the official cause of death as sudden cardiac arrest. Matthew called it by the non-technical name—his mother had died of a broken heart.

"It was peaceful. It was painless," explained TJ. "What wasn't painless was what she had gone through since your father left us. She put on a brave face but, as you well know, she was never the same. The parole experience was more than her body and mind could handle, I guess. There was a hole in her heart that never healed. I'm sorry I couldn't do more for her. Matthew, can you forgive me?"

"No need. I'm the one to blame. I should've been here. I should never have gone away to college and medical school. I should've stayed here after the hearing. I should have—"

TJ dismissed Matthew's self-blame with a wave of his hand. "Matthew! No more of that! Your mother positively shone whenever we talked of your accomplishments and how you had gotten on with your life. She was grateful to God that you had not let your father's death consume you." Matthew almost choked on that absurd sentiment.

"She talked with such pride about the fact that you had developed and matured into an amazing man, and that you had gone out of your comfort zone to go away to school. In fact, I daresay that her only real source of contentment these last years has been seeing the passion with which you have attacked life."

TJ continued "And knowing my sister, she will come back and haunt you if you start laying some sort of guilt trip on yourself."

Before Matthew could respond, his cell rang.

"It's Torrey calling, I'm sure to say she is boarding the plane in San Jose. Last night I invited her to come today." He let the phone go to voicemail. "What should I do? Should I call her back and tell her not to come? She doesn't know what happened."

TJ didn't have to think hard. "Let her come. Call her back and tell her you'll pick her up from the airport. You can tell her about your mom when you're face-to-face. She was coming to help comfort your mom. Now she can comfort you. Torrey will want to do that."

Matthew said, "I don't want to leave you here to deal with everything by yourself."

TJ simply said, "Go. Call her. I can handle things here. I've already put the funeral arrangements in motion. You have enough on your plate. Let me do the heavy lifting for now."

When Matthew met Torrey at LAX, Torrey immediately sensed that Matthew was very troubled. He looked like he hadn't slept and was even more reserved than normal. The first words out of her mouth were, "How's your mom doing today?"

Matthew just said they would stop for lunch on the way home and talk about it. He was in no hurry to get back to the house. He stopped at a nondescript café nowhere near the beach.

After they were seated, Matthew whispered, "She's dead."

Torrey gasped.

"What? What do you mean? When? What happened?"

With a quivering voice, Matthew slowly recounted the details of the last twenty-four hours. He thought he had cried himself out already, but the tears rolled down his cheeks as he spoke. He did not try to stop them. Neither did Torrey attempt to hide her emotions. By the time Matthew finished, Torrey wept until her shirt collar was soaked with teardrops.

They sat catty-corner from each other and held hands in silence until the waitress appeared. The grandmotherly server gently asked, "Are you two okay? Is there anything I can do?"

Torrey didn't want to force Matthew to speak so she replied. "Thank you. We just had a death in the family."

"Oh kids, I am so sorry."

Soon thereafter, food quietly arrived that neither remembered ordering. Both Matthew and Torrey moved their food around on their plates but neither ate more than a bite or two. They passed another two hours just staring at each other before a resigned Matthew said, "I guess we better get going." Matthew, always a generous 25% tipper, left the kind waitress an extra $100 for the extended use of her table.

Torrey stayed at the Preston home for a week. True to his word, TJ took the laboring oar on the funeral arrangements. There really wasn't much to do because Mary's wish was to be cremated and her ashes scattered in Santa Monica Bay.

One evening when TJ was at the house for dinner, he announced that he had found a copy of Mary's will in her bedroom desk drawer. He was surprised, but happy, to see that she had added a handwritten codicil to her will before she died. Matthew was in no mood to talk about wills or codicils, but TJ insisted on sharing the news. "Matthew, you know that when your father passed, you, your mother, and I went out on my boat and scattered his ashes. He had said to your mother, in no uncertain terms, that he did not want any public service or burial if he should predecease her. Just a cremation and to be spread randomly into the ocean. Family only. Your mother said to me after that event that she wanted the same thing if she were to die before me."

Torrey was feeling uncomfortable with TJ's remarks. She started to get up from her chair as she said, "I should leave you and Matthew to discuss these private family matters. I will go upstairs and do a little reading."

"No," said TJ. "This concerns you as well as Matthew." TJ gestured for her to sit.

A puzzled look descended on Torrey's face. Her mouth half-opened to protest further but she sat back down without further debate. Matthew raised his eyebrows and shrugged his shoulders at her and then focused his attention back to TJ. "Mary's original will is with the lawyer and has been for years. She kept a copy here at the house and she obviously left it where I would be sure to find it." TJ gestured to Matthew as he continued. "The will specifies that she wanted you and me to give her the same burial at sea that we gave your father, so she could be with him in body and spirit.'

"But, according to the codicil, which is dated two weeks ago, she wanted to expand the family-only ceremony as follows," said TJ as he raised the will close enough to his eyes to read verbatim, "'I, Mary Preston, wish to amend my will to invite Torrey Jamison to participate with Matthew and TJ in spreading my ashes. Torrey is the closest I have ever come to having a daughter and I know how she has changed Matthew's life for the better. If I should pass before Matthew comes to his senses and marries her, Torrey is most welcome at this and any other family occasion.' And then she drew a little smiley face," said TJ as he turned the paper around for Matthew and Torrey to see.

Torrey gasped sharply. "Oh my god!" She looked at Matthew and TJ. "If you'll let me, I would be honored to go with you!" Torrey and Matthew both stood up at the same time and drifted towards TJ at the head of the table where they spontaneously engaged in a tight three-person hug.

TJ selected a sunny cloudless day for the burial at sea. The three of them took TJ's boat about two miles directly offshore from Pacific Palisades. Matthew held the urn with both hands. TJ cut the engine and they drifted in silence for a good hour until Matthew gave the word that he was ready.

Matthew then passed the urn to TJ who whispered a private prayer. He passed the urn to Torrey who did the same. She carefully handed the ashes back to Matthew. He spoke quietly to the urn as he leaned over the edge of the boat and opened the top. Ever so gently, he emptied the urn after which each of them tossed a bouquet of pink roses. They all watched as the ashes disappeared under the surface of the sea, leaving only rose petals to mark the spot.

TJ poured them each a glass of the most expensive champagne he could find. He raised his glass through wet eyes. "To Mary Preston. The best sister, mother, and wife that ever lived."

They all drank. Then another group hug.

Chapter Forty

Both Matthew and Torrey were looking forward to the third year of medical school, but for different reasons. The strict coursework and classroom learning of the first two years were behind them. Now they were going to get to do the clinical curriculum that allowed interaction with and treatment of actual patients at teaching hospitals and clinics. Each clerkship was three weeks in duration. The idea was to expose the students to various medical specialties so that an informed choice could be made when selecting the longer fourth-year rotations and, of course, ultimately selecting a career specialty.

At Stanford, the required third-year disciplines included pediatrics, internal medicine, neurology, psychiatry, pharmacology and obstetrics. Most important to Torrey, however, was the surgery rotation. She couldn't wait to scrub up and be admitted into the sacrosanct operating room with accomplished surgeons and residents. She probably would just shadow and observe, being at the bottom rung on the personnel hierarchy, but she hoped she could at least sew up an incision or two. Everyone told her that her stitch work was now second to none.

For Matthew, the third year meant he was one step closer to walking into San Quentin as a physician. Additionally, the mandated pharmacology clerkship caught his eye because that is where he could learn the practical details about deadly adverse drug reactions in Lambert-Eaton Syndrome patients.

But most remarkable of all, Stanford permitted each student to sign up for an introductory elective rotation to allow a head start on the student's primary area of interest. Matthew wasn't surprised that Stanford not just allowed, but affirmatively encouraged, its students to do an outreach stint at the San Quentin medical facility to show willingness to help in *under-served* areas.

Despite his distaste for the type of virtue-signaling programs that would gain him access to the prisoners, he knew he needed to show his interest in prison medicine as a third-year student so that he could justify a three-month long service project at the prison as a fourth-year student. So, he spent an afternoon in the Stanford law library researching Stanford's attitudes towards criminals and victims. As he expected, he found hundreds of books dedicated to the plight of prisoners and the effects of incarceration—but noted with disgust that there were virtually no books or publications concerning the victims of violent crimes.

Matthew's long-range plan was to get the lay of the land as a third-year student and then to learn the nuts and bolts of the prisoner care system as a fourth year. Surely, he would discover a foolproof method to cause one small obscure fatality among the astronomically large and motley group of prison patients.

Matthew and Torrey had prearranged to meet in Matthew's dorm room at 3:00 p.m. to discuss their third-year options. They had to register online by 5:00 p.m. and they figured two hours would be plenty of time to coordinate classes. "So, Matthew," said Torrey with a thoughtful expression on her face, "I was thinking that we might harmonize our schedules to take the same clinical rotations at the same time. And we need to decide on which two elective rotations we want to do. I noticed that one of the offered electives is a rotation with a world-famous heart surgeon in San Francisco. I heard through the grapevine that a student who took that clinic last year got to hold a human heart during an open-heart surgery. How about that! Shall we sign up for that together?"

Matthew commented dryly, "I'm not sure I'm up for holding living organs in my hands." Then he nervously added, "What if I were to drop it? I once dropped a routine fly ball that cost my high school a game in my junior year. That was bad enough. But a human heart?"

Torrey scoffed. "You played four years at Stanford with no fielding errors. I'm not worried about a fumble in the operating room. Besides, if we're there together and a human heart needs a pair of hands, I'll jump in and offer mine."

Matthew still looked skeptical, so Torrey laughed and changed tactics. "Well what about you? What electives do you want to do? I'll tell you what. You pick out whatever you want, and I'll do it with you. In exchange, you take the heart surgery elective with me. Deal?"

He supposed that he might as well put it out there, so he said in a carefree voice, "I'm going to do the San Quentin elective to learn more about the life of a prison doctor." Matthew had always envisioned that his plans for Ted Nash would be carried out in a solitary fashion. "I'm sure that wouldn't interest you."

Torrey groaned and gave him a penetrating stare to see if he was kidding. "Are you still serious about that? You haven't mentioned it for a long time, so I thought, actually I hoped, you had abandoned that course of action in favor of something more—" she paused and furrowed her brow while searching for the right adjective— "*uplifting*. No such luck?"

Matthew shifted his weight and gave her a lopsided grin. "I guess I'm just a sucker for those less fortunate. But really I just want to check it out."

Torrey wasn't sure what was going on, and she certainly had no interest in prison medicine, but she resolved that she needed to keep an eye on him to figure out what he was trying to accomplish. "I'll tell you what. I guess I could expand my horizons a bit if you could. And I suspect that medical students get significantly more hands-on experience in a prison than in a typical hospital setting. Who knows what legitimate health issues we might get to treat? Let's confirm the deal," she urged while extending her hand to shake.

Matthew paused for a long moment. This was not part of his plan. But as Torrey stood there with her hand out and an impatient look on her face, he could think of no reasonable grounds upon which to refuse.

"That's no way to seal a deal," said Matthew as he grabbed her and pulled her into his arms. He laughed uneasily as they embraced.

Just before the clinical rotations were set to begin, Matthew got a call from Joe Cook. Matthew had received a beautiful bouquet and a nice note from Joe after Mary's death was made public, but the investigator had waited a respectful period to contact Matthew about the results of his George Rincon investigation.

"Hi Matthew, Joe Cook here. I hope I didn't catch you at a bad time. I wanted to give you an oral report about my probe into this Rincon fellow. We can talk now or at a later time if that would be better for you."

"Now works. I'm back at school, but I haven't started my first rotation yet. And by the way, thank you for the flowers you sent when my mother passed. They were much appreciated."

"You're welcome. I was so sorry to hear about her."

Matthew took a deep breath. "So, what did you find out?"

"I can tell you that Rincon is one sick hombre. It's a poor reflection on our society that he is not sitting in a jail cell."

Matthew's mouth tightened. "What do you mean? What's he done?"

"The better question is 'What hasn't the creep done?' Not even sure where to start. But first of all, that whole bit about him quitting his teaching job due to dire health complications is nonsense. That was just a convenient excuse he gave to the principal, or the principal knows the truth and he was sworn to secrecy at the expense of his job. In any event, Rincon actually left because of a rape claim by a student at his high school." Matthew gasped involuntarily.

Joe told Matthew all about the employment records that documented the Vicki Post allegation that Rincon raped her after school hours in his office. And that Joe had seen the sealed records showing that if Rincon agreed to leave the school district then there would be no prosecution. "Matthew, because this deal sounded so fishy, I checked into family connections to law enforcement. It turns out that Rincon's brother is an FBI agent based in Los Angeles so that explains how this episode was swept under the rug. With the help of the teacher's union of course."

Matthew could feel his breathing go shallow. He asked coldly, "What else did you find on this guy?"

"Lots," Joe said grimly. "He has a confidential criminal file which shows that his 23-year-old daughter took out a restraining order against him just six months ago. He is barred from contact with her or her two little kids. The order doesn't specify 'why' but in light of Vicki Post and what I'm about to tell you, I think we can assume the restraining order is based on molestation.

"A few years back he was caught doing a Peeping Tom on the next-door neighbor girl. Again, there was no prosecution, but I tracked down the girl's mother and she was very convincing. I have ten bucks that says the FBI stepped in there too in order to keep Rincon out of jail."

A new rage was burning inside Matthew. "What is wrong with this country! These criminals, these animals, are allowed to remain free at the expense of their next victims. I hope and pray that this FBI agent has daughters and that—"

"Whoa! Let's not go there. I know you are just frustrated with the system, but—'"

"I'm sorry Joe. You're right. No reason for children to suffer for the sins of their parents," Matthew said apologetically.

"No need to apologize to me, Matthew. I know where you are coming from, of course." Joe let a moment pass and then said, "You also wanted me to find out about this guy's medical situation. He has Crohn's disease for which he gets regular treatments at Kaiser in San Diego. I have copies of his most recent medical records that have the details of the drug infusions he receives. Do you want them?"

"Yes. Can you black out his name and identifying information and then email the records to me under the caption 'Crohn's?' I'll recognize the email from that title."

"Sure. Matthew, you're being a little mysterious. Why are you so interested in this Rincon fellow?"

"Oh, I just want to keep tabs on him for a friend. And I might want to have a talk with the guy at some point."

"Is there anything else I can do for you regarding Rincon? I don't want you to be in over your head with something where my expertise could help you." Matthew did not immediately reply, so Joe added, "C'mon, put me in coach!"

"Thanks for your offer, Joe. I'll let you know if I need you again."

Matthew had hardly hung up the phone when the email arrived from Joe Cook. Rincon's medical records showed that he was receiving regular treatments for Crohn's disease at the Infusion Center at Kaiser. The records revealed that Rincon's immune system was attacking his gastrointestinal tract. His chronic inflammatory disorder was causing him abdominal pain and bloody diarrhea. He was regularly undergoing Remicade infusion therapy to reduce inflammation in order to minimize the chances of bowel obstruction. Matthew wasn't sure what to do with this information, but it pained him that modern medicine was keeping someone alive who was undeserving of the privilege. He took a deep breath and pondered how and when he should tell Torrey.

That evening, Matthew and Torrey were having their last meal before the start of their third year of medical school. Matthew did not feel right about knowing Rincon's story and keeping it from Torrey. And he figured that a huge distraction during a clinical rotation would be unkind to Torrey and unfair to their patients. Rather than having pizza in a dorm room, Matthew decided to have the conversation over a nice dinner at a swanky waterfront restaurant in San Francisco. "What's the reason for all of this?" said Torrey as they were seated. She teased, "Are you trying to ply me with good food and drink so you can ask for a loan?"

"Oh, just wanted to mark the occasion of starting the second-half of our journey towards becoming real doctors," said Matthew sarcastically. "Besides, how often do we get a warm evening in this city where we can actually see the bridge without a shroud of fog? I wanted to share it with you."

Torrey blushed, but was quick to respond. "Okay, now I know something is up. What is it you have to tell me? Are you pregnant?"

Matthew belly laughed. "I guess you know me too well. As a matter of fact, there is something I want to discuss."

Just then a bubbly young waitress arrived and took their orders. After she left, Torrey studied Matthew expectantly. Matthew tried to avoid looking agitated, but he was worried how Torrey would react.

"I got a call today from my private eye, Joe Cook, who has been investigating George Rincon." Matthew paused and searched her eyes for physiologic response. There was none. "He confirmed our suspicions that Rincon is bad to the bone." Matthew told her everything—the rape claim, the spying on the neighbor girl, and the restraining order by his own daughter. "And he is now living the good life down in San Diego where he gets infusions at Kaiser every couple of months for his Crohn's disease." Matthew tried to decipher the look on her face. He couldn't. Torrey didn't start to cry. Neither did she laugh at the absurdity of it. She just sat there and gazed out the window at a passing ferry.

Torrey wasn't as indifferent as she appeared. She was frozen in place. Her heart was racing as Matthew spoke. Her stomach was turning. But she was still as a statue. Finally, she spoke. "Thank you for looking into that for me. So, how are the desserts here?"

Matthew got the message. Torrey was not ready to talk about it.

Chapter Forty-One

Matthew was disappointed that his San Quentin rotation was not until the beginning of December, but he was pleased that his pharmacology clinic was first up. Matthew felt that he and Torrey were fortunate to be assigned to Dr. Fred Peters, a world-renowned scientist and clinician who was a Nobel prize nominee thirty-five years ago for his work on new drug treatments for rheumatoid arthritis. Torrey was nonplussed. She did not doubt the professor's intellect, but she found it difficult to overlook the fact that Dr. Peters appeared old enough to have worked with Dr. Banting, the true genius who, in 1921, used the principles of clinical pharmacology to discover insulin for the treatment of diabetes.

The small group of students who were in the clinic knew from Dr. Peters' opening remarks that he was a no-nonsense, old-school academic whom you did not want to disappoint. He started speaking at 10:00 a.m. exactly, even though two stragglers were barely through the door.

"The purpose of Clinical Pharmacology is, at its core, to understand and design drug therapy regimens for patients. What we do at my clinic, which is essentially an inpatient research center, is identify and test therapeutic interventions on people who have not been helped by traditional drug treatments. These patients might have any number of different disorders and my team, which now includes all of you, must find unique or novel ways to improve their quality of life. This means you have to know the mechanisms of how drugs are absorbed and distributed in the body. How to determine proper drug dosage and interaction depending on the characteristics of the patient's disease. How to know the difference between expected side effects and unexpected adverse reactions. And how to identify and manage those toxicity reactions."

Matthew's ears burned as Dr. Peters continued his talk on the dangers of administering the wrong drug, an improper mix of several drugs, or even too much of the right drug.

"A fair number of our beds are taken up by folks whose bumbling general practitioners overdosed the patients on too many medications or on a drug that was contraindicated by the patient's disease. And lately it is increasingly frequent that community doctors bereft of common sense will prescribe a medication for an off-label use that they might have read about on the internet, in *Readers Digest*, or in some other non-medical publication."

Matthew raised his hand. Dr. Peters was not a fan of interruptions, but he allowed the question as he impatiently drummed his fingers on the lab bench. "Professor, could you give us an example of a disease where the primary physician gave the wrong drug? And how did you determine in your clinic that the patient's symptoms were being caused by an unsuitable medication?"

"Last year we had a case where a primary care doctor just out of medical school inherited a young female patient with lupus who had been on steroids for years. The doctor saw her one time and decided her symptoms had improved and therefore took her completely off her steroid medication. The woman developed adrenal insufficiency because her adrenal glands had stopped producing cortisol during her steroid use. She presented here with fatigue, muscle weakness, and severe weight loss. It took us a while to diagnose and treat her because we couldn't imagine she had been made to stop her steroids cold turkey.

"And that case makes me think of another patient, Mrs. Carruthers, who is in the clinic right now. She suffers from rheumatoid arthritis which causes severe joint pain and swelling in her hands, wrists, and knees. Her doctor, we think, prescribed an overdose of her Methotrexate medication which caused vomiting, gastrointestinal bleeding, and bone marrow suppression. He denies it, but Mrs. Carruthers almost died, and we need to figure out why. And how to get her better. Perhaps you, Mr.—"

"Preston, sir."

"Mr. Preston, perhaps you would like to focus on Mrs. Carruthers for your case study in this rotation. You and a partner will have three weeks to design and implement a drug therapy protocol for her. You will work with my team of doctors and will be allowed to suggest any diagnostic tests you deem appropriate. At the end of your rotation, I will expect a short paper detailing your opinions regarding her exact disorder, what caused the exacerbation of her symptoms, and what you propose should be done for her. How does that sound?"

"That sounds incredibly challenging. I would love that."

"One other thing, Mr. Preston. And this goes for all of you. Mr. Preston asked for an example of a disease that we treated in our clinic. I want you to *not* fall into the trap of referring to these patients by their diseases. I don't want to hear you say that today you treated a kidney, or a liver, or a gallbladder. These patients are real people. They are fathers, mothers, parents, and children. Often their family members will be present when we are discussing their case with the patient. Put yourselves in their position," he admonished. "Don't become jaded and lose the altruistic attitude that caused you to go to medical school. Don't dehumanize them. Be human yourself."

Over the next few days, Dr. Peters took the group along on his rounds and introduced them to each of the clinic patients. Then Matthew and Torrey concentrated on Mrs. Carruthers. They found a room to themselves and studied her voluminous medical chart. Matthew couldn't help but notice the similarity between Ted Nash's Eaton-Lambert Syndrome and Mrs. Carruthers' rheumatoid arthritis. Both are auto-immune disorders in which the immune system attacks healthy cells in the body by mistake. Both disorders can be fatal if the wrong drug therapy is administered. Torrey noticed that Matthew seemed more than academically interested.

As it turned out, Dr. Peters had to take a medical leave of absence after the first week of rotation and none of the experienced doctors on Dr. Peters' team took the medical students seriously enough to let them do anything of consequence for the patients. Matthew was a little perturbed about that but Torrey, frankly, was relieved. She figured she would have an entire surgical career to bungle something that could cause a patient's death—she was not interested in having that responsibility as a student. They wrote up their paper based on the test results, data, and research available to them. In their paper, Matthew had insisted that they investigate and emphasize the myriad of drugs that could cause the adverse medical issues from which Mrs. Carruthers suffered. They were not kicked out of school, so they guessed that their conclusions, assuming they were even read, were satisfactory.

Chapter Forty-Two

The rest of the fall rotations dragged. Matthew felt like he was just marking time until his December clinical clerkship at San Quentin. Even the elective surgery rotation that Torrey had coerced Matthew into taking turned out to be a bust. There had been no holding of a human heart. Apparently, that was an urban myth passed down each year to overeager second-year students. There had not even been any opportunity for Torrey to show off her suturing skills. The medical students had been relegated to watching surgeries from elevated viewing areas above the operating rooms. This time it was Torrey, not Matthew, who was disappointed with the failure of the rotation to deliver any practical experience. Matthew was fine with—if not relieved by—watching surgeries from a safe distance.

For Matthew, the only upside to the intermediary rotations was that he got to spend more and more time with Torrey. Ever since his mother's written wish that Torrey become an official member of the Preston family, Matthew couldn't help but look at Torrey in a different light. Maybe more alluring? More captivating? Whatever it was, he didn't mind. In fact, he had been so closed off to personal relationships in his life, he never imagined he could fall under the spell of any woman, much less an idealistic computer brain. Even if wrapped in a cute package. As he confronted his own feelings, he reluctantly admitted to himself, "Torrey has made it clear that she is opposed in principle to the concept of revenge, whereas my primary goal in life is to avenge my father's death. How can this do anything other than blow up in my face?"

Finally, December arrived. Matthew would have three full weeks inside the San Quentin Medical Center. Torrey assumed the two of them would make the one-way, ninety-minute commute every day from Palo Alto to San Quentin. However, Matthew called her on Sunday when she was visiting her parents and said, "Hey, while you're at your parents' house, grab a big suitcase for yourself and any clothes you have there that you might want between now and December 21."

"Why?"

"No time to talk right now. Just do it," he said with a chortle. "And when you get back to campus, call me and I'll come over to help you pack up all your essentials. You'll not be coming back to your room before the end of the rotation."

"Matthew, what—"

"Sorry! Have to go now! See you soon!" With that, he hung up and Torrey was left staring blankly at the phone.

"Honey was that Matthew?" asked Torrey's father.

"Yes."

"Give him a message for me, will you?"

"Sure. What is it?"

"Tell him if he's looking for a quiet place to study that he should go to Dodger stadium after the seventh inning in a close game. He'll be the only one there!" and he roared with laughter.

Torrey ate dinner as quickly as possible and then announced she had to get going to get ready for her next clinic. She called Matthew the moment she drove into her Stanford parking spot. "So, what's happening?"

All Matthew said was, "I'll meet you at your room. Bye!"

Matthew picked up the papers he had printed out from the internet and walked excitedly across campus. Even though it was Sunday evening, he had to dodge all of the crazy helmetless bicyclists that zoomed around without the slightest thought for the safety of themselves or others.

A grinning Torrey opened her door after the first knock and slugged Matthew playfully in the shoulder.

"What's going on with you?" she giggled.

"Oh, not too much. Only that I made the executive decision that spending three hours on the road each day during this rotation would be a colossal waste of our time and energy." As he waved his paperwork with a flourish, he announced, "We're going to be living for the next three weeks on a Sausalito houseboat only fifteen minutes from San Quentin! And get this, the houseboat was once an actual working ferry up in Washington State. It's called the Yellow Ferry."

"I've heard of it!" said Torrey. "There was a write-up in the local paper a few years ago. It sounded pretty cool."

"That's the understatement of the year." Matthew started reading from his printed brochure materials. "It was originally launched in 1888 as the *City of Seattle* paddleboat ferry. It has been converted into a luxurious rental property with lots of original features. It even still has the paddlewheel!"

Torrey seemed less excited than Matthew expected. With a quizzical look and some surprise in his voice he asked, "Are you okay? I know you hate driving in traffic. I thought you would be more enthusiastic."

Torrey looked a bit sheepish and said, "I'm not sure about us living together like that."

With his trademark disarming grin, he added, "And it has three full bedrooms and two bathrooms. The place is so big, we probably won't even see each other!"

Torrey turned beet red and stammered, "I'm sorry. I didn't mean to assume—"

"No need to say another word. We are on the same page. It sounds like we both grew up with the same strictures about staying pure until marriage. Do you think your parents will be okay with us sharing the 2600 square foot place? It's so big that they could come and stay with us on the weekends or anytime they want."

"Thank you, Matthew." She gave him a huge hug. "Thank you for understanding."

Bright and early the next morning they were off to Sausalito and the Yellow Ferry. Torrey used her Waze app to guide them to the Yellow Ferry dock. While Matthew drove, she acted as unofficial tour guide by reading aloud from various websites about the history of the Ferry and its amenities. "Listen to this," Torrey said as they were about to cross the Golden Gate Bridge. "The Ferry has been used as a film set for several movies and has been written about in tons of magazines. Julie Christie, that beautiful woman from Dr. Zhivago, lived there for a while during the height of her popularity." Torrey looked over at Matthew, "This site says the daily rent is really high." After a brief pause, she added with a snort, "I keep forgetting that you're rich."

Matthew glanced at her with a smile, "That's one of your many charms."

They found the Yellow Ferry at the end of a long wooden walkway. As impressive as it was from the outside, it was even more magnificent inside. The main living area was like a giant solarium with jaw-dropping views of the Bay. The original wooden deck had been beautifully restored. They wanted to dawdle but a complete tour would have to wait. So, they just dropped their bags and made the short drive north to the nearly 300-acre San Quentin prison complex.

Chapter Forty-Three

They had been there before, of course, but this was going to be the first time seeing the medical facility. They were met by one of the resident physicians, Dr. Giselle Gerard, who had graduated from Stanford two years earlier. As a relative rookie at the hospital, she was charged with greeting duties and familiarizing the medical trainees with the rules and procedures.

"You must be Torrey Jamison and Matthew Preston. How do you do? I'm Dr. Gerard," she said with a light expression. "I'll be showing you around and will act as your supervisor while you are here. We normally have five or six third-year students at a time but, I guess with the holidays approaching, you were the only ones willing to make the trek." She started walking into the labyrinth of hallways as she talked. Matthew and Torrey quickly followed so as not to be left behind.

As Dr. Gerard nodded to the ancient-looking guard who was sitting next to the clinic entrance, the set of heavy locked doors opened as if by magic. They found themselves in a large atrium, with a giant overhead skylight providing natural light for the many plants. The waiting area, similar to what one would see at any major hospital, had nice padded chairs, vending machines, and two big-screen TVs. The primary difference was the existence of two bored—but armed—guards standing on either side of the room. No one paid any attention to Dr. Gerard or her charges as they strolled through the lobby to the next set of vault-like steel barricades. Dr. Gerard looked through the small safety glass window and waved to the guard in a booth on the other side. The electronic sound of the bolts unlatching signaled that they were free to enter the inner sanctum of the clinic. They entered the hallway and the door loudly clicked shut behind them. They were locked in. Startled, Matthew jerked his head back at the sealed door and then at the uniformed guard. The heavy-set man with a bulbous nose tipped his hat at Matthew and chuckled, "Get used to that sound, rookie!" just loud enough for Matthew to hear.

As they walked in silence towards the physicians' lounge, which doubled as an orientation conference room, Matthew absorbed the surroundings. Most of the examination room doors were closed, but through the wire-reinforced windows he could see inmates in various states of prison garb undress with a doctor or nurse. Other than the guard at the corridor entrance, he saw no other security personnel.

Entering the lounge, Matthew surveyed the spartan furnishings. There were five round metal tables, one of which was being used as the refreshment station, which consisted of an old Mr. Coffee, a stack of white Styrofoam cups, and small packets of sugar. There were flimsy, molded-plastic chairs around the tables, and there were two oversized, well-worn sofas. No TV or magazines. Matthew couldn't help but notice that the prisoner reception area was far more luxurious than what was provided for the doctors. He felt no need to verbalize the obvious.

None of the three doctors in the room acknowledged their entry. One briefly looked up, but just as quickly went back to his newspaper. Dr. Gerard nodded towards an empty table and the three of them sat down. Torrey deadpanned in a whisper, "Friendly group you have here."

Dr. Gerard peered around, lowered her voice, and said with a knowing smile, "If you're looking for a workplace full of comradery and fun, you are in the wrong place. Most of the doctors who choose this career path do so because of regular but flexible hours, good pay, and relatively low stress. I fall into that category. I'm the single mother of a two-year-old. I work a 7:00 a.m. to 4:00 p.m. shift so I can pick up my daughter at daycare at 4:30. I couldn't swing that schedule in private practice. Plus, did you know we get free malpractice insurance? And maybe best of all, we don't have to comply with all that nightmare administrative paperwork that has caused so many primary care doctors to retire."

Matthew and Torrey exchanged glances as Matthew said for Torrey's benefit, "Wow, being a prison doctor sounds like a pretty good deal!" Torrey gave him an elbow poke and an exaggerated roll of the eyes.

Dr. Gerard looked down at her outline and got back to business. "Sorry to say but I'm obliged to start this orientation with some safety information. First, every so often the entire prison goes on lockdown for one reason or another. If that happens, stay where you are in the hospital. Don't panic or try to leave. If there is an escape attempt or a riot in any part of the prison where you happen to be, you will be escorted by guards to safety. So, stay put and wait for instructions.

"Second, you are both surely wondering about your own personal safety while you are here. It's true that there have been prisoner attacks on medical staff, including doctors. And Torrey, you need to know that females are the usual victims of such attacks. But assaults are rare and are usually sexual in nature rather than being physically violent."

"I'm not worried," said Torrey in an even voice.

"Of course you aren't," said Matthew.

"Well, you needn't be frightened, just aware. And when you give it some thought, it is arguably safer here than at most public hospitals where people high on drugs arrive in emergency rooms with concealed weapons. No such problems here. Moreover, there is a video camera in each exam room. I'll show you the video center later where a guard monitors the patients during treatment.

"Now for some good news." Dr. Gerard scanned the room. The other doctors had left, but she talked softly anyway. "All of the physicians here, even us newbies, get to have full responsibility for patient care and treatment. I've been able to do more hands-on medical practice in two years here than I would have in ten years elsewhere, including minor surgeries. Except for maybe one or two old-timers, no doctor here cares about hierarchy. No one cares if you are male or female. No one cares about your race. You get autonomy without someone looking over your shoulder every second. It's actually better than I imagined it would be."

As Dr. Gerard spoke, Matthew's eyes lit up. He could envision being alone with Ted Nash with no physician oversight.

Dr. Gerard continued, "Now as far as medical students are concerned, I will tell you that a few of the doctors here are tired or bored—and certainly some are just lazy. So, they let the medical students do more than they really should. I'm not talking just about giving routine shots and taking vital signs. Last session, one of the fourth-year clinical students was allowed to be the first assistant on an inmate puncture wound surgery. She did scalpel and suturing work. We see a few of those punctures each month from one inmate using a homemade shiv on another."

Now it was Torrey's chance to get excited. "That sounds great!" exclaimed Torrey. Dr. Gerard gave her a quizzical look. "Oh, I didn't mean that shiv puncture wounds are great," said Torrey with a sheepish look. "Just that we might get the opportunity to treat them."

Matthew jumped in with an amused peek at Dr. Gerard, "We know what you meant."

Dr. Gerard showed them the surgery center, the pharmacy, and the small offices assigned to the doctors. Next, they went into an empty exam room where Dr. Gerard proudly unlocked and opened the supply cabinets and drawers to show how well stocked they were. "Look at this," exclaimed Dr. Gerard. "These rooms are better equipped than those in most public hospitals. We have all the bandages, syringes, needles you'll ever need. And, if you ever see that something is low, just let the nurses know and they will reorder."

She was about to announce that the grand tour was over when Matthew reminded her about the video center where the exam rooms were monitored. "Oh, right. Let me take you upstairs to show you." They used the employee elevator, which Dr. Gerard activated with a card key and a punch code. When the elevator doors opened, Matthew scanned the area for guards and saw none. "Why no security up here?" asked Matthew.

"This floor is off limits to inmates and even if one gained access to a key card and a current code, guards from other floors could be here before the elevator arrived. Did you notice how slow this elevator is?"

Dr. Gerard passed a few closed doors until she came to one marked 'Video Center.' She knocked as she stuck her face up against the small, but thick, square window. A moment later, the door buzzed open and Dr. Gerard and her charges walked in. "Hi Ed. How's your day going?"

Ed was leaning back in his black office chair with a cup of coffee in one hand and a jelly donut in the other. "Hello Dr. Gerard," he said with a grin. His teeth were smeared with red jelly. He put down his donut and waved. "Hi there, young people! I guess you're here to see where the magic happens." He held up his fingers to indicate that they were too sticky to shake hands.

Dr. Gerard thrust her chin in the direction of the guard and said without a hint of sarcasm, "This is Ed Steed. Everyone calls him Mr. Ed, for reasons unknown to me."

Mr. Ed seemed to enjoy the nickname and guffawed, "And my middle name is Wilbur!" Like Dr. Gerard, neither Matthew nor Torrey were familiar with 1960's television, so they both gave a shrug and a polite chuckle.

"Ed has been in charge of clinic surveillance for five years. He is the go-to guy for anything technical concerning the surveillance system here at the prison."

"Enough about me!" beamed Mr. Ed. "Let me give you my spiel and the ten-cent tour of my domain." The room was only the size of a single car garage but, to Ed, he was a king in his castle, albeit a diminutive king. He was barely 5'6' and 140 lbs. His hair was short but fashionably cut. He sat at a long, narrow metal table, behind which was a bank of twelve black-and-white monitors. Each screen was only a foot square. On the adjacent wall was another identical table and set of monitors. Ed's chair had wheels which allowed him to easily move around the room. He scooted from one group of monitors to the next as he spoke. "We have sixteen private examination rooms, each with their own video camera. Six other monitors are for cameras situated in various hallways in this building." Ed pointed as he talked, showing how each screen was clearly labeled by exam room number or corridor location. "And there is one camera in the reception area that I saw you walk through, and one camera showing the front of the pharmacy."

Dr. Gerard clarified, "FYI, there is another video center for the fifty-bed hospital ward, and another one for the small specialty clinics, but you will be spending most of your time here in this clinic."

Mr. Ed thought Dr. Gerard's unnecessary interruption slowed his momentum, but being the professional that he was, he let it pass without comment. While Ed droned on about how quickly the guards can rescue any doctor or nurse that he determines is being threatened, Matthew was busy watching the doctor-inmate interactions that were happening in front of him. "You have all these monitors, Mr. Ed," said Matthew. "How can you simultaneously watch what is going on in each room?"

"Well, I can only look at one screen at a time, but I've been doing this for so long that I can spot trouble before it starts. Unless something unusual is happening, I look at every monitor at least once every 60 seconds."

Torrey had a different concern. "Ed, I was watching exam room 4 and I saw the patient lying down on the exam table where the doctor was listening with his stethoscope. Then the doctor walked away and disappeared from the video screen. He came back a few seconds later with a blood pressure cuff. What—"

"Good observation, young lady. I was going to get to that, but as you've noticed, the video cameras in these exam rooms are a bit inadequate. Someone budgeted incorrectly when this place was designed and so instead of two cameras per room, which would give complete coverage, we have about three feet of dark space around the perimeter of each room. They could have at least used wide-angle lenses, but I guess they decided to cut back on safety technology in favor of more prisoner amenities." He added with a hint of sarcasm and a reproachful look, "Have you seen the new drama workshop they just constructed for the prisoners? My daughter's public school has its theater program after school in the teachers' lounge."

"Isn't that a problem?" asked Torrey. "I mean the lack of coverage in the exam rooms."

Dr. Gerard cut in, "Not really. Most of the perimeter of each exam room is taken up with counters, storage closets, and drawers full of medical equipment. There are only one or two spots of dark area in each room where you are invisible to the camera."

Torrey nodded, and made a mental note to keep close to the exam table. While Matthew and Ed debated the technical merits of the video system, Dr. Gerard motioned to Torrey to join her in the hallway. Once outside the video room, Dr. Gerard turned her back to the hallway camera so that her hands were shielded from Ed's view. She leaned in close to Torrey and whispered, "I don't know about you, but I don't want to put my life in Mr. Ed's hands. At least not exclusively. So, I carry with me a little extra protection against an attack by a patient." With that, she opened the inside pocket of her lab coat. Torrey stared down at a surgeon's scalpel. "The administration would go berserk if they knew I carried this around. But I'm the one putting myself on the line with any miscreant who comes in for treatment. I probably will never have to use it, but I will if I have to. It's up to you, but you can *borrow* one from the surgery center if you are so inclined. We women need to stick together," she said with a smile.

When the two women stepped back into the room, Ed and Matthew were still babbling technical jargon. Matthew wondered about audio. "What about sound? Can you listen in when you think it is necessary?"

"I wish I could. It would take some of the guesswork out of my job. But the legislature in its wisdom has decided that doctor-patient conversations are privileged, and we cannot eavesdrop. The only thing I can do is use my loudspeaker to communicate with the entire floor in an emergency."

Matthew allowed himself a fleeting smile.

Chapter Forty-Four

Torrey was assigned to shadow Dr. Daryl Digby, a surgeon, who, at age 64, was near mandatory retirement. It didn't take Torrey long to figure out that Dr. Digby should have been pushed out years ago. The overriding problem, Torrey thought, was that Dr. Digby was living in the past as many in his generation were. He had started working at San Quentin when all inmates were thought of as zoo animals to be caged. Dr. Digby explained his philosophy in between patients.

"Ms. Jamison, don't ever forget that these inmates are the lowest of the low. They do not have the same regard for human life as you and I."

"What about the ones that were wrongfully convicted? Surely there are some innocent inmates who deserve our compassion."

Dr. Digby snorted derisively. "You work here long enough, and you will realize that they are *all* innocent. Everyone here was wrongfully convicted! Oh, there are some decent ones who just got involved with the wrong crowd. I'm the first one to say that. But most of them would just as soon knife you in the back as shake your hand. So, don't ever be in an exam room alone with one of them. I know that Mr. Ed is watching from his perch upstairs, but a vicious criminal can do a lot of harm to a small girl like you in just a few minutes."

Torrey let the *small girl* comment pass. But things continued to get worse. Dr. Digby obtained his license to practice medicine back in the days when women interested in health care were relegated to the nursing profession. He took every opportunity to let the female medical students know that the good old days were the best days.

"Now, Ms. Jamison," said Digby as they walked from patient to patient, "what is going to be your area of specialty?"

"Surgery."

"Oh really," replied Digby as he lowered his glasses to the end of his nose to peer at her, highlighting his bald head and weak chin.

"Yes. Brain surgery, to be precise."

Digby towered over her small frame. He looked her up and down, spending a fraction too much time below the neck. "Young lady, do you think that's wise?" he said with a smug smile. "In my experience, patients, even felons, want a surgeon who exudes power and authority. And brain surgery—do you realize you would be required to use a power tool to drill into skulls?"

Torrey batted her eyelashes, flicked her hair back as much as it would flick, and demurely inquired, "Oh, I didn't realize a power tool was involved. Maybe I could get someone to turn it on for me." Torrey opened her eyes as wide as they would go. "Dr. Digby, do you think dermatology or pediatrics would be a better choice for me?"

"Absolutely! Or maybe obstetrics? Any of those would be a good fit for you," he said with a self-satisfied smirk. "And if you are set on surgery, perhaps a pediatric surgeon? I think you would get along great with young kids."

Torrey was finished with the charade. "Dr. Digby," she bristled as she stopped in front of him, squared her shoulders, and used her hands-on-hips power pose, "that is absurd. I'm no startled fawn. Are you an elitist in general or only a misogynist? Next you'll be saying I need a binky. Rest assured, I'm not only going to be a brain surgeon, I'm going to be a damn good one," she said crisply. Dr. Digby gaped and started to stammer, but Torrey held out her right hand in the universal stop sign. "I understand that I, like the brave women who came before me, will have more to prove than my male counterparts. So, I will. I daresay that I would compare favorably to you right now with my scalpel and suturing skills. Shall we arrange a contest?"

Dr. Digby was not used to being chastised or challenged. Especially not by a medical student acting in complete disregard of decorum and convention. And especially not by one who looked younger than his granddaughter. But before he could fashion any sort of rejoinder, Torrey took another breath and continued. "And perhaps you are unaware of the recent study by the Harvard School of Public Health which concluded that patients treated by female surgeons tended to have more favorable outcomes than do the patients of their male counterparts. I'll tell you what. I will forgive your sexism if you forgive my assumption that your age is dictating your outdated and inappropriate comments." Digby's eyes registered the rebuke, but no coherent sounds came out of his mouth. Torrey turned on her heel, went into exam room 12, and started reviewing the next patient's chart. Digby shuffled in a few minutes later. He hardly deigned to acknowledge Torrey for the rest of the day—and the rest of the rotation. And that was just fine with her.

Matthew's rotation mentor was nothing like Torrey's. Dr. Davis Goodwin was neither a rookie nor a tired old timer. Although a bit naive for Matthew's taste, Dr. Goodwin was an excellent physician who obviously wanted the best for his patients, even if they were murderers and rapists.

Their first joint patient was Frank Billings, convicted of armed robbery of a grocery store in Palm Springs, California. His take from the cash register was a whopping $58. He might have gotten a mere slap on the wrist from the legal system except that he took the pregnant store clerk hostage at gun point after another customer attempted to restrain him. The checker screamed as Billings tried to push her into his get-away car. He pistol-whipped her on the face and head. She suffered permanent brain damage and lost the baby. Somehow Billings was sentenced to only eight years. Of course, Matthew was not privy to this background. The chart for Billings, like all inmate patients, provided only the information needed to treat his particular conditions. And Matthew had been admonished already that he was never to ask any patient what they had done to be incarcerated.

Dr. Goodwin had been treating Billings for five years and Goodwin took some pride in the fact that he and Billings had become friendly. Before Billings walked in the door, Goodwin had given Matthew an idealistic speech about the basic goodness of humans. "Matthew, I'm so glad you are considering this career. Correctional institutions need good young doctors to help these wayward men. It doesn't matter what they did to be sent here, they still deserve a touch of kindness. I like to be sociable with my patients. Treat them right and they will do the same to others." Matthew gave a robotic nod while turning his head away to hide his sneer.

"Good morning, Frank. How are you today?"

"Just living the dream," said Billings with a trace of contempt.

"Frank, this is Matthew. A medical student at Stanford. He'll be working with me. Do you mind if he listens in today?"

"No problem, Doc. Anything you need."

"Matthew, Frank is one of many here with a liver hepatitis C infection. We're having some good success in his treatment."

"How? I thought hepatitis C was incurable without a liver transplant."

"That has been the case, but these days facts have a half-life of about two days. Recently two new drugs, Sovaldi and Harvoni, have been made available. Frank's liver is improving."

"I heard about those drugs in my pharmacology class, but we were told those new medicines are very expensive and hard to get."

"True. A twelve-week treatment costs about $100k in the outside world, and no insurance will pay for it, but we can get it at no cost for our inmates. Isn't that wonderful?"

Matthew was speechless. Violent degenerates were receiving life-saving treatments that were unavailable to law-abiding citizens. To avoid responding to Dr. Goodwin, Matthew buried his head in the chart and pretended that the question was rhetorical.

Dr. Goodwin and Matthew had plenty of time to talk in-between patients. Matthew was surprised that so many of the prisoners had chronic diseases. Dr. Goodwin noted that Matthew's confusion was not uncommon.

"I was the same way when I first started here. Too many misleading prison movies, I guess. We all tend to think that we will spend our time treating wounds from fights, wounds, and accidents. But in truth, many of these inmates arrive here with infectious diseases like HIV, STDs, MRSA, TB, and hepatitis. And some contract diseases while they are incarcerated. Perhaps most importantly, we have two mental health practitioners on staff who help those inmates who came here with deep emotional problems."

Dr. Goodwin charged Matthew with the job of scribing notes on each patient's chart detailing what was done in the visit and when the next appointment would be. He was then to place the completed chart at the nurses' station where a young nursing trainee would put the chart back into an alphabetized row of file cabinets. Matthew noted that the fourth cabinet over had three drawers devoted to prisoners whose name started with an 'N.' The cabinets were not locked.

It took six days, but Dr. Goodwin and Matthew finally treated an 'N' patient. His name was Mo Norton. After the consultation, Matthew surreptitiously picked up the next chart from the nurse's station without returning Norton's file. During his morning break, he wandered over to the file cabinets. When he saw that the filing nurse had left the floor, he opened the top 'N' cabinet drawer. His eyes were quickly drawn to the Ted Nash file. He pulled it out and carefully read the top sheet. Just as he stuffed the folder back in its place, he felt a tap on the shoulder. "Hey, are you angling for my job?" asked the young nurse flirtatiously.

Matthew turned and held out the Norton file. "I'm sorry," he said as he held out the Norton file to her. "I forgot to return this file earlier, so I was just trying to put it back where it belongs." Matthew gave her his brightest smile as he read her name tag, "I'm glad you are here so that I don't screw it up, Nurse Watson."

She lit up and giggled, "I'm sure you would have done just fine. Let me know if you need anything."

"Thanks," said Matthew. "I have everything I need for now."

Chapter Forty-Five

By the time the short San Quentin rotation was completed, Torrey was more than ready to say goodbye and never return. Dr. Digby remained condescending and boorish the entire three weeks and Torrey could well imagine that the written review of her work was going to be less than stellar. She didn't care. She only hoped that karma would catch up to Digby sooner rather than later. Nothing too bad. *Maybe just have the good witch Glinda drop a house on him?* She had to laugh to herself. *Maybe Matthew is onto something about revenge!*

The best part of the rotation for Torrey was that her parents came up to stay with them on the Yellow Ferry for two weekends. Her parents had never been to Sausalito despite being so geographically close. They had a wonderful time seeing the sights and experiencing the Ferry. Matthew was the consummate host, showering her parents with hospitality and good cheer. Even TJ came up for a midweek visit. He said he had a meeting in San Francisco but both Torrey and Matthew suspected that TJ just wanted to see how they were doing, and to see the Yellow Ferry for himself.

Matthew also was happy that the rotation was over, but for an entirely different reason. Knowledge was power, and now Matthew had the information necessary to move forward with his plans. More than just the general layout of the clinic, he now knew where the guards were posted, where the cameras were located, and where Mr. Ed was situated. He knew where the medical charts were kept. Most important of all, he now knew Ted Nash's appointment schedule and his treatment protocol. Things were falling into place.

While Matthew had been busy surveilling San Quentin, Ted Nash's parents had not been sitting on their hands. They had met twice with attorney Murtaugh in the last month and they had been quietly selling assets in order to accumulate as much liquid cash as possible. They were worried, with good reason, that the governor would lose his reelection bid. Since the governor had become an outspoken proponent of California's sanctuary state policy, there had been a spate of random killings by illegal aliens. And jihadists yelling 'Allahu Akbar' had pipe-bombed a popular concert venue. The aftermath showing bloody body parts and crying parents had gone viral on social media. Most experts were predicting that more attacks against the California citizenry were likely. The politicians, insulated in their gated communities and protected work buildings, didn't worry about the murders, but everyday families did. Working taxpayers did. Voters did. The governor's poll numbers were dropping like a stone.

The Nashes were afraid that contributing to the governor's campaign in exchange for a post-election pardon might be a fool's errand. They needed to ensure Ted was freed *before* the election. They decided that if the governor agreed to sign the parole by next Christmas, then they would funnel $5 million to the governor's reelection campaign.

Murtaugh was willing to act as the go-between with the governor, for a healthy fee. He proposed the deal to the governor's chief-of-staff, Martin Barrows, over dinner and drinks at the exclusive Polo Club in Sacramento. After the obligatory feigned wounded surprise at the idea that the governor might lose the election, Barrows dutifully listened to Murtaugh's pitch. Murtaugh knew it would never fly but he started off the negotiations by insisting that he personally watch the governor sign the parole papers before he turned over the Nash offshore bank account numbers that the campaign could access. As Murtaugh expected, Barrows was insulted and said with an irritated voice, "That is offensive to me and to the governor. You have my word that the governor will sign the parole as soon as you hand over the money."

"Martin, it's not that I don't trust you. It's Mr. Nash. He's putting a good chunk of his family fortune on the line and he needs to be sure that his son's freedom is not dependent on the fickle will of the voting public. My hands are tied on this. Mr. Nash is adamant that he has the signed parole in his hands before you take his money. Surely you can understand that."

Barrows was well aware of the governor's falling poll numbers. He also knew that the governor's pandering to the open borders crowd—specifically his stance on keeping the southern border open to undocumented aliens—could cause the numbers to plunge even more, especially if a band of illegal gang members raped a school girl like had just happened in Arizona. Not to mention the fact that there were several grandstanding mayors who were harboring illegals who had committed violent crimes in their communities. It was Barrows' job to get the governor reelected so he was going to agree to whatever it took to procure the much-needed campaign funding. He just didn't want to concur too quickly or do anything that might prove embarrassing to the governor.

After a protracted back-and-forth, Murtaugh and Barrows agreed that the Nash campaign contribution would be made by next December 15. The public's attention would be diverted during the holiday season and the governor would have eleven months before the election to combat the fallout from victims' rights groups. The funds would be placed into an offshore escrow account that

Barrows could access immediately upon handing over the signed parole. Barrows also negotiated a confidentiality provision so that the parole would be made public only at the discretion and timing of the governor's office. They shook on the deal over a cherries jubilee that was prepared right at the table.

Chapter Forty-Six

Matthew and Torrey had big plans for the Christmas break. They were going to do nothing, and then some more nothing. Matthew invited Torrey and her parents to spend the Christmas holidays with him and TJ. The idea was to have the older generation get to know each other while the youngsters relaxed. But, as is often the case, the best laid plans are seldom realized.

On December 27, Matthew and Torrey decided to take a trip up the coast. Matthew had not driven up Highway 1 since high school. Torrey had never visited any of the coastal towns between Los Angeles and San Francisco, so they were both excited about the adventure. They laughed and held hands as they experienced the beauty of the coastline. They stopped for lunch at a quaint seaside diner in Pismo Beach. Just as they sat down on the outside deck overlooking the sand, Matthew's phone buzzed. Before he had a chance to look at the caller ID, Torrey pleaded, "Do you have to answer that?"

Matthew had no intention of picking up, but he glanced at the screen out of habit. It was TJ. "It's TJ," smiled Matthew. "He probably wants to know how to turn on the cable TV. Let me take this really quick." Torrey sighed and nodded.

"Hi TJ, what's up?"

"Matt, I'm sorry but I have to ask you to come home, right now."

Matthew frowned and glanced over at Torrey. Before TJ could say another word, Matthew said, "Why? What's wrong? Is everyone okay?"

"Yes, we're all fine. It's something else. How long will it take for you to get back here?"

"Uncle TJ, tell me what's going on. Now!"

After an uncomfortable pause, TJ said in a resigned tone, "I'll give you all the details when you get here, but the bottom line is that I got a call from Carly St. Cere. She heard from a source in the governor's office that the Nash family and the governor have struck a deal to get Ted Nash released by next Christmas."

In an instant, Matthew's good mood evaporated. "What? Everyone was telling us that the governor would not let Nash out until after the next election, and that's almost two years away!"

"Yes, that's what we were told. But apparently, Mr. Nash made a monetary offer that the governor could not refuse."

Torrey was looking at Matthew with puzzled eyes as she mouthed "What?" over and over. Matthew scowled and waved his open hand in her direction to suggest she needed to hold her horses so that Matthew could concentrate on what TJ was saying.

TJ concluded the call with a plan of action. "Try to get back by tonight. Carly normally takes this week off, but she is willing to meet with us tomorrow at her office. I'll tell Torrey's parents that we'll have to go out briefly, but they can have the run of the house. See you soon."

TJ hung up. Matthew's faced darkened as he stared at the silent phone. He looked up at Torrey. "TJ says that Ted Nash is going to be paroled before the end of next year!" Matthew silently added to himself, "Before I am a doctor!" Matthew slammed his fist on the table. The sound caused the alarmed waitress, who looked like a young high-school student, to scurry over.

"Sorry for the delay, sir. May I take your order?"

PART V

Chapter Forty-Seven

The three-hour drive back to Pacific Palisades was torture. Neither noticed the scenery. Every stop light and traffic delay were maddening. Torrey tried to engage Matthew, but he drove stone-faced with both hands gripping the steering wheel. She had never seen him remain silent for so long. He looked as though his head was about to explode. When they stopped for gas, Matthew filled up at the self-serve island while Torrey sat in the car. He was so preoccupied that he drove away without putting the gasoline hose back on the pump. The hose tore off and fell to the ground. Matthew did not stop. He just shrugged and swore under his breath as he headed back to the highway.

As they sped along mile after mile, Torrey tried to imagine what Matthew was thinking. Actually, she thought she had a pretty good idea. Almost involuntarily, her computer brain started to compile a checklist of behaviors and statements that, taken separately, were meaningless. But taken together … wasn't there only one logical conclusion?

First, there was the ever-present anomaly of Matthew claiming he wanted to become a prison doctor. It made no sense in general for someone with ambition, and it made even less sense in Matthew's case because his father was murdered by someone now in prison. And why was he adamant that the prison be San Quentin where his father's killer was incarcerated?

Next, Matthew had stated several times in different contexts that Ted Nash would never get out of prison. Before and after the parole hearing, Matthew had as much as guaranteed that Nash would be in prison for his entire life. How could he know that?

Finally, Matthew had talked freely about the necessity and righteousness of revenge. Was it farfetched to imagine that he wanted to become a prison doctor simply to gain access to Ted Nash for an act of revenge? She thought back to the papers she found in his desk drawer concerning effects of contraindicated drugs. Was a medicinal drug going to be the weapon of choice?

Torrey shuddered and looked over at Matthew. He had a faraway look in his eyes. "Matthew, where are you right now?"

As if snapping out of a trance, Matthew glanced over at Torrey and saw the concerned look on her face. "I'm sorry," he replied. "I haven't been good company." He reached across the center divider and grabbed her hand. "I was just taken aback by TJ's call." He smiled at Torrey. "I'm fine now."

Torrey remained skeptical but played along. "I'm sure the news was shocking. Do you suppose there is anything Carly can do?"

"No. Now that I have thought about it, I don't even know why we are coming back from our trip. There's no point in going to see Carly. It's going to be a 'sit around and wring our hands' meeting. I don't need that. TJ can go if he wants to, but I'm not going."

Torrey's puzzled expression contrasted with Matthew's renewed look of confidence. Matthew had concluded that there was only one thing to do—move up the timetable.

Chapter Forty-Eight

When they got to Matthew's house, Torrey's parents were packed and ready to leave. TJ had given them a heads-up about the parole, and they didn't want to intrude on the family grief or planning. TJ had tried to talk them out of going, but to no avail. Matthew had no better luck. It was up to Torrey. She took her parents aside and explained that everyone wanted them to stay. That no purpose would be served by leaving. When that plea failed, Torrey went for the heartstrings. "Look, Mom and Dad. If you leave, I'm leaving. And I don't want to leave. I need to be with Matthew right now. He needs me. He is my spirit animal. I want to stay as planned through New Year's Day." Torrey grabbed her mother's hand and looked her in the eyes. "Please stay."

Mrs. Jamison knew what her daughter was saying. This wasn't about Torrey staying for a few more days. It was about her staying forever. Mr. and Mrs. Jamison unpacked. Matthew saw to it that the rest of their stay was wonderful, culminating in grandstand seats at the Rose Parade.

TJ had gone alone to meet with Ms. St. Cere. He reported afterwards that Matthew had been right. Carly had no realistic legal means to prevent the early release. She could not even go to the press because that would entail revealing her source in the governor's office. TJ was surprised at Matthew's stoic reaction.

He chalked it up to Matthew's growing closeness to Torrey. He was glad that Matthew was putting Ted Nash behind him.

The remaining months of Matthew's third year of medical school were meaningless to him. He went to class, studied with Torrey, and presented himself as a dedicated doctor-in-training. In reality, his mind was constantly working towards the only goal that mattered to him—the death of Ted Nash.

Most details of his scheme were finalized. Without telling Torrey, he had already signed up for the three-month 'underserved population' rotation at the prison. He didn't want Torrey there if things went south. He was able to reserve the September through November rotation so that he would be at San Quentin before Nash was released. He knew that fourth-year students were allowed to give injections to inmates, and he was confident he could talk his way into the role of Nash's provider on the day Nash was scheduled for his shots. He had researched the treatment that Nash was receiving, and he figured that he could switch out the syringe containing the proper medicine with a drug that would cause death. And he had decided that that perfect replacement was the drug rocuronium.

Rocuronium was ideal for several reasons. First, it is a common drug used by doctors everywhere to relax muscles during surgery. The medicine blocks nerve impulses to muscles so that muscles do not move during delicate surgical maneuvers. He considered swiping a small bottle from the prison surgery center, but the inventory log would eventually show that it was missing. A better source might be TJ's medical office. Matthew knew from listening to TJ over the years that TJ kept all kinds of drugs in his office. With the many surgical procedures that TJ performed in his clinic's small private surgery center, he certainly would have a supply of rocuronium. And Matthew knew that TJ was not a stickler for record keeping. He just reordered when he saw he was running low. Matthew planned to visit TJ soon.

Second, rocuronium was the perfect medicine for the job because it is specifically contraindicated for patients with autoimmune diseases such as Eaton-Lambert Syndrome. Matthew had read case studies where normal doses of rocuronium injected into *healthy* patients caused death from paralysis of respiratory muscles and cardiac arrest. In *unhealthy* patients like Ted Nash, a small dose of rocuronium would cause a severe aggravation of his symptoms. A large dose would certainly be fatal. Matthew intended to use the highest dose that he could pilfer from TJ's stock.

Torrey wasn't dumb. She could see that Matthew was preoccupied. That his mind was not on his studies. That he could barely muster up the enthusiasm for exams. That he was spending every waking moment devising a scheme to ensure Nash did not leave San Quentin alive. She was not sure how he intended to do it, but she was pretty sure he had a plan. And the plan had to include doing the three-month rotation at the prison at the beginning of their fourth year.

She had asked Matthew about his fourth-year schedule several times and had received back vague platitudes about his uncertainty over which electives he wanted to take during his last year of medical school. Torrey knew that Matthew was trying to protect her from conspirator status, but she did not appreciate the sentiment. She was unclear about what she could do to keep him from his self-destructive path, and, truth be told, she was uncertain whether she should try to stop him. She only knew one thing for sure—she wanted to spend the rest of her life with Matthew, and so she needed to be with him during this crucial time. She did the only thing that she could do—she signed up for the same three-month rotation.

"You did *what?*" Matthew looked incredulous when Torrey nonchalantly mentioned over coffee that she had selected the elective stint at San Quentin.

"It shouldn't surprise you. I remembered what they told us about fourth-year students getting lots of responsibility and I couldn't find anything comparable. And," she said with a sweet smile, "I remembered that you said you planned to do the clerkship as an entrée to becoming a prison doctor. I was hoping we could do the three months together."

Matthew protested. "Surely you could find a surgical elective that would be more helpful to your career. Of course, I would like to be with you for that time period, but you need to think about your own self-interest. Being a prison doctor certainly isn't your goal."

"That's true. But I think serving the prison population will stand me in good stead with the administrators who are in charge of public hospital residency applications. Those folks love a do-gooder. And I'll be competing for surgical residencies with students who probably will have nothing comparable on their applications showing they want to help the downtrodden." Torrey's face lit up with another big smile. "Besides, it's a done deal. I already have my confirmation and it's too late to sign up for anything else."

Matthew was torn. Naturally he had hated the idea of not seeing Torrey for a few months. He didn't want to admit, even to himself, the depth of his feelings for Torrey for fear that he might become distracted from his ultimate goal. On the other hand, if she were doing the rotation with him, he would have to figure out a way to keep her in the dark. He would have to make certain that she was not involved in any way with Nash's death. If his plan worked, neither she nor anyone else would ever know what happened to Ted Nash. As he told himself repeatedly, he was not trying to make a global statement or even a statement about California's screwed-up criminal justice system. At this point, he was simply meting out justice in the microcosm of his own personal world.

Chapter Forty-Nine

During the summer before their last year of medical school, Matthew and Torrey spent nearly all their time together. They used Matthew's house as a home base and explored Southern California's many wonders. California was losing its luster as the land of economic opportunity, but the natural beauty would last forever.

While the emotional bond between Matthew and Torrey was already profound, they both found it more and more difficult to resist the physical attraction. Of late, they had been spending more time kissing and less time talking. They both knew where the line had to be drawn, but the line was starting to blur.

Matthew insisted that Torrey's parents come visit for a week. He secured box seats at the Hollywood Bowl for one evening and they spent a day at the Santa Monica beach and pier. TJ took everyone out on his boat, and they cruised over to Catalina Island. A good time was had by all.

With only two weeks left before the start of their shift at San Quentin, Torrey announced she was going home to spend the remaining days of summer at her parents' house. She wanted to sleep in her own bedroom for a change. This suited Matthew just fine. He needed to visit TJ's office, alone.

"Hi Ms. Zimmerman, this is Matthew Preston calling. How are you today?"

"Well goodness gracious! Matthew, it has been forever since you called the office! Are you trying to reach your uncle?"

"Actually, I wonder if you could check his schedule to see when he might be in the office this week. I want to come by and see him." After a short pause, Matthew added, "And you too!"

"Aren't you the sweetest thing. A perfect gentleman, just like always."

Mavis Zimmerman had been TJ's office manager for as long as Matthew could remember. Some would call her officious, but she was protective of TJ's schedule, his reputation as a doctor, and his personal well-being. Although TJ scoffed at the idea, Mary always used to say that Mavis had a huge crush on TJ. Mary had wondered aloud if someday TJ would return the affection. However, TJ seemed quite content to keep the relationship on a purely business level. That is not to say that TJ didn't have a soft spot in his heart for Mavis. He did. She had started with TJ when she was a twenty-something looker. But after a messy divorce from an abusive husband, and a grown son who was nothing but trouble, Mavis was now fifty pounds overweight and a chain smoker. She never lit up in the office, but the smell of tobacco on her ill-fitting clothes was sometimes overwhelming. Despite an appearance that was less than consistent with a professional doctor's office, Mavis had a job for life. TJ would never let her go. She needed employment. She was quite competent. And, it was good to have an employee who had your back.

After more pleasantries were exchanged, Matthew learned that TJ was going to be making rounds at the local hospital on Thursday between 8:00 a.m. and noon, after which patients were scheduled in the office beginning at 1:00 p.m. Mavis penciled Matthew in for noonish and said she would order in sandwiches for the two of them. Matthew's plan was simple. Arrive early, find the medicine storage cabinet, and snatch a bottle of rocuronium.

On Thursday morning, Matthew walked into the reception area of TJ's office at 11:30. Mavis was at the front desk explaining to a millennial patient why his insurance was useless because his deductible was more than the cost of the treatment. Mavis looked up, smiled at Matthew, and waved him into the inner sanctum of the office. Matthew could not believe his good luck. Not only was Mavis preoccupied with the disgruntled patient, Matthew could hear the conversation while he looked around. He knew that Mavis would monopolize him as soon as she could break away.

He chuckled as he heard the patient raising his voice to Mavis. "So, what's the point of having this insurance if I can't use it?"

Mavis was acting the part of the wise elder. She had heard this complaint many times. "Yes dear. It is a dilemma."

"But they said that our premiums would go down! That health insurance would be more affordable!"

"Yes dear. I know they did."

Matthew had looked in every open room by this time. No drug cabinet. There was a physician's assistant doing some paperwork, but he couldn't ask her. He was on his own. And he could hear that Mavis was trying to end the conversation at the front desk. "Oh, you don't know who your congressman is? Perhaps you can find out and—"

Mavis's voice faded away as Matthew reached the far end of the hallway where there were two closed doors. He knew one was the entrance to TJ's personal office. He tried the other doorknob. It wasn't locked. He slowly opened the door and looked inside. There were two brooms, a mop, and some cleaning supplies. Matthew was dejected. The drugs must be in TJ's office, but he couldn't go in there, at least not without an invitation.

Just then Mavis appeared and cornered Matthew in the hallway. After being asked all about school, his future plans, and whether he had a girlfriend, Matthew knew he only had a few minutes before TJ arrived. "Mavis, do you think it would be alright if I waited for TJ in his office? I need to return a call on my cell."

"Of course. I'll send your uncle in the moment he gets here."

"No rush. I know I was early," Matthew replied.

"I'm going to check on your lunches. The food should have arrived by now." With that, Matthew entered TJ's office and closed the door behind him. He scanned the room. He saw several bookcases filled with medical texts, two closed credenzas, and of course, the obligatory cluttered large-wooden desk. Nothing that looked like a medicine storage cabinet. Knowing TJ might walk in at any moment, Matthew quickly checked the credenzas. More books. He hated to do it, but he even opened each desk drawer to take a quick look. Just office supplies and personal items. He was resigned. He would have to get the rocuronium from San Quentin. It would be tricky, but he resolved that he would find a way.

Once he changed his focus, he noticed the many photographs on the walls. One entire collage was devoted to TJ's boat. As Matthew walked around the office, he saw that some of the photos were of his grandparents. Some were of Matthew's father and mother. And a few were of Matthew alone from various significant events, including high school and college graduations. He grinned as he saw a photo of himself hoisting the Stanford championship baseball trophy over his head. And directly below the picture was Matthew's MVP trophy, a present from Matthew to TJ for all his support. The trophy was resting on a what appeared to be a dorm room fridge that was covered on top with a decorative piece of cloth. Matthew thought a soft drink would hit the spot, maybe even a beer if he was lucky. He pulled open the small door. The inside was stuffed with medicines.

Matthew went down on one knee and searched through the small boxes and bottles, trying not to make a mess or undue noise. On the top shelf, he found seven or eight loose vials of rocuronium bromide. Most of the small glass bottles were labeled as 50 mg, which Matthew knew was a typical dose for a healthy adult. He found two vials labeled as 100 mg. Suddenly he heard TJ's voice. He was talking to Mavis about something, but his voice was getting progressively louder. Matthew liberated a bottle of the 100mg drug and shoved it in his jacket pocket. He closed the door to the fridge and quickly stood up. When TJ burst through the door, Matthew was studying his trophy.

"There he is—my favorite nephew!" exclaimed TJ. Seeing the trophy in Matthew's hands, TJ laughed, "I see you're trying to relive your glory days. Time to move on son!"

"Hi TJ," Matthew grinned. "I didn't know you kept this trophy and these photos in your office."

TJ slapped Matthew on the back. "And where else would I put them so I could look at them every day?"

"Ha! So, tell me, how's it going? Everything okay at the hospital this morning?"

"Oh, just the usual." TJ nodded to the chairs. "Let's sit. I've been on my feet for hours." Matthew sat in an uncomfortable client chair across the desk from TJ's leather throne. TJ leaned back and sighed.

"Of all these pictures, do you know which one is my favorite?" mused TJ. Matthew shook his head.

"This one right here." TJ picked up a small framed photo that was facing away from Matthew. TJ turned it around so that Matthew could see. It was a photo of Matthew standing at the White Coat Ceremony reciting the Hippocratic oath. Matthew picked up the photo and held it close to his face. He examined it carefully. It was three years ago but he remembered it like it was yesterday. *Above all else, do no harm.* He put the photo back on TJ's desk. He reached into his jacket pocket and fondled the bottle of death serum. He smiled at TJ and thought of a different oath. An oath he had sworn on the memory of his father. An oath of vengeance.

Chapter Fifty

Matthew booked a two-bedroom, two-bath, kitchen suite at a chain hotel near Sausalito for the three months he and Torrey would be working at San Quentin. The Yellow Ferry had been a fun diversion, but now they just needed a clean place to decompress each night, with complimentary breakfast in the morning. And Matthew knew he would have too much on his mind to enjoy anything but the basics.

Torrey had never been prone to bouts of apprehension or nervous anxiety, but she was preoccupied with concern for Matthew. As they made the drive from Stanford to Sausalito, she could see that he was deep in thought. Torrey studied the side of his face as Matthew drove through the maze of San Francisco streets. She searched in vain for some sign of confirmation, or validation, of her theory. Self-doubt crept into her mind. *Maybe she was wrong. Maybe Matthew really did want to be a prison doctor. Maybe this rotation had nothing to do with Ted Nash.* She grimaced to herself as she thought how hollow her own words sounded. She knew in her heart she was right. But what could she do? What *should* she do? Killing was morally wrong, *wasn't it?* But she well knew Matthew's views on the necessity of punishing wrongdoers. On his obsessive devotion to revenge. She thought back on Matthew's passionate desire to have the death sentence imposed for drunk drivers who have killed innocent bystanders. She recalled that when she told Matthew about George Rincon, Matthew's immediate solution was to get a gun to shoot Rincon. She knew that Matthew was in favor of vigilante law. He had every reason, and every justification, to want Ted Nash to remain in prison until his death. If the corrupt system was going to set Nash free, of course Matthew was going to try to stop that injustice.

And who was she to try to stop him?

Just someone who didn't want him to be caught and executed, or to be caught and sentenced to prison.

Just someone who wanted to spend her life with him.

That was all.

Chapter Fifty-One

As they maneuvered into the San Quentin parking lot for their first morning, Matthew and Torrey both stared up at the guard towers. A steel-gray fog was rolling in which made the facility even more ominous than usual. The guards stood like ghostly statues with their rifles resting across their arms. Because of the advancing fog, the eerie sentinels were unmistakable one minute, and invisible the next.

Even though Matthew had been inside the prison already for the parole hearing and the three-week rotation, he knew this time was different. This was the last-chance culmination of Matthew's lifelong plot.

The ending would go one of two ways. He could have a triumphant success with Nash dead. No autopsy. No investigation. And no concern over how or why he had suddenly passed away.

The other possibility was scary. Whether Nash died or not from the injection, Matthew could be caught and imprisoned. With his mother gone, he told himself he could live with those consequences if it meant Nash was dead. But he wasn't so sure he could live with the penalty of losing Torrey forever.

Unlike the third-year orientation which had been conducted by a low-level doctor in the clinic's spartan doctors' lounge, the fourth-year initiation was headed up by the chief of medicine, Dr. Kristin Remington. She realized that any student who voluntarily signed up to spend three months at the prison might well be willing to come on-board permanently after graduation. And she needed more full-time doctors on staff.

There were four students in the group. In addition to Matthew and Torrey, there was Martin Bower, an African American man, and Martha Wong, a Chinese woman, both from UC San Francisco. Bower and Wong had done their third-year rotations at the prison in the spring. After the obligatory pat-downs and backpack searches, they were all led to Dr. Remington's bright spacious office on the first floor of the hospital. Although she had a hundred other things that demanded her attention, Dr. Remington knew that recruitment of new doctors was high on her list. The funding for more doctors was in place, but she still had to find some candidates.

"I have studied your resumes. What an impressive group you are! Let me introduce myself and then we will go around the room so that you can get to know each other. As you likely know, I graduated from Stanford Medical School twenty years ago. I did a clerkship here at San Quentin before my surgery residency at Harvard and my spine surgery fellowship at Yale. I came here from being chief of surgery at UCSF. I have been here for four years and I expect to stay for many years to come. My goal is to make medical care at San Quentin on par with that of the best private institutions."

Mr. Bower cleared his throat and raised his hand a few inches. Dr. Remington looked at him. "Dr. Remington, is it realistic to think that prisons can ever provide quality medical care to inmates? I saw a news story that said—"

Dr. Remington cut him off with a wave of her hand. "I know that some in the news media are on a crusade to suggest that conditions at San Quentin and

263

other prisons are abysmal. If you believe what they say, things are no better now than they were in 1860. I am confident that you will see for yourselves while you're here that our ambitious objectives are within reach. We simply need the help of bright young minds, like yours."

After a pause and a smile, she gestured to the walls of her office like a game show hostess revealing a prize. "Plus, there is another important factor at play. As you can see from my photos, you can actually have a private life as a doctor here. I spend most of my free time sailing on the bay."

The four students silently glanced around the room at the large photographs of a smiling Dr. Remington on the deck of a catamaran that looked big enough to operate as a sunset cruise sailboat for tourists in Maui. The centerpiece of the collage was Dr. Remington sailing past San Quentin's walls. Matthew's mood darkened as his eyes fell upon a different photo—one of the governor wearing a noble expression. The photo was captioned 'Standing for Truth, Integrity, and Justice.'

Dr. Remington continued, "We'll have a sailing party at the end of your service project. There is nothing as awe-inspiring as looking up at the Golden Gate Bridge from the water." After a polite round of oohing and awing, the students looked back at Dr. Remington as she asked, "So who wants to go next?"

After each student gave his or her introductory spiel, Dr. Remington got back to the business of preparing the group for the *experience of a lifetime*. "You all know from having done short clerkships here already, that safety is our first priority. You also have probably heard that in last few months we have seen a spike in inmate fighting and rioting. Several guards have been injured and the warden has had to put the prison on lock-down seven or eight times this past summer.

"I don't mean to make it sound like your lives are in danger, but most of these prisoners are angry. Angry at the world, at the system, and themselves. No doctors have been injured by inmates for several years and the rioting is typically in the yard or inside one of the cellblocks. And even though things have gotten unruly lately, this place is like a church compared to how things used to be. You have to keep in mind that San Quentin was built in 1852 by inmates who were temporarily housed in a prison ship moored in the bay. Many of California's most notorious criminals have been housed here. As doctors, we treat them all, even those that are injured while fighting or rioting."

The four students nodded. Matthew looked over at Torrey. She seemed to be tuning out Dr. Remington. He expected that at any moment Torrey was going to blurt out, "I'm not worried." Matthew wasn't worried either, at least not for himself. He was now up to reason number 11 why he wished Torrey was not here with him. But Dr. Remington was just about to give him reason number 12.

"One thing that the warden insisted I mention to you is San Quentin's long-time policy against negotiating for hostages. If a one or more prisoners grabs a guard, an administrator, a member of the public, or even a doctor, the prison will not accede to prisoner demands in exchange for the release of the hostage. The hostage is on his or her own." Dr. Remington looked at the faces of her audience. She added in a singsong voice, "So the takeaway is?"

Torrey offered the first, and only, response, "Don't get taken hostage."

"Correct young lady. So, it really comes down to staying aware of what is going on around you. If you feel unsafe or if you think something isn't right, tell a guard.

"Now if there are no questions, I am going to be your guide today. I want you to see a cellblock, the exercise yard, and where you'll be working." Dr. Remington looked at her notes. "I understand that Mr. Bower and Ms. Wong have asked to be assigned to the hospital. And Mr. Preston has requested the clinic. Ms. Jamison, do you have a preference?"

"The clinic, definitely."

Something seemed wrong about walking through the yard among the inmates just after hearing about the unrest in the prison population. But they did it. Even though a weathered, tough-looking guard with knife-scarred hands escorted Dr. Remington and her charges, Matthew noted that they were badly outnumbered. There were hundreds of inmates wandering about with only a handful of guards in the exercise yard. Matthew looked up at the tower sentries who were supposed to be the eyes and ears of the folks on the ground. He assumed the guards were up there, but the fog was too thick to see them or their automatic weapons. He mumbled to himself, "If we can't see them, how can they see us? What could they do if a group of inmates decided to overpower us?"

Fortunately, although he felt the raw energy in the yard, he observed that few prisoners paid them any mind. Mostly, the inmates were in clusters based on race. On closer examination, there seemed to be no mingling among the Blacks, Whites, or Hispanics. Torrey must have noticed it too because she questioned Dr. Remington about it. "Ms. Jamison, you will find this self-segregation at all prisons. Much of it has to do with gang affiliations. The surest way to find yourself getting beat up is to try to socialize with another race. That is one of the unwritten rules that the prisoners learn to follow very quickly. And the second surest way for an inmate to be attacked is to squeal on another prisoner, regardless of race."

Dr. Remington elaborated as they continued walking but Matthew was too distracted to listen. He watched the inmates exercising on shiny, state-of-the-art weight-lifting equipment. He saw others playing basketball and tennis on beautiful courts suitable for private country clubs. From the baseball field in the distance he heard the sounds of grown men laughing and yelling over a missed umpire call.

He thought back to the elementary school next to Torrey's house in East

Palo Alto. He pictured the old, rusted playground equipment. The bent basketball hoops with no nets. The play fields overgrown with weeds and dead grass. And the flaking paint on the metal merry-go-round. The voice in his head rang out, *Criminals over children. Sounds about right.*

On the way to one of the four massive cellblocks, they passed through the Education Center where inmates could sign up for free classes on everything from college credit courses, to theater, to Pilates. Matthew kept his thoughts to himself, but Torrey could read his mind.

The cold stone façade of North Cellblock belied the hot chaos inside. As soon as they entered, the stench of confined men was overwhelming. Immediately, the hooting and hollering started. The cacophony was white noise until they were walking between the rows of cells, and the individual voices could be isolated. Dr. Remington was old news, but Martha Wong and Torrey were fresh meat. Cat calls, wolf whistles, and vulgar shouts rang out. Torrey kept her eyes forward, looking neither right nor left. Matthew looked cautiously around and instinctively moved closer to her. He nudged her along with the slightest touch of his hand on the small of her back. 'Hey baby, whatcha doin tonight?' and 'Let's do this thang' were common refrains. A more-clever inmate went with a variation, 'C'mon bitches, come over and gimmie a little something,' as he exposed himself.

The odor and noise abated the moment the heavy steel doors clicked closed behind them. As they exited the cellblock, Martha had tears in her eyes. Torrey did not. Dr. Remington stopped the group and explained. "I'm sorry to put you through that, but this job is not for the faint of heart. It is important that you see where these inmates live and who you will be dealing with for the next few months—and for your career if you choose this path. They are in those cells about twenty hours a day so any diversion from the normal routine is exploited." She looked directly at Martha who was still trembling and was making sounds like she couldn't breathe. Dr. Remington sighed, knowing that she just lost another candidate.

"Are you going to be okay?" Martha nodded, but no one was convinced. They all were certain that Martha would be looking for a different career path, starting immediately.

They stopped by the hospital and had a look around. The beds were full, but no one looked as sick as Martha. Martin and Martha stayed behind when it was time to take Matthew and Torrey over to the clinic. Matthew was glad to be going back to where Ted Nash would be treated.

As they walked through the yard, Matthew noticed a number of small cages, each holding a single prisoner. "What's with the guys in those cells?" asked Matthew as he pointed.

Dr. Remington explained that those inmates were in protective custody for their own safety. "Those who have committed crimes against children, especially molesters, are targeted by the other inmates. The men in those outside cells are entitled to an hour a day in the great outdoors but they cannot be released into the general population. Even murderers look down upon child molesters."

Just before they reached the yard exit, Dr. Remington was recognized and hailed by a grandfatherly inmate who looked like the Charlton Heston version of Moses. As no threat was posed, the guard let Moses approach to renew his longstanding and recurring complaint about the prohibition against conjugal visits. Dr. Remington smiled as she let him argue. Even the burly guard was grinning.

While Dr. Remington was occupied, Torrey spoke in a low voice to Matthew.

"That was bad, but can you imagine what it would be like to be crammed in those cells like sardines? To have no privacy? To have someone watching your every move, every second of the day? That might be the worst part about being in prison. Other than the bad food and the mind-numbing boredom."

Matthew's top lip curled. His voice was thick with disgust. His reply was succinct.

"They made their choice."

Chapter Fifty-Two

Everything looked pretty much the same in the clinic. The same doctors, the same nurses' station, and the same medical chart filing cabinets. When Dr. Remington announced that they were going to go up to the video room, both Matthew and Torrey said they had already been briefed by Mr. Ed.

"About that," said Dr. Remington, "there is something you need to know that is a change from last year. Let's duck in here," she said as they followed her into a small empty office. When they were seated, Dr. Remington explained. "About six months ago, Mr. Ed began the paperwork and the procedures in order to become *Mrs. Ed.*" Dr. Remington paused to let that sink in. Matthew gave a puzzled look at Torrey, who smiled in response. Both waited for the doctor to continue.

"Ed is hoping to become the first prison guard in the country to have taxpayer-funded sex reassignment surgery." Matthew gasped and tried to interrupt. Dr. Remington waved him off as she further explained. "You two are too young to remember this, but back in 1980, Rodney Quine murdered Shahid Baig, a young father of three. Quine was convicted and sentenced to prison. After years of incarceration, Quine claimed that he self-identified as a woman, so he sued California to require the State to provide him with a sex change operation. The State sanctioned the request in 2015 despite opposition from many, including Baig's daughter. She argued that she, as a taxpayer, should not have to fund such an elective surgery for her father's killer. The daughter's pleas fell on deaf ears."

While Dr. Richardson talked, Matthew imagined all of the people suffering in the State of California. All of the poverty and homelessness. The lack of sufficient police in crime-ridden neighborhoods. And finite tax revenues are funding sex change operations for criminals? *What next?* When Dr. Richardson appeared to be finished with her story about Quine, Matthew asked the obvious question. "What does Quine have to do with Ed?"

"When Ed came to me and asked for my support, he argued that if the State is going to pay for inmates to have the operation, then why not for guards? I counseled him on the medical ramifications of his decision, but at the end of the day, he was adamant. And I had to admit that his logic was sound. So, Ed is in the process of transitioning while his case winds its way up the administrative ladder. He has started hormone therapy, body hair removal, and he has had some facial feminization surgery on his face. We are hopeful that the transition will be complete within the next six months. He says his new name will be Edwina, but that we can call him Mrs. Ed."

"How are the other guards reacting to the new Ed?" asked Torrey.

"As you might expect, Ed is taking some abuse, but he says it's worth it. He still has the same happy demeanor. And there is no sign that his work has been adversely affected. So, don't worry. Ed will still have your backs while you are in the clinic."

Before she left, Dr. Remington explained that they were unusually shorthanded in the clinic because Torrey's "mentor" from the previous year, Dr. Digby, had finally retired. His replacement had yet to be hired. Torrey couldn't help herself. She burst out laughing.

Dr. Remington said goodbye to Matthew and Torrey at the doctors' locker room. Each was given a picture ID on a lanyard, a padlock for a personal locker, a keycard for the doors in the clinic, and a white lab coat. As Matthew stored his personal belongings in his locker, he reflected on his plan to smuggle his vial of rocuronium into the prison. Stealing it from TJ's office had not been easy, but in light of the scrutiny for banned substances at San Quentin, he knew that the more difficult task was going to be avoiding detection by the X-ray machine at the entrance to the prison. He couldn't just carry it in his pocket, and any liquid, especially medicines, were strictly prohibited. As he stared into his open locker, Matthew replayed in his mind the call he had made a month ago to his private investigator.

"Joe, this is Matthew Preston. I have to ask for your help again."

"Hi Matthew. Anything for you. You know that."

"I hope you feel that way after I tell you what I need. I have a delicate situation that requires an item that can't be purchased at the neighborhood Walmart. I'm hoping that with your connections you might be able to obtain it for me with no questions asked."

"Well c'mon, what is it?"

"I need to get a small item through a metal detector. The item is a two-inch vial of medicine. The glass bottle has a strip of metal around the cap. I'd like to conceal it inside of a personal-sized coffee thermos. Is such a thermos available that would get my small item past an X-ray machine?"

There was quite a long silence on the other end of the phone. Joe would have refused such a request from anyone else. But he trusted Matthew. And Matthew wasn't asking to conceal a gun. It was just medicine. "As it happens,

I know a guy who works at the CIA. He once told me about a fellow in Germany who fabricates a hard-shell liner that can be used to shield weapons from X-ray detection. The liner can be incorporated into everyday items. I know the CIA special orders from him, but I suspect he also sells to whoever is willing to pay. The products he fabricates are very expensive because he uses a rare material called Osmium, which is twice as dense as lead."

"Joe, for this, money is no object."

"Let me call my friend. He owes me a favor. I'll get back to you when I have some information."

Less than a week later, Joe had called back and told Matthew that the order had been placed—and the amount of the outrageous bill. The turnaround time would be three weeks.

The day Joe delivered the thermos to him, Matthew had carefully wrapped the vial of rocuronium and placed it in the bottom of the thermos for safekeeping. He planned to bring it into the prison a few days before Ted Nash was scheduled for his next injection. He would keep it hidden in his personal locker until D-day.

Torrey watched Matthew lingering outside of his opened locker. What could be so interesting inside his new locker? Was he hiding something in there? She tried to sneak a peek, but his solid frame was blocking her view. She wondered if he somehow had a weapon in there.

After donning their blindingly white new doctor coats, Matthew and Torrey hung their nametags around their necks and walked down to the doctors' lounge where they were to get their assignments from Dr. Gerard. She confirmed what Dr. Remington had said—they were short-staffed and therefore Matthew and

Torrey were going to be functioning more as first-year doctors than fourth-year medical students. There would be less supervision and more autonomy. That suited Matthew just fine.

As Dr. Gerard was explaining their duties, Matthew made a production out of getting himself a cup of coffee from the ancient machine in the corner. He took a sip and spit it back into the foam cup. "That is the worst coffee ever," he scowled. "I'm going to start bringing my own coffee with me to work."

And he did. Every day for a week he filled up his special thermos with coffee. The gate guards pulled the thermos out of his backpack and checked inside for the first two days. After that, they just waved it through. The next couple of days after that, Matthew left the thermos empty. No one checked inside. Then he tested whether metal inside the thermos would trigger the metal detector. He put a small screwdriver inside. If the screwdriver showed up on X-ray, he was prepared to say that he needed a jeweler's screwdriver to fix a loose screw on his exam room overhead surgery light—he didn't want to bother anyone by asking for help.

His elaborate precautions were unnecessary. The screwdriver was not detected.

The next morning, he placed the vial of rocuronium in a small padded box and then carefully wedged it inside the thermos. He stuck the thermos inside of his backpack just as he had done every other day. He calmly drove Torrey to San Quentin. They talked about nothing important. Matthew held up his end of the conversation.

As they approached the doors leading into the clinic security checkpoint, Matthew knew that this was the point of no return. They joined the queue and shuffled along. He started to second guess his entire plan. *How could he expect this to work? What if he is caught? What would TJ think about him? What would Torrey think?* As he placed his backpack on the X-ray machine belt, he became more and more nervous. Torrey was standing right next to him. *How would he explain any of this to her if the guard chose today to look inside his thermos?* Torrey sensed his unease. "Are you okay Matthew? You look funny."

Matthew was afraid of what sound would come out of his mouth if he tried to speak. So, he just forced a smile and tried to look natural—but it was challenging. He glued his eyes on his backpack and then on the guards on the other side of the metal detector. Torrey and then Matthew were ushered through the walkway opening while the backpack travelled along the belt. Matthew glanced over at the guard manning the computer screen. Matthew had never seen him before. Suddenly the belt stopped. The guard bent down to look more closely at the screen and then yelled out to the guard standing opposite Torrey and Matthew. "Hey Frank, you will want to take a look at this backpack."

The belt started up again. As soon as Matthew's backpack came out of the chute, Frank grabbed it and stated, "Whose bag is this?"

"Matthew raised his hand and said lightly, "That's mine, sir."

"Step over here please," said the guard as he carried Matthew's backpack to the table at the end of the belt. The people in line behind Matthew silently stepped around him and kept moving. "Where did you get this backpack?"

"What do you mean?" asked Matthew.

"I mean where did you get it? I've been looking for this model backpack for months! My son is going on a hiking trip to Yosemite and he asked me specifically for this model. I've been to every camping store around and I can't find anyone who carries it. So, where did you get it?"

Flooded with relief, Matthew grinned broadly. "I think I ordered it online from REI. You might try them."

"Thanks, buddy. I will." Frank handed the backpack back to Matthew. "You have a good day now."

Matthew could not wait to get up to his locker and unload his valuable contraband. He hid the vial behind his extra change of clothes.

Chapter Fifty-Three

Most of the work in the clinic was relatively routine—required monthly checkups, shots, minor scrapes and pains. Matthew requested and was assigned to examination rooms 2 and 3 where patients received regular treatments for long-term diseases, while Torrey was at the far end of the hall in rooms 13 and 14 where minor surgeries were performed. Torrey quickly determined that most of the injuries she treated were self-inflicted out of anger, such as punching a concrete wall when denied parole or smashing a head against a cell door when a wife or girlfriend did not come on visiting day.

Licensed doctors supervised their work for the first few days, but the shortage of physicians, combined with no decrease in demand for service, allowed the medical students more autonomy than they could have imagined. Dr. Gerard had taken a strong interest in Torrey's development and well-being. Three or four times a day, Dr. Gerard would drop in on Torrey and her patients, especially if Torrey was tending to a historically unruly inmate. Torrey was always happy to see Dr. Gerard, but she felt no need for extra supervision or protection.

Matthew only saw Dr. Gerard as they passed in the corridor. They were pleasant enough to each other. Their interactions were cordial, but no special bond existed. That was fine with Matthew. He was delighted that Torrey was nurturing a friendship that would help her in the next step of her career.

Besides, Matthew had the idealistic Dr. Goodwin looking over his shoulder, whether Matthew wanted his guidance or not. At the beginning of each day, and at every break like clockwork, Dr. Goodwin would search out Matthew to give him unsolicited advice on the best techniques to interact with the prisoners. "I'm telling you Matthew, the key to this whole doctor-patient thing in a prison is to treat the inmates with respect. In here, respect is everything. They are just people like you and me. They simply made some regrettable mistakes. They deserve our compassion."

Say what? Matthew said to himself.

"There really is no reason to treat them any differently than if you were in private practice. These inmates know you're here to help them. So, most of them will be quite friendly. Return the sentiment and you'll do just fine."

Matthew quickly grew tired of Goodwin's bleeding-heart speeches, but he knew there was no point in debating the merits with him. He recognized that nothing he could say would undo Goodwin's programming. And he would have bet the farm that neither Goodwin nor his family had ever been the victim of a violent crime. So, he just listened and nodded every few minutes.

Matthew had been waiting for a chance to steal a look at Nash's current chart, but no luck. In the interim, each morning he made a beeline to the nurses' station to check the calendar to see if Nash was scheduled to be a patient that day. Any changes to the schedule were delivered throughout the day to each exam room.

He was getting frustrated. The filing nurse seemed to be constantly hovering near the filing cabinets where the charts were kept, and Matthew hadn't had one patient yet with a last name starting with *N*. As Matthew pondered how long he could afford to wait for the perfect opportunity, he was blessed with a fortunate break—a riot in the West Cellblock.

Just after mid-morning, the loudest alarm Matthew had ever heard sounded throughout the entire prison. Within seconds, a loud and commanding voice sounded over the intercom. "This is a Code 3 alarm! All prisoners stay where you are until escorted back to your cells by a uniformed guard! All available guards report to West Block!"

Matthew and Torrey both hurried from their examination rooms into the corridor and looked around. The hallway in both directions was empty. The nurses had disappeared to who knows where. The doctors had remained in their exam rooms. Everyone except Matthew and Torrey knew the drill. They caught each other's eye and gave a shrug. Matthew looked up at the nearby video camera and mouthed, "Ed, what's going on?"

Ed responded over his private PA system. "Nothing to worry about Preston. There is fighting in one of the cellblocks. The general alarm goes off anytime a lockdown is imminent. The alarm will go probably go off in a few minutes. Then it will be back to business as usual."

Torrey heard the explanation and retreated into her exam room where her patient was stoically waiting for his boil to be lanced.

Matthew noticed that he was alone and that he had walked out of his exam room with the patient's chart. Even if Ed were watching, he wouldn't know or care whose chart was in Matthew's hand. Without a moment of hesitation, Matthew strode over to the cabinet containing the N patient charts. He opened the drawer and easily spotted Nash's file. Matthew assumed that Ed was busy keeping tabs on the prison emergency but, just in case Ed was watching, he used his upper body to shield his actions from view while he scanned the top sheet. Nash's next appointment was scheduled for September 29—almost three weeks away. In exam room 2. Perfect. Matthew would be ready.

Unbeknownst to Matthew, Torrey was also getting ready. Having figured out that Matthew could not carry out any sort of plan without knowing Nash's appointment schedule, she decided that she needed the same information. She couldn't bring herself to articulate *why* this was important, but she knew in her gut that it was.

Torrey shunned the cloak-and-dagger approach. One day she simply walked over to the patient file cabinets and searched out Nash's file. If any of the nurses noticed or cared, no one said anything. It took just a few seconds to see the appointment date. She saw that Nash was on a three-month injection schedule. September 29 at 1:30 p.m. was going to be Matthew's one and only encounter with Ted Nash.

Chapter Fifty-Four

Despite everything on his mind, Matthew looked forward to spending every minute of every evening and weekend with Torrey. Somehow, she could make him forget, if only for a few hours at a time, what lay in front of him. And if his days as a free man were numbered, he wanted to take full advantage of each one remaining.

Most evenings after work the two of them picked up some grass-fed beef or free-range chicken, with all the fixings, to take advantage of the fully equipped kitchen in their hotel suite. They enjoyed the camaraderie of cooking together and the closeness of eating their creations at the small dining table. They talked mostly about who had the weirdest or wildest patient that day. Torrey usually won because her group of inmates were more varied in their maladies. One evening, Matthew thought he might win because he had a man come in whose face had been badly disfigured during a teenage knife fight. He was grossly overweight and was missing two fingers. Yet what he wanted was a drug to grow hair on the small bald spot on top of head.

Torrey said, "Why don't we make this interesting? Loser does the dishes."

"I'll take that bet," said Matthew with an air of confidence. "You go first."

Torrey grinned. "Get ready to do dishes." After a dramatic pause, she continued. "Have you ever heard of *keistering*?"

"No, should I have?"

"Well, if you're going to work in a prison, yes, you should be aware. Keistering is a timeworn scheme for smuggling contraband. You insert the item into the rectum to avoid detection by security personnel. Drug mules have used this method to bring heroin into the country, but prisoners have taken this artform to a whole new level. Today I had a guy who inserted a homemade shank to hide it from the guards who were searching his cell. It worked. The guards didn't find it. But then the guy couldn't get it out. Guess who got that lovely job?"

Matthew had never welched on a bet in his life. He didn't say a word. He just got up from the table, cleared the plates, and proceeded to work until every dish was spotless. Torrey enjoyed watching.

The weekends were devoted to fun. They visited local tourist destinations like Fisherman's Wharf, and they rode the cable cars, but strangely enough, neither had an interest in taking a tour of Alcatraz. One Sunday, Torrey suggested a hike through the Muir Woods National Monument, less than an hour away. Torrey said that when Leia was alive, her family had hiked through the park almost every summer weekend. She had not wanted to return since then. Until now. Matthew had never been. Once there, he wished he had known about it sooner. Matthew was stunned by the splendor. It was mindboggling that this pristine beauty was so close to the ugliness of San Quentin.

As a part of the Golden Gate National Recreation Area, Muir Woods had trails of every length and difficulty through towering primeval old growth coast redwoods, the tallest trees in the world. The literature at the front entrance explained that all of the trees were at least 400 years old—some were more than 1000 years old.

Matthew let Torrey select their trail. They started on a wooded walking path that skirted Redwood Creek. Old wooden bridges crossed the creek at varying intervals. It had been years since Matthew had been surrounded by nature. He was thunderstruck. He grabbed her hand as they stood next to a stand of redwoods that blocked out the sun. He pulled her close so that he could look in her eyes. "I had no idea that this peaceful oasis existed. Thank you for bringing me here. I know it must bring back memories, some of them painful."

"Actually, I thought coming here would make me cry. But being here with you brings only happiness. I'm glad we came." She kissed him sweetly.

From a distance, they heard musical instruments. Matthew was no student of chamber music, but it sounded like a flute and maybe a violin. "Let's go check it out," he said.

They walked another hundred yards where they spied a group of twenty-five or thirty people in a cluster. Some of the men were wearing black hiking shorts, white long sleeve shirts, and black stovepipe hats, and some of the women were wearing matching light-yellow spring dresses. As the flautist started playing Canon in D, Matthew and Torrey realized they were watching the start of a wedding.

As they got closer, the crowd parted slightly, and they could see the bride and groom standing just inside of a giant hollow redwood. They were in the process of saying vows and exchanging rings. The setting was magnificent.

Matthew did not want to intrude on the moment, but he was mesmerized. He couldn't pull himself away. As he stared, he imagined Torrey and himself as the wedding couple. And what being married to Torrey would be like. He knew it would be wonderful. It was what he wanted. He wished he could propose right then. He thought to himself. "If things go according to plan, Nash will be dead, and Torrey will be my bride."

Just as quickly, he remembered why he was here. Why he had gone to medical school. That it would be totally unfair to Torrey to broach the subject of marriage until Ted Nash was dead. Either he would get away with it or he would be sent to prison. He couldn't think about the future until he knew which it would be.

Chapter Fifty-Five

Matthew was mentally checking off the days on the calendar as September 29 approached. So was Torrey.

If Matthew was conflicted about his plot, Torrey wasn't able to discern it. There was no break in their routine. There was no change in his behavior. When they visited her parents on Sunday September 27, Matthew was his usual polished and funny self. He had even read up on Bobby Thompson's homerun to impress her father. If she didn't know better, she would have concluded that September 29 was just going to be another day.

Matthew knew better. September 29 was the going to be the climax of his life. He had dreamt about killing Ted Nash for so long, and now he was on the cusp of success. He knew he was prepared. He knew his strategy was sound. Why shouldn't he be calm? And he was, until the evening of September 28 when he felt a fleeting moment of self-doubt.

He and Torrey had finished dinner. The dishes were done. It was time to retire for the night. He gave Torrey a long hug and kiss. Matthew then went into his bedroom and shut the door. After a long hot shower in his *en suite* bathroom, he stood in front of the medicine cabinet mirror and rubbed off the steam with a hand towel. He stared at the mute reflection in the mirror and had his final internal debate.

As he looked deeply into the mirror, his own face disappeared and was replaced by his mother's soft face. Then by his father's visage. He knew that his parents were in heaven together. They were watching over him. His thoughts jumbled together. *What will they think of me? Will they understand? Does that matter anymore? For so long my life has been black and white. Torrey introduced color. Can I take the risk of getting caught and losing her? But I won't be caught. No one will be suspicious enough to order an autopsy. No one will care about Nash's death. But even if I get away with it, what will it be like keeping this secret from Torrey forever? How will I feel afterwards? I'm not some special forces agent who can kill someone eleven ways with his bare hands and never think twice about it.*

He closed his eyes, ran his fingers over a day's worth of stubble, and allowed the deliberation to continue for several more minutes. When he opened his eyes again, he saw in the mirror his dead mother lying in her bed. He saw his father's body falling backwards as bullets crashed into his head and chest. The familiar anger roiled up inside. The debate ended as he knew it would. Ted Nash had less than 24 hours to live.

Chapter Fifty-Six

Matthew woke up refreshed. He had wondered if he would have trouble falling asleep. He didn't. He had never been more ready for a day to begin. With a little luck, it would all be over in a few hours. Then he could get out of the hellhole known as San Quentin.

On the other hand, Torrey hardly slept at all. Last night she had given Matthew every opportunity to open up, and to disclose his plan. To stop trying to protect her from the truth. At every turn, he had deftly changed the subject. If he had noticed the disappointment on her face, he didn't mention it.

Unbeknownst to Matthew, he wasn't the only one with big ideas for the day. In South Cellblock, a 25-year-old, 6'7", 250-pound albino, whom Ted knew by the moniker *Big Whitey,* had set the wheels into motion to use his scheduled visit to the clinic as a means to escape. Big Whitey had been locked up since he was twenty. He had learned two weeks earlier that his six-year-old son was terminally ill. He was committed to getting home at any cost.

He had emptied his modest bank account to pay a ragtag group of troublemakers to start a diversionary riot in the exercise yard at 10:30 a.m. His appointment with Dr. Goodwin was at 10:25. He planned to take Goodwin hostage during the riot. Big Whitey's mental functioning was at the level of a fourth grader, but he was confident that his plan was foolproof.

When Torrey and Matthew left their hotel, it was drizzling. Traffic was slow. By the time they arrived at the prison at 9:00 a.m., the rain was coming down in torrents. The wind was gale force. Despite having two oversized umbrellas, the two medical students were soaked, and late, by the time they walked from the parking lot to the clinic. With no time to do anything but change into scrubs and lab coats, they hurried to their respective exam rooms.

By 10:00 o'clock, Matthew already had seen three unremarkable patients in exam room 2. No muss, no fuss. Torrey, down the hall in Exam Room 13, was still on her first patient because this day she had been assigned to shadow Dr. Goodwin, who spent more time chatting with the inmates than actually treating them.

At 10:15, everything changed. Everyone on the floor would forever remember the next twenty minutes.

While Matthew was just starting on his next patient, Nurse Gonzales walked in. Not wanting to interrupt, she quietly put a piece of paper on the counter by the door, and casually announced as she left, "Here are the changes to the patient schedules for today."

It didn't occur to Matthew to immediately check out the revised schedule. He should have.

Torrey's patient was just leaving when Nurse Gonzales dropped off the new

schedule. Torrey scanned the changes. Her eyes were drawn to one name—
Theodore Nash. His new appointment time was 10:30.

Nash knew that that his doctor appointment was scheduled for 1:30, so he
was surprised when an ancient guard with a large permanent knot on his
forehead showed up at his cell mid-morning to escort him to the clinic for his
shot. "Hey, you're early. My appointment isn't until this afternoon."

"What do I look like, your personal secretary? They told me to get you over
to exam room 2, so that's what I'm doing. Move it."

Just as Nash was leaving his cell at 10:25, Big Whitey was arriving at exam
room 13 where Dr. Goodwin and Torrey were waiting. For weeks Goodwin had
been treating Big Whitey for a nasty infection on his leg from a brawl in the
dining hall. They started chatting like old friends.

At the same time, Matthew took a perfunctory look at Nurse Gonzales' revised
patient schedule. For a moment, he was shocked into inaction. The rocuronium was
in his locker. He had planned to retrieve it over the lunch break. Without a word to
anyone, he bolted out into the corridor, ran past exam rooms 3-16, and shouldered
open the exit door. He would be a couple of minutes late for Nash, but he could still
do it. He checked his watch every few seconds as he worked the combination on
his metal locker. He reached in and grabbed the crucial vial.

In exam room 13, Torrey looked at the clock on the wall—10:30. She imagined Matthew was now in the same room with Nash. *What was happening?* She had to find out. She excused herself and racewalked down the hall towards exam room 2. Ted Nash was advancing from the other direction very slowly, as he was being escorted by an elderly overweight guard, soaked to the bone, who walked like he had a wooden leg, maybe two. The guard, double chin wobbling, breathing hard, stopped a few steps from the doorway. His belly hung over his uniform belt as he stared at Torrey with sad sack eyes. As he retreated, he simply panted, "Here is your 10:30."

Big Whitey was also looking at the clock. The riot was supposed to have started by now. But no alarm. Only silence.

Matthew slammed his locker shut, sprinted out of the locker room, and headed back towards the clinic floor. If he hurried, he would be back in exam room 2 before anyone missed him.

Torrey stared slack-jawed at the guard as he walked away. Nash simply wandered into the exam room, leaned up against the table, and took off his wet shoes. Matthew was nowhere to be seen. *Where is he?* she wondered.

Big Whitey was getting anxious. While Goodwin droned on about his weekend plans, Big Whitey was listening for one thing only—a Code 3 alarm. Finally, at 10:31, the siren blasted. Big Whitey sprang into action.

When the alarm sounded, Matthew was just a few steps away from the clinic floor doorway. He knew that there were only a few reasons for a lockdown alarm, all of them bad. He heard the loud urgent order over the loudspeaker for all available guards to report to the exercise yard.

Torrey stood in the open doorway to exam room 2. She looked up and down the hallway. No Matthew. She looked inside the room and saw Nash eyeing her. He rubbed his hand on the exam table as he said in an oily voice, "Come on in here honey. My name is Ted, but you can call me anytime."

Torrey stepped into the room and let the door close behind her. She stared with unblinking eyes, daring him to say more.

Before Goodwin knew what was happening, Big Whitey had grabbed

Goodwin's surgical scissors and had pinned him up against the door. "You're my ticket out of here, doc."

When Matthew burst through the exit door and entered the clinic corridor, the first thing he saw was Dr. Goodwin and a huge ghost-white albino standing behind him. Goodwin's face was contorted with fear. His eyes were unnaturally wide, and his face was blood red. His mouth was open in a silent scream. Matthew understood when he focused his attention on the giant. A tree trunk of an arm encircled Goodwin's neck. At the end of the other arm was a ham-sized hand holding a blade against Goodwin's chest. Matthew directed his gaze up from Goodwin's face to the albino's features. He had a drill sergeant crewcut and a long stringy red beard. His pink eyes bulged, and his nostrils flared. A lightning strike had relieved him of his eyebrows when he was fourteen, which served to highlight the large pulsating vein on his forehead. Sweat was beading on his upper lip. The cobra tattoo on his neck stood out against his milky skin.

Nash knew that a riot in the yard meant no one was going to be paying any attention to the inmates in the clinic. He was immediately primed to take advantage of the situation. He leered suggestively at Torrey. "You're one sweet looking honey. Come hop up on the exam table." There was lust in his eyes. Torrey knew that look.

The albino and Goodwin were between Matthew and where he was desperate to go. Matthew pictured Nash alone and waiting in exam room 2. Then he focused on

Goodwin's pleading eyes. "Get out of my way, doc," growled Big Whitey. Matthew did not bother to correct the elevation of his status from medical student to doctor. Instead, he tried using his calming voice as if he were talking to a troubled child.

"C'mon guy. Put down the knife and let's talk about it." Matthew's attempt to smooth over the situation didn't work. Big Whitey's reply was far from conciliatory.

"Nothing to talk about. Out of my way or I am going to cut him! And you too!" Matthew didn't doubt the albino's word.

Nash blathered on. "You scared of being here during a lockdown? You need to relax, honey. Come over here and lie down. I know what you need." Suddenly, Torrey flashed back to high school. To George Rincon. To lying down in his office.

Nash would not shut up. "And I'm getting out of this dump soon. We could get together then too. What do you say?"

A hard truth struck Torrey. Matthew was right all along. *This lowlife murderer does not deserve to take another breath.*

As he squeezed Goodwin's neck, the albino bellowed, "Tell them to open the doors! I have to get out of here!"

Matthew knew that his opportunity to kill Nash was fading away, but he had to stay and try to save Goodwin. "Guy, you know they can't open the doors. They won't. We all know it. Just let him go and I promise we'll help you in any way we can." Big Whitey's response was to slowly press the scissor tips into Goodwin's chest. A blot of blood seeped through Goodwin's white lab coat.

A steely resolve enveloped Torrey. She knew what she was going to do. What she *had* to do. Her hands were shaking, but not enough to dissuade her. The next thirty seconds played out like a slow-motion movie to Torrey. She was repulsed by Nash, but she forced herself to keep her eyes locked on him as she backed away from the center of the room. She flashed him a seductive smile. When her spine was up against the wall, she knew she was invisible to the video camera and beyond the reach of Ed's prying eyes.

Matthew knew it would be a fruitless mission, but his adrenaline was pumping, and it took all of his self-control not to blindly rush forward. His feet were rooted to the floor as he considered his options. Suddenly, out of the corner of his eye, he saw a flash of movement behind Big Whitey. Someone was creeping up from behind. Then, like a whirlwind, Mr. Ed launched himself like a missile into the small of the Big Whitey's back, knocking the giant to the ground. Matthew heard the unmistakable sound of bone cracking.

Torrey ripped open her lab coat. The buttons fell to the floor. Nash stared but did not move. In the most provocative manner that she could muster, she lowered her scrub pants to her thighs revealing her panties. "This is what you like, isn't it?" she purred. Nash pushed himself away from the table and opened his mouth to speak. Before he could say a word, Torrey put a finger to her lips and whispered, "Shush. Don't say a word." She softly touched the front of her panties. "Just come and get it."

With adrenaline coursing, Matthew's martial arts training kicked in. He gritted his teeth and barreled forward. He pushed Dr. Goodwin to safety. While Ed locked his legs around Big Whitey's neck, Matthew used every ounce of strength to wrestle away the scissors and then he delivered three quick blows to the albino's face. Within seconds, Big Whitey gave up. He stopped fighting or defending himself. The only visible movement was the shaking of his shoulders as he cried, "I'm sorry!" His face twisted as he wailed over and over until his voice was just a whimper, "I just want to go home."

Nash did not have to be asked twice. He charged toward Torrey. When he was close enough, she grabbed the front of his shirt with her left hand and pulled him up against her body. With her right hand, she reached into the pocket of her lab coat and pulled out the scalpel that Dr. Gerard had recommended that she always carry for self-defense. In one brutally smooth stroke, she plunged the knife into his throat. She pulled the blade sharply to the left to ensure the vocal cords were severed in case he did not bleed out immediately.

While Nash was clutching at his neck and blood was filling his chest cavity, Torrey stared at his pasty face and into his blank, bulging eyes. She stabbed him in the heart. "That is for Matthew Preston." She stabbed him again. "That is for Grant and Mary Preston." With the final puncture, she left the scalpel imbedded in Nash's heart. Her last words were simply, "That is for me, and the rest of the women of the world, you disgusting psycho!" Covered in blood, Torrey stepped to the exam table, looked up at the camera, and started waving for help.

Chapter Fifty-Seven

Medical School Match Day has been a rite of passage for medical students since 1952. In February of their fourth year of school, students submit a ranked list of preferred residency programs. The U.S. accredited teaching hospitals where resident physicians will train for the next three years simultaneously rank their preferred list of students. The National Resident Matching Program runs the data through a unique computer program which matches the students to the hospitals. The sealed results are made available to all students in the country at the same date and time.

On March 18, Matthew and Torrey were with their graduating class at Stanford's Berg Hall, everybody anxiously waiting to find out where they would spend the next few years of their lives. Having gotten engaged at Christmas, the two of them had gone into the system as a couple, expecting that at least one particular institution on their joint list would want both of them.

Matthew was one of the few students without either parent present for the occasion. As much as he missed them, he was surrounded by goodwill. He and Torrey were huddled with TJ, Torrey's parents, and two special invitees. Matthew's guest was Mrs. Ed, officially now known as Edwina. She had completed her transformation surgery and looked amazing. Matthew and Edwina had formed a special bond that would last forever.

Torrey's guest was Dr. Gerard, to whom Torrey would be eternally grateful for her advice on self-protection.

Matthew had also sent a courtesy invitation to Dr. Goodwin, but he knew that Goodwin was still recovering from his wounds. Matthew heard through the grapevine that Goodwin had resigned from his position at San Quentin, so that he could find an administrative hospital position with no direct patient interaction.

Before the ceremonial opening of the envelopes containing the match results, the Dean of the Medical School went to the microphone. "Hello everyone. Thank you for coming to this momentous and festive event in the lives of these wonderful and dedicated soon-to-be doctors." He spoke for five more minutes about the timeless ritual of physician training, about the importance of compassionate healing towards the less fortunate in our society, and about the necessity of following the Hippocratic oath. If Matthew had been listening to the speech, he would have been amused. But like most everyone in the room, Matthew's group was whispering among themselves and counting down the minutes before they could rip open their envelopes.

Despite the building anticipation, the room fell silent when the Dean started talking about a special recognition for an extraordinary person. They all knew the story, but everyone listened with respect and awe. "Ladies and gentlemen, it is my great pleasure to announce the creation of the first annual Courage Award. As most of you know, one of our students, Torrey Jamison, singlehandedly fought off an attacker in the San Quentin prison clinic—"

As praise was heaped upon Torrey from the podium, Matthew squeezed Torrey's hand, leaned in close, and whispered something in her ear. She squeezed his hand in reply.

After the award presentation, the countdown began. As one voice, the entire room shouted out the last ten seconds. Matthew and Torrey calmly opened their envelopes and smiled at each other.

"Well?" said TJ. "So where are you two headed?"

"Yes! What's the news?" asked Mr. Jamison.

Matthew picked up their match sheets and slid them across the table to his uncle. "We matched at our first choice, Uncle TJ!"

TJ's grin faded for a second as he did a double take at the name of the institution.

"Kaiser?" he said. "In San Diego?" TJ thought that with their grades, test scores, and recommendations, they would have chosen a residency hospital in the bay area or in Los Angeles where they would be close to family. He was genuinely perplexed at their choice, but seeing how happy they looked, he just smiled and gave them both a hug. He figured they must have a good reason.

Made in the USA
Middletown, DE
08 October 2020